# The Innocent

ROBERT TAYLOR

# The Innocent

Fithian Press
SANTA BARBARA • 1997

Printed in the United States of America

Design and typography by Jim Cook
Cover design by John Daniel

Published by Fithian Press, a division of Daniel & Daniel Publishers, Inc.,
Post Office Box 1525, Santa Barbara, California 93102

This is a work of fiction. Any resemblance between characters in this book and real persons, living or dead, is a coincidence.

LIBRARY OF CONGRESS CATALOGING-IN-PUBLICATION DATA
Taylor, Robert
The innocent / Robert Taylor.
p. cm.
ISBN 1-56474-230-X (alk. paper)
1. Vietnamese Conflict, 1961-1975—Fiction. 2. Gay men—Vietnam—Fiction. I. Title
PS3570.A9516I5 1997
813'.54—dc21 97-11655
CIP

Second Printing

*For Ted*
*who has made it all possible*

# FOREWORD

Dear Reader:

Look carefully at this first novel by a friend of mine whose dedication to his craft and singular accomplishment I admire. If there is another fiction quite like it in subject matter and straightforward, unembellished manner of telling, I do not know of it.

Sympathetically, it deals with a young intelligence officer stationed in Vietnam during that terrible war, a story of love, homophobia, and the suffering of a man whose service record was exceptional, but whose sexual choice is suspect.

I think a novel of this quality can well be lost in the confusion and loud hype of "big books" that deafen readers to quieter, thoughtful fictional sounds. I do not have to remind the sensitive reader how difficult it is for a first novel that is not a blockbuster to make its way on today's publishing scene. In your hands now is such a book and I wish to lend a hand to its passage.

One last note: some first novelists have trouble with the

resolution of their fictions. They ride speedily through their story and then balk at the finish. I like Robert Taylor's original and most satisfying coda. I urge you to read *The Innocent* to discover for yourself how right my judgment is.

—Doris Grumbach

# The Innocent

# 1

The big Pan-Am jet leaving San Francisco could have been going anywhere. Anchorage. New York. Mexico City. When we boarded, a flock of stewardesses, all smiles and makeup and carefully tended hair, fluttered up and down the aisles passing out pillows and magazines. After we leaned our seats back and settled in, the pilot talked to us about cruising altitudes and possible turbulence along the way. It couldn't have been more ordinary.

But our plane wasn't headed somewhere sane. It was going to Vietnam.

Looking around, I was struck by how young we all were. I wondered how the older ones, the sergeant-majors and the colonels, got over there. I couldn't see anyone much over thirty on our flight.

Enlisted men and officers had been separated, of course.

Officers up front where I was, enlisted men to the rear. The front of the plane was noisier by far, a long, twenty-six-hour fraternity party. The stewardesses spent most of their time with the rowdiest group of all. The ringleader, a first lieutenant with a blond crewcut, kept putting his hand up inside the skirt of a tall brunette. She would laugh, toss her shiny hair, and hit at his *other* arm to make him stop.

We had meal after meal, movie after movie, and drink after drink. We stopped briefly in Hawaii, a little longer in the Philippines. I read a while, listened to the captain beside me talk about Utah, and slept some. Mostly I watched the carousing. Hannibal crossing the Alps it was not.

Late at night, about ten o'clock, on either the day after or the day before, I couldn't get straight which one, we were told we were about to land. At Tan Son Nhut Air Base just outside Saigon. The same calm voice that had discussed oxygen masks and flotation devices with us now explained about dive-bomb landings.

"To avoid mortar and rocket fire," she said soothingly, "we will be making an extremely steep approach to the runway. Do not be alarmed. This is standard procedure."

The hush that filled the plane threatened to pop out the windows. My heart was beating fast, and I felt an urgent need to pee.

"Please be *sure* your seatbelts are securely fastened. Place your forehead against the seat in front of you. Clasp your hands behind your neck."

We did. And the plane went straight down.

At the last possible moment, it leveled out and settled onto the runway. My ears had had no chance to pop, and my eardrums ached. I could barely hear the voice continue.

"Move as quickly as possible down the stairway and follow the guides to the bunkers at the edge of the field. Speed is essential, both for your own safety as well as that of the aircraft and its crew. We will be taking off as soon as the last of you has deplaned. Thank you for flying Pan-Am, and we hope you've enjoyed your flight. It was our pleasure serving you."

We ran down the steps, our carry-on luggage bouncing beside us. It was so stifling, even late at night, that just walking would have been an effort. But we kept on running, gasping for breath, and followed the guides into a row of bunkers. The plane roared away. Seconds later, incoming rockets began to explode around us.

For maybe ten minutes, we crouched on the floor waiting for them to come whining in and burst. My ears finally popped, and as I listened, I found I could tell by the pitch of the whistle whether the next rocket would hit close by or further away. Bright orange flashes lit up the bunker a fraction of a second before the sound of the explosion arrived. I heard someone off to my left whispering Hail Marys. For me, fear was so completely mixed with fascination I couldn't tell which was which.

We waited through another ten minutes or so of silence before we were led outside and separated into groups. My group of young officers followed a private to a screened-in dormitory a few hundred yards away. We peed, gratefully, at an outdoor latrine, took off our khaki uniforms, and lay down on squeaky cots in our underwear. It was hot and muggy, but I slept surprisingly well.

We were awakened at five and washed up at sinks hanging off the outside wall of the latrine. Later I would see the exotic sights that let me know I was on the other side of the world—small brown people in cone-shaped woven hats, water buffalo in rice paddies, a jungle canopy like nothing in Mexico or the Caribbean. That first morning, though, I was amazed at how familiar things were. I had expected a totally foreign world. What I found was air that went in and out of my lungs just like the air back home. Water that tasted like water. A sunrise the same rosy pink as in a Texas sky. I didn't realize how different I thought it would be until I saw that it was very much the same.

I had a hard time believing I was really there. I'd never expected to wake up in a war zone. Well. I'd never expected to be a soldier at all. It just happened. A simple bargain, really. I needed money for college, and the Army was eager to oblige. Sign up for ROTC, the recruiter said, and we'll give you a monthly check your last two years. You help us, we help you. Fair enough, I thought.

My timing was bad, though. When my three years at the Pentagon were up and I applied for release, they told me I must be joking. A war was on, and they needed officers with my training and experience. The answer was no. My promotion to captain that next year was a kind of consolation prize, I figured, followed soon by orders to report to Vietnam.

I thought I'd enjoy being home in Texas with my family before I left, but the visit was strained. No one knew what to say. The women patted me on the arm and fixed mountains of food. The men talked about Normandy and Guadalcanal.

Then, after a long, surrealistic flight and a short, nightmarish attack, there I was. I didn't want to be, but not going would never have occurred to me.

We ate a big breakfast and filed into a room to learn our assignments. Someone somewhere had made decisions that would mean life or death for each of us. All we could do was sit there, listening to a high-pitched voice reading from a long list.

Cu Chi. First Cav. Danang. Nha Trang. 101st Airborne. Chu Lai. Words that would become as familiar to us as our own names we heard for the first time.

"Captain Matthew Fairchild. Headquarters, U.S. Army Vietnam. Saigon."

I closed my eyes and took my first real breath of the morning. A reprieve. That's all I could think of. A reprieve. Not sudden death in some infantry unit. Saigon. Civilization. A chance to live.

I knew what had happened. All those years in Washington

with the Assistant Chief of Staff for Intelligence had saved me. Had looked far too good on a resume to pass up. Just a matter of being in the right place at the right time. Luck, pure and simple.

First they would issue me my jungle fatigues and combat boots. Then they would show me where I was going to live. Army Headquarters was on the base at Tan Son Nhut. The Bachelor Officers' Quarters there were all full. Temporarily. The buildup was coming faster than expected. Too many officers, too few rooms. I would live in Saigon for a while and be shuttled back and forth by Army drivers. The men I'd spent the night and morning with went off in helicopters to steamy jungle encampments. I went in an air-conditioned staff car to a lovely old home on the outskirts of town.

Five officers were already living there. Three captains and two first lieutenants. I filled out the quota, two to a room in three large sunlit bedrooms. I moved in with a captain named Larry on the second floor. Two other captains, Gregg and Ross, lived on our floor. The lieutenants, Keith and Donnie, lived upstairs. I met them all late in the afternoon when two staff cars brought them home and they tumbled up the stairs, laughing and talking.

Ross poured Scotch for all of us from a bottle he brought from his room, and we sat around on the beds in Larry's and my room getting acquainted. That consisted mostly of listening to Donnie and Ross trade wisecracks, with Larry turning to me to explain. The group was fun. We laughed a lot and decided to go into town later on for dinner. My luggage had arrived in mid-afternoon, so I had civilian clothes to change into. Off duty in Saigon, Larry told me, we were always to wear civvies. Fatigues with names and insignia only to go to and from work. Larry, like the others, had been in-country for several weeks. I was grateful for all the tips they could give me.

We rested a while and left around seven-thirty. They

showed me where to hail a cyclo, a funny kind of mechanized rickshaw with a seat up front and half a motorcycle behind. We went off two by two—Gregg and Ross, Keith and Donnie, Larry and me. Larry gave our driver, a wrinkled but smiling old Vietnamese man, the name of a restaurant in Cholon, the mostly Chinese suburb of Saigon. The driver smiled and smiled and bobbed his head.

It was a wild ride. Our knees were way out on the leading edge where a bumper ought to have been. Traffic was chaotic, a confusion of shouting and honking and noxious fumes, and we were right there in the middle of it. Nothing between us and it, not even a pane of glass.

A smell like garbage rotting in stagnant water stayed with us the whole way. Other smells came and went. Sweet ones like cloves or cinnamon. Acrid ones like fermented cabbage. And one so sharp and pungent it made my eyes water. But the rotten garbage smell was constant.

Barefoot women in conical hats woven from rattan trotted along, balancing enormous loads on both ends of a long pole. A child or a chicken would dart unexpectedly into the street, and the stream of traffic would divide to miss them and then merge again on the other side. None of the thousands of mopeds that swarmed around us seemed to have a muffler. All of them coughed and sputtered. Cheap gas or poor maintenance? I wondered. Probably both. I would have asked Larry which he thought it was, but the noise of the traffic made conversation impossible.

Business was brisk along many of the streets. Crowds on the sidewalks moved in and out of little shops and stopped to buy food being cooked by women squatting flatfooted along the edge of the curb.

Most of the vehicles passing by were small. Not the American jeeps. They loomed up suddenly, filling the narrow streets. Cars, mopeds, and cyclos had to swerve onto the sidewalks to let them pass, scattering vendors and buyers alike. But the drivers and pedestrians all smiled and nodded and waved. "Yankee GI!" they shouted. "Numbah one! Numbah one!"

# 2

The next morning, we all gathered on the sidewalk in front of our house. The cars were to come for us at six. We were out chatting by five-forty-five.

I had breakfast at the Officers' Mess and took a bus to the Headquarters building, a three-story structure made of gray cinderblock. A major named Sinclair showed me around the area on the second floor assigned to G-2, the intelligence staff. Our boss was Colonel Dunhill, whose large office was next to the main stairway. The Commanding General was up on the third floor.

All Major Sinclair could give me was a general orientation. My assignment was a hush-hush project he knew was in the works, but he hadn't been told what it was about. He was careful, by his look and the tone of his voice, to let me know he was offended to think there were going to be things I would know that he would not.

He left me at a desk and gave me a stack of briefing books. I sat there flipping through them until midmorning, when the sergeant-major came to get me, ushered me into Colonel Dunhill's office, went out, and closed the door. The colonel, a short, stocky man with a bald head and a thick brown mustache, was reading some kind of report. He looked up and motioned to a chair. I sat.

"No preliminaries, Captain," he said. "No formalities. I'm a busy man, as you will soon find out. I say what I have to say and move on to the next task at hand. So. We're about to set up a new facility here at Headquarters, and I'm thinking of asking you to take charge of it. What do you say to that?"

"I'm flattered, sir."

"We're real excited about it, the CG and I. Think it will be a big help in getting a handle on what's what in this godforsaken place." He stared at me and pulled on his mustache. "It won't be easy, Captain, getting it set up and running. But your efficiency reports say you're good at organization and detail work. That so?"

"Yes, sir. I think it is."

"Also that you can write pretty decently. We'd be asking you to prepare a number of reports. Travel around the country. Put pieces together for us. That sort of thing. Sound like something you can handle?"

"Absolutely, sir."

"There's one drawback, Captain. You'd have to work in a sealed-off room down the hall. Entered by pressing a combination known to only a few of us. No windows. No daylight. But air-conditioned, of course. As befits an officer and a gentleman."

He chuckled.

I chuckled.

"Any of that bother you?" he asked.

"No, sir."

"We'd be able to give you a sergeant to help out. The two of you would be responsible for working out the details, getting it set up, keeping it absolutely up-to-date, and giving any special briefings we might ask you to do." He stared and rubbed at his mustache. "I like your look and your manner, Captain. I pride myself on being a good judge of men, and I think you're just the one I'm looking for. What do you say? Yes or no?"

"I say yes. I appreciate your confidence, sir, and I'll try to live up to it. When do I start?"

"Soon as you've been polygraphed. The team's up-country right now. Rush job. Take two or three days is my guess. They should be back on Tuesday. We can get you in and out Wednesday morning, and you can start that afternoon."

My heart was pounding, and I couldn't swallow. A lie detector test. Jesus. The last thing I'd expected.

"What's the point of a polygraph, sir?" I asked. "I thought I had every clearance the Pentagon could think up."

"You do. Just about. But this stuff you'll be handling is special. Real sensitive. No one sees it without a recent polygraph. Just a formality for you, though. You've been tested plenty of times already, I expect."

"Yes, sir. I have."

Plenty of times. Back when I had nothing to hide.

The colonel stood up.

"We're all set, then," he said. "Polygraph as soon as possible, and you hit the decks running right after. This project is dear to my heart, Captain. Don't disappoint me."

I hesitated. But it was no use. What bigger red flag could I wave than saying I'd decided to reconsider?

"Thank you, sir," I said.

I walked out of the colonel's office and straight into Major Sinclair.

"How'd it go, Fairchild?" he asked.

"Fine, sir," I said.

"Let me know if there's any way I can help."

"I will, sir."

I went outside and sat on the steps.

It's over, I thought. Just like that. Less than a week in Vietnam and I go right back home with a dishonorable discharge. I'd had those tests all right, and I knew what they liked to ask. And I knew that when they asked it, I'd send the needle right off the page.

They'd ask, and I'd remember an afternoon in Washington. Ten minutes, fifteen at the most, that had turned my life upside down.

I was leaving for Vietnam in a couple of months, and the woman I was dating, a pretty blonde named Joanne, was being kind and sympathetic. For some couples our age, I guess, kindness and sympathy would have included sex. But not us. She was a well-brought-up Southern girl I'd met at church, and I, at twenty-six, was the oldest male virgin in the United States. It wasn't something I'd intended, but there it was.

I remembered that afternoon with absolute clarity. Joanne and I were going to the Officers' Club for dinner and dancing, and I'd gotten it into my head that I wanted to look especially nice for her. I went downtown, in civilian clothes since it was my day off, to buy a new shirt and tie. I couldn't find anything I liked at Hecht's, so I went over to Woodward and Lothrop's, a more upscale store.

My luck improved. I found an Oxford button-down and a paisley tie that satisfied me. After I paid for them, I stopped by the men's room on the third floor. An older man in an expensive-looking suit was standing at one of the urinals. His short gray hair had been carefully trimmed, and his face was deeply tanned.

I went and stood at the urinal next to him. I glanced over. His penis curved outward in a heavy graceful arc. I glanced again. Instead of trying to block my view with his hand, he turned toward me. I was so startled I moved backward a little.

"I don't mind your looking," he said. "Quite the contrary."

He had a deep resonant voice. Comforting.

I looked back down at his penis and felt my own, also hanging exposed, begin to quiver.

"Do you want to touch it?" he asked.

That wasn't something I would ever have thought of, but as soon as he asked, I knew it was exactly what I wanted to do.

I nodded.

He reached out and guided my hand toward it. It was amazingly alive, soft and smooth at first, then hard and insistent. My own stood out straight toward him. His hand moved toward it and touched it. I saw the glint of a wedding ring on his finger. I was excited and terrified.

I looked up. He was watching my face.

"Not used to this?" he asked.

"No," I said.

"At all, or in places like this?"

"At all."

He put his hand on the side of my neck and rubbed his thumb up and down. "Want to keep going, or stop? It's up to you."

I felt a rush of affection for him.

"Keep going," I said.

"Lucky me. Come over here, then."

He led the way to the furthest of the stalls. We went in, and he latched the door. He hung his suitcoat on the little hook on the back of it. I leaned my package against the wall. We unbuckled our belts and let our pants slide to the floor. He pushed my shorts just down around my thighs, then his. He put his arms around me, and I felt their strength. He rested his chin on my shoulder and caressed the skin of my buttocks. I reached up under the tail of his shirt to find his. They were firm underneath but silky on the surface. I loved touching them more than I could comprehend.

I heard a noise and froze.

"Relax," he whispered in my ear. "There won't be much traffic this time of day. But if someone does come in, we'll just wait quietly. All right?"

"All right," I said. I relaxed and let my hands do what they seemed to know they wanted to do.

After a few minutes, he sat down and pulled me toward him. I laid one hand on his left shoulder and ran the other through his hair. He put my hard penis in his mouth and started moving his head in and out. I had never imagined anything could feel so good. Not just the intense physical pleasure, which sent tremors all over my body, but the sense of absolute rightness. I knew what was happening: I was being sucked off in a public toilet by a complete stranger. If ever there was sin in the world, this was it. I should have been paralyzed with guilt, but instead I was exhilarated by it.

When I realized I was about to come, I tried to move his head away. I couldn't believe he would want that stuff in his mouth, but apparently he did. I shot into him with an exuberance I wouldn't have guessed was possible. My knees were weak, but I knew I was smiling.

He moved his head back and stood up.

"Shall I try to do that for you?" I asked.

"Sure you want to?"

I hesitated. "Not exactly."

"Then don't. Let this be enough of an initiation."

Relief and disappointment fought inside me. Relief won out.

We pulled up our pants, zipped our zippers, and buckled our belts. I reached for my package, unlatched the door, and went out. He followed me. I turned to look at him once more, and he smiled.

"Thank you," I said.

He looked startled.

"Oh, my god," he said. "Thank *you*."

I walked out the door and around to the escalator. On the way down, I realized how eager I was to do that again. Soon. Maybe I'd even be brave enough to reciprocate. Christ! I thought. You idiot! You don't know how to find him.

I ran down the last few steps of the escalator, around the corner, and back up to the men's room.

He was gone.

# 3

As I sat there on the steps of the Headquarters building, I couldn't be sure what it was I was feeling. Either my life had been basically uncomplicated until recently, or I hadn't been paying real close attention. Whichever, I was not very good at looking below the surface of things.

The physical signs were clear enough. Beads of sweat were sliding down my forehead, and my hands resting on my knees were so wet they were soaking through my brand-new fatigues. Shame was a big part of it, an overwhelming sense of shame, but there was more. Just like that afternoon at Woodie's. Only that time, along with the shame I'd felt pleasure and excitement. And I'd also felt stupid. If only I'd thought to give him my phone number, or ask for his, we could have done that miraculous thing again—somewhere. Surely he would have known how to arrange it.

Well, *there* was an important clue. Doing it once, even enjoying it as much as I knew I had, could have been explained away as an accident. A momentary lapse. But lying awake night after night thinking about the heaviness of that man's penis and the smoothness of the skin on his buttocks was no accident. I was a queer. I had to be. There was no other explanation. Did I mind? Not much. Which was even more shameful than if I'd had sense enough to hate it.

No, *being* queer wasn't the worst thing. I could find a way to live with that. The worst thing would be everybody else knowing. The thought of it made me shiver. All the relatives and friends who'd been so proud as they watched me go off to war would be horrified by the circumstances of my sudden return. For the rest of their lives, my parents wouldn't be able to look at me without pain in their eyes. My grandfather would get up and walk out whenever I entered a room, and my grandmother would make special trips to church to pray, with a heavy heart, for my redemption.

The prospect of all that scared me more than anything else ever had. That was it. That's what was mixed in with the shame this time. Fear. I'd assumed I would be afraid over here. Probably a good bit of the time. But not like this. Not *of* this. I'd thought many times of the possibility that I'd be wounded—or killed—by a bullet or a rocket or a mine. But for my life to be destroyed by the truth of who I was, that had never occurred to me. The truth? I hadn't given much thought to what that might be when it came to the interiors of people's lives. Particularly my own.

So what was the truth about me? I had a secret I was just beginning to understand and that I wanted no one else ever to know. Except for others like me, whoever that might be. In a way, I could see, I'd been lucky. By a trick of physiology, my secret could be hidden quite easily. I'd been given an advantage that made living a lie not only a natural but surely a wise thing to do. People looked at men who swayed their hips or flapped their hands and nodded knowingly. They looked at me and didn't have a clue. Now, technology was about to change all that. A stupid, mindless machine was going to look deep inside me and tell everyone watching it that what I seemed to be and what I was were two very different things.

I thought of one of the briefing books I'd been reading that morning. There'd been a discussion of "friendly fire," a term they used when, through ineptness or inattention or "honest" mistake, our own blasts hit our own men. I laughed. My god. I was about to be wounded by friendly fire. And, to make it even more unbearable, I knew that it was coming, and there was nothing I could do but sit and wait for it to flatten me.

Or was there?

Did they always work, those polygraphs? Not always. It wasn't that the machine could tell the difference between truth and untruth. The important thing was that *I* would know the difference, and the machine would be trying to detect the subtle changes in my body's functioning this knowledge would create. So it was the friendliest fire of all that was going to damage me. I was being asked to shoot myself.

I could lie! I was quite sure I *would* lie. Admitting it, like trying somehow to avoid the test, would be certain disaster. Lying might give me a fighting chance.

Bubbling up through my fear and shame came something just as strong—my instinct for self-preservation. I was not about to just give up. They'd have to work for everything they managed to learn. No way was I going to make it easy for them. I stood up, wiped my wet hands on my back pockets, and went to see if Major Sinclair had any more briefing books.

Those next few days, I was proud of myself. I played my role calmly and confidently. Inside I was a wreck, but to everyone else I was just another officer waiting for his assignment to begin. Food didn't have much taste, though, and I slept fitfully, if at all.

On Wednesday afternoon, Colonel Dunhill called me into his office. Sweat soaked through my clothes and ran down my sides. For nothing. The polygraph team had been delayed. The new facility up-country was a big one, and lots of men had to be cleared. The team would be here on Saturday for sure. Polygraph on Sunday, start work on Monday. In the meantime, help Major Sinclair with the weekly briefing for company intelligence officers.

Yes, sir, I said.

Another gut-wrenching trip to Colonel Dunhill's office on Sunday morning. He was looking out the window. When I closed the door, he spun around. I saw the muscles of his jaw working up and down. He couldn't stop pulling at his mustache.

"Two things I can't stand, Fairchild," he said. "People who

can't get a job done, and people who go back on their word. The polygraph team assured me—*assured* me—they'd be here yesterday. Now they say it may be another week. Screw that. I'm supposed to sit here with my thumb up my ass while they diddle around on a job they could damn well've wrapped up long ago? Not fucking likely. I got a project here can't wait any longer.

"I'm waiving your test, Fairchild. Come on back. I'll show you the combination and the secure room where you'll be working."

# 4

The project was interesting, no question about that. All day and all night, around the clock, highly sensitive and sophisticated electronic equipment was listening to every radio transmission throughout North and South Vietnam. We knew the codes for all the North Vietnamese and Viet Cong units, so we could pinpoint their locations and their movements. The sergeant assigned to me and I were to work out a system for plotting those locations and movements. Once the system was in operation, we would receive continuous reports by secure teletype of these electronic eavesdroppings and keep whatever graphic representation we came up with absolutely up-to-date. I would analyze the texts of any messages we overheard and prepare daily briefings on that information for a highly select group of Headquarters personnel. I would brief the Colonel. The Colonel would brief the Commanding General.

"Any questions, Captain?"

"None, sir. It's very clear."

"Good. Then get to work. I'm counting on you."

He left. I heard the heavy steel door shut and the combination only we knew click into place.

That's *it*? I thought. All that secrecy, all that anguish, just to keep people from knowing we were eavesdropping on enemy broadcasts? It was insane. Hell, I *assumed* we were listening to everything said within range of what I *assumed* were extremely sensitive listening devices. Every war movie I'd ever seen had gone on and on about radio silence and codes and using Navajos to transmit critical information because no one else knew what the hell they were saying. Christ, if I asked my *mother* how the Army knows where enemy units are, she would say, "Oh, they probably listen to them talking to each other on the radio."

I slammed my fist into the wall. I mean, what *was* this? A bunch of paranoid bastards had actually been willing to sacrifice me without another thought just so they could keep secret the fact that whenever an enemy unit goes on the air we know where it is?

I pulled out the brand-new chair from behind my brand-new cheap metal desk, sat down, and wrapped my handkerchief around my bloody knuckles. I had never before trembled with rage. I'd always thought it was one of those literary exaggerations. I found out it wasn't.

Starting the next morning, my sergeant—First Sergeant Kevin Anderson, called Boots—and I worked hard. We requisitioned big maps of every province in North and South Vietnam. We mounted them on the walls, covered them with heavy acetate, and worked out a system of assigning a different color of eighth-inch tape to each major unit. Every morning, I would rip the previous day's locations off the teletype machine and sit at my desk calling out coordinates while Boots cut off a small piece of colored tape with his pocketknife and stuck it at that exact spot on the acetate overlay. When units stayed put, a little mound of red or chartreuse or fuchsia would begin to grow. When they moved, a little colored trail wandered around on the surface of the map.

Everyone was thrilled. Colonel Dunhill was thrilled and patted me on the back. The CG himself, who stopped by to see this wonderful new thing, was thrilled.

"Fine work, Captain," said the general. "Tell your sergeant I said 'Fine work.'"

"Thank you, sir," I said. "I will."

The messages we intercepted were far more interesting, to me, than lists of coordinates. Loose-lipped enemy soldiers chattered on about where they were, where they were going, what they were going to do when they got there, and what they were going to do it with. Troop movements, weapons, tactics. Everything about their conduct of the war poured out into the air. And we listened and wrote it all down.

No wonder they were losing, I thought. They just didn't have a chance. A bunch of possibly well-meaning but hopelessly outgunned, outmaneuvered, and outeavesdropped Third-World peasants who blabbed day and night about what they were up to and were too blind to see that we had the technology and they didn't have a chance.

# 5

Army Headquarters, I soon learned, was a hotbed of patriotic fervor. Everything was simple. The U.S. military was the one hope of the free world, and global communism was the relentless enemy. We were in Vietnam to stop the spread of a way of life that was far worse than death. Did I believe that? Of course I did. Nothing in my life up to that point would have caused me not to.

I'd never thought much about politics until the fall of my junior year in college. Before then, I'd read newspapers mostly as a way to do well in current events discussions in civics classes. Suddenly it all became real, and I, along with other young Democrats, attended meetings, rang doorbells, and talked earnestly to anyone who, unlike us, was old enough to vote.

The wave of enthusiasm John Kennedy aroused in us was like nothing else I'd ever experienced. Everything that had seemed old and tired now looked young and fresh. Life was full of one thing above all others—possibility. And I and my friends came to take for granted something we had never thought of till then, that we, with our zeal and our confidence in a young man and his view of the world, could make what had been merely hoped for in the past actually happen.

Lubbock, Texas, wasn't an important enough place for a full-blown appearance by the candidates, but they stopped once at the airport on their way to someplace else. We were there, waving our banners and screaming louder than at any pep rally, no matter how important the game. John Kennedy—young, self-assured, more handsome than we could have imagined—stepped out of the plane onto the platform at the top of the portable stairway. Lyndon Johnson, with his big ears and big smile, stood just behind.

We screamed and moved our banners up and down in time to "The Eyes of Texas" being blared out by a high school band. The two men up on the platform waved and nodded but mostly smiled. Johnson stepped forward to introduce his running-mate. After his twangy voice, Kennedy's sounded remote and aristocratic. We couldn't make out much of what he was saying since the wind was blowing his words across to the other side of the runway, so we just yelled every time we realized he'd stopped for a breath. We handed our banners back and forth to each other so we could all take pictures.

Johnson waved and went back inside the plane. Kennedy stood for a minute with both arms raised above his head. Then he went inside, the stairs were rolled away, and the plane was gone.

When Kennedy won, we were uncontrollable. We may not

have been much of a deciding factor, but we'd been a part of it all the same. They'd called us idealistic, the old cynics, for thinking the world could be a better place. Well, we'd shown them. The old farts—that's what all of us called them—the old farts had had their day. Now it was our turn.

The black-and-white television set in the dormitory lounge was too small to contain the enormity of that cold, bright January day in Washington. Eisenhower looked properly old and of another age. Kennedy looked properly young and full of vigor and ideas.

"Let the word go forth from this time and place," he said, in a speech I quickly memorized, "to friend and foe alike, that the torch has been passed to a new generation of Americans—born in this century, tempered by war, disciplined by a hard and bitter peace, proud of our ancient heritage—and unwilling to witness or permit the slow undoing of those human rights to which this nation has always been committed, and to which we are committed today, at home and around the world.

"Let every nation know, whether it wishes us well or ill, that we shall pay any price, bear any burden, meet any hardship, support any friend or oppose any foe to assure the survival and success of liberty."

Yes, that's it exactly, we all thought. We may be young and idealistic, but we know as much about liberty and what it requires as any old fart. Just get out of our way. What we were watching that day, we were convinced, was the dawning of a new era, in which the young and the bright and the undaunted, bolstered by compassion and firm resolve, would create a world full of opportunity and prosperity for all its people.

"Let the word go forth" indeed.

His death, horrifying in its unexpectedness, only made our burden that much greater. I stood in line all night, with thousands of others, to walk by his casket, lying still and majestic in the Capitol rotunda. And I went out to Memorial Bridge to watch him roll slowly across to Virginia to his final resting place. I didn't say it to myself in so many words, I wasn't self-aware enough for that, but I did feel the heavy weight of his legacy. It was up to us, the young and still-living, to keep working for what he had believed in.

# 6

It took Boots and me nearly three weeks to get the secure room set up and operating. I'd ridden in every morning with the group from Le Van Duyet Street but had usually gotten a special car to drive me home late at night.

A couple of evenings, two or three of the guys took me to different restaurants in Saigon or Cholon. Each time, the others ended up at one of the brothels on Tu Do Street, but I begged off and took a cyclo home by myself. Said I was really tired from all those long hours. Next time, I said. Maybe they believed me, maybe not.

I enjoyed sharing a room with Larry. At first, we exchanged information in short spurts. He'd majored in accounting and was eager to get this over with and start his career. His wife was an operating-room nurse who'd gone back to work after their daughter was born. His wife's mother, recently divorced, had moved to Dayton to help take care of her granddaughter while Larry was away.

One night I was in bed with the light out when Larry came tiptoeing in, trying hard to be quiet.

"It's okay," I said. "I'm still awake."

I flipped on the bedside lamp. He put his shoes, which he'd been carrying, on the floor.

"Can't sleep?" he asked. "Or just started trying?"

"Can't sleep."

"Want to talk, or keep trying?"

"Talk."

"Good," he said. "I could use a little soul-baring."

"Why's that?"

"Because I'm a shit, that's why."

"For going to Tu Do?"

"Yeah. I wish I'd never started. Like you. It'd be easier to not go the first time than to stop once you've been."

"Guess so."

He took off his shirt and pants as he talked.

"I love my wife, you know." He laughed, a little too loud at first, but he caught himself. "God. Listen to me. The oldest line in the books. I'll bet every married soldier on Tu Do Street would say that. Even the ones who don't mean it."

"But you mean it."

He sat on his bed in his underwear.

"I do. Susan's great. Maybe that's one reason I go. Because I've gotten so used to being close to a woman. And these women are so sweet and pretty, Matt. They chew gum and you can't have a serious conversation with them, but they're so soft and cuddly. Oh, god! Every time I come home like this, I tell myself that's the last time. The absolute last time. Never again. What I'll do when I'm tempted is think of Susan and all I owe her, and I just won't go. But. . . . like tonight. I get downtown, someone says, 'How about a drink with the girls?' and I think, 'Sure. One drink won't hurt anything. I'll laugh with them a little and feel a little less lonely and come right home.' But I don't."

"So *are* you less lonely? Afterwards?"

He hesitated.

"Not really," he said. "So I go right back again."

He was quiet for a minute. "You know what really bothers me, don't you?"

"No, what?"

"I keep praying I won't pick anything up. They say the girls are clean. Regular check-ups and all. But who knows? A lot of guys go in and out of there in a week."

"You can get shots, can't you?"

"Sure, if you catch it in time. God. I just hope I don't get anything that takes a long time to treat. Because Susan, who's a damn good nurse, would spot the symptoms right away and give me hell."

He sighed. "I just want to get this over with and go home. Start living my life."

"I wish I could help, Larry. I honest to god do."

He smiled. "Thanks, Matt. Just keep listening when I get maudlin like this."

"Promise."

He went off down the hall to brush his teeth.

# 7

Most of what I knew about my other housemates I learned in the mornings while we waited for the staff cars to take us to work. Donnie was the most talkative. He usually arrived out on the sidewalk first and would hold court while the rest of us straggled out. He was from Seattle, had finished pre-law, and was headed for Stanford as soon as he got back. We heard all about his fraternity (Kappa Sigma), his girlfriends (all expecting to marry him on his return), his family (large and gregarious), and his dog (at home with Donnie's parents and youngest sister).

Ross and Donnie talked football a good bit. Ross had been a star on his high school team in Arkansas and then played, with distinction, from what I could tell, at West Point. Donnie was in awe, as was Gregg, a farmboy from North Carolina who went through ROTC, got stationed in Germany, and decided the Army might not be a bad career. His wife, a German girl from Garmisch, was lonely in the States and wanted to go home for a few months. Gregg kept telling her no. He was afraid she wouldn't come back.

Keith didn't say much. He was small and blond and had a pretty face. He listened to the others talk, laughed at their jokes, but never tried to interrupt with talk about himself. After that first night, he didn't go out to dinner with us again. He was from Phoenix, he told me in the car once on the way to work, but that's about all I knew.

I talked some about the Pentagon, showed them pictures of Joanne, and listened to tired jokes about Texas. But I was far more interested in what they had to say.

One morning, Donnie and Larry and Ross were arguing about some baseball team. Keith was daydreaming at the edge of the curb. I had just come out the front door and was talking to Gregg. Someone, it must have been Larry, yelled "Grenade!" I looked fast, saw something dark coming over the top of a van parked in front of the house next door, and dove into the alley. My elbows and knees hurt like hell. I heard the explosion behind me, and the ground shook.

I had no idea what to do. How long to lie still. Who might be waiting on the street for me to stick my head out and look around. I kept lying there until I heard voices behind me. Someone said, "Jesus, Mary, and Joseph." I stood up and leaned against the alley wall of the house. I couldn't put any weight on my right knee. I limped around the corner.

Donnie and Ross were over by the front door. Gray smoke drifted down the block, and a bitter smell hit my nose. Blood covered the sidewalk. Gregg lay face down, his back a mass of raw meat. Pieces of Keith and Larry, ripped out of them by jagged shards of steel, were scattered across the sidewalk and out into the street.

The three of us left standing were useless. We just stared and kept saying, "Jesus Christ." I don't know who called the ambulance or the MPs. They arrived about the same time as the staff cars.

Gregg was alive, barely. Two corpsmen rushed him into the ambulance, and they wailed off down the street. One staff car took Ross and Donnie to Headquarters to begin making a report. The other took me to the hospital to have my elbows and knees seen to.

Before we could get by to visit him, Gregg was flown to a trauma care unit in Japan, where he recovered. Larry and Keith, friends for a short time but friends nonetheless, were gathered up into long dark bags with zippers and sent home to their families.

# 8

The next morning, all the officers assigned to Headquarters reported to the big briefing room on the first floor. There were hundreds of us, and we were jammed in together. It was hot and stuffy as a colonel from security talked for a long, long time.

"You've got to understand the kind of war we're fighting here, men," he said. "It's not a classic confrontation of two conventional military forces. Far from it. It's a guerrilla war, fought from the inside as well as the outside. The enemy is everywhere. Right here on this base. All over the BOQs. Working in our mess halls. Driving our jeeps.

"We do our damndest to root out the sympathizers, and we're getting better at it all the time. But we can't do it with a hundred percent accuracy. These gooks are clever. Much cleverer than we realized at first. And their minds work different from ours. They have no concept of loyalty, the way we understand it. Just because we hire them and pay them good wages doesn't mean they give a damn about us. They're perfectly capable of taking our money, smiling at us, making those funny little bows, and running right off to Viet Cong headquarters to report all they've seen."

He looked from one side of the room to the other. He held a pointer in his right hand, though he had nothing to point at, and kept slapping it into the palm of his left.

"Worst of all, men—and this is what we're here about this morning—they have no respect for the sanctity of human life. It's part of their culture. Living and dying are all the same to them, so they don't have the sense of every individual being sacred that we've all grown up believing.

"Two of our finest young officers were killed yesterday on the streets of Saigon. They were not engaged in battle. They were not even armed. They were standing on a sidewalk waiting for a car to bring them here. Some traitor in our midst hid behind a van and threw a grenade at them. This was the act of a coward, unwilling to show himself and fight a fair fight.

"It was a terrible act, and we are all justifiably outraged, but in a way, although he never intended it, this bastard has done us a favor. He has given us the opportunity to remind ourselves what kind of an enemy it is we're fighting.

"He is sneaky. He is everywhere. And he can't be trusted. I want each and every one of you to remember those three things. Especially the last. You have to operate on the assumption that there is not one Vietnamese you can trust. Not the ARVN soldier who works alongside you. Not the mama-san in the BOQ who shines your shoes."

I saw Donnie and Ross sitting together up near the front. I wished I'd thought to wait for them by the door.

"I know all this is discouraging and makes you wonder what the hell we're here for. Why should our boys die to bring freedom to people who don't understand it or appreciate it? There are two answers to that. The first is that freedom is what we stand for. It's what our country was founded on, and we have dedicated our national treasure and the blood of our finest young men to spreading it around the world.

"The second is that global tyranny is on the march. The communists are armed and dangerous. And they will stop at nothing. Their goal is nothing less than the subjugation of every man, woman, and child on this planet. Much as we would like to stay home with our wives, tend our gardens, play a little golf, and watch our children grow up, the men of America have said 'No' to tyranny. We have said 'Enough. This far and no further.' Communist aggression has already engulfed half the globe. We cannot afford to let it go one inch further."

He was right. Why was I wishing I were someplace else?

"Vietnam is a small country. It is of little importance in the world community in and of itself. It makes nothing the world needs. It has no oil, no uranium, no natural resources to speak of. But what it represents is of paramount importance to all of us. It represents a line drawn in the sand by brave men willing to lay down their lives in the cause of liberty. However ungrateful or uncomprehending the recipients may be, the gift of freedom is America's legacy to the rest of humanity.

"Well, so much for philosophy."

Good, I thought.

"What we've really asked you here for today is some nitty-gritty. We're involved in a war like no other we've ever fought. We're surrounded here by treachery. Every gook in the street is a potential enemy. How do we protect ourselves? Two ways. With our brains, and with our anger. First of all, we've got to realize that these people, though clever, are not smarter than we are. Far from it. We just have to learn to think the way they do. What they look for is routine. Those officers made the mistake of establishing a routine. Every morning they gathered in the same place at the same time. It was like an open invitation. The way to counteract terrorism is to vary your schedule. Never do the same thing twice. Meet the car one day at five-thirty, the next at seven, and the next at six-fifteen. It plays hell with efficiency, but if it saves lives, which it does, it's well worth it."

Sure, I thought. Who told us when to meet the cars and where? Who waited to give us this lecture until Larry and Keith were dead?

"Now, we're not going to ask you men to stop going into Saigon for some food that's not cooked by a mess sergeant and for some pleasant company." He winked. "But we *are* asking you to be more careful. Don't expose yourself to danger. Don't wait out on a sidewalk. Wait inside the building. Present no target if you can help it. Look up and down every street, behind every parked car. Be alert all the time. You hear me, men? *All* the time. And the most important thing of all: trust no one who's not an American. No one. They'll kill you without a second thought. Use your brains.

"But also use your anger. Use it to your advantage and to the advantage of our effort over here. Let your outrage at the deaths of these fine young men fuel your resolve to fight on, as long as it takes. When we win, as we surely will, Captain Laurence Ford and Lieutenant Keith Richards will not have died in vain."

The assembled officers rose and cheered.

# 9

The two deaths concentrated the attention of the housing officers admirably. Within days, the three of us left on Le Van Duyet Street were absorbed into the BOQ. I moved into a third-floor room with Captain Brent Cameron. The room was large and pleasant, two twin beds, two wooden armoires, and two chairs. Three big windows looked out toward the runways at Tan Son Nhut. One end of the long narrow tiled bathroom served as an uncurtained shower stall.

Brent was a combat intelligence officer, one of Major Sinclair's stable of briefers who performed with vu-graph slides and pointers at Friday morning sessions. Company intelligence officers, or their representatives, came in from the field to find out what was going on.

All the briefers had been carefully selected, but Brent was the acknowledged star. I'd been to several of those briefings, and I could see why. People waited for his turn to talk. He was tall and muscular, and his rugged, not quite handsome features were compelling. He was Army manhood at its most admirable. An officer who looked and talked and acted like an officer.

He was clearly from the deepest of the Deep South. I found out later it was Mississippi, a fact of which he was inordinately proud. I'd grown up around Southern accents, of course, the twangy Texas kind primarily. Never met a person without one, in fact, until I went to college. But Brent's was the most liquid I'd ever heard. It poured out like heavy molasses.

The trouble was he was loud, in a way I found offensive. He talked loudly and laughed loudly, often at what seemed to me like inappropriate times. He liked to sit on the corners of desks and tell raunchy jokes, most of the ones I overheard having to do with sex or excretion. Brent was a man's man, and the other officers loved him.

He was in the room when I hauled up my two suitcases late in the afternoon, my knee aching all the way. He came toward me with his hand outstretched. I set down the suitcases.

"Fairchild," he said. "Brent Cameron. We haven't really met." He laughed.

My aim was bad, and his hand closed around the ends of

my fingers. They folded up when he squeezed them. Damn, I thought.

"Roomie who just left had the bed by the windows. I'll move over there now, if you don't mind." He laughed.

"I don't mind," I said. "So this is my armoire?"

"All yours. I just finished moving my stuff. Fellah left this morning for Danang. Lucky shit."

"Why is that?"

"You kidding? Out of this candy-ass place to where something's actually happening?"

"Meaning you wish you'd gone instead."

"You bet your sweet life I do."

"Career Army?"

"Absolutely. With a job to learn and tickets to punch. HQ looks great on the resume, but there's no point in overdoing." He laughed. "Two months? Fine. I'll give 'em that. Now get me the fuck out to the field."

"To each his own," I said.

"ROTC tourist, right? Just passing through? I forgive you."

"Thanks."

He laughed. "With that grenading, though, you've seen a hell of a lot more action than I have. So you're the real veteran in this room. But I'll catch up soon, you can bet on that."

"I hope so," I said.

He looked at me hard for a second. Then he laughed.

"I'll head on down to the bar and get started on the evening's drinking," he said. "You join me there when you're settled, and we'll do some catching up over dinner."

After my first drink and what I guessed was Brent's third, he suggested we go to Cholon for Chinese food. The sense of danger and apprehension I'd been feeling the past few days was waning and the fatalism of the rest of the guys seemed to be a better way to proceed. Brent and I climbed into a cyclo and careened off toward town.

Brent's favorite restaurant, the Golden Dragon, was noisy and crowded, but after a short wait, maybe ten minutes, we were shown to a table. Brent ordered for both of us—whole steamed fish and Peking duck.

"You don't mind if I take over, do you?" he asked.

I did mind, but what was the point? He obviously knew more about Chinese food than I did, so I said, "No, not at all."

As we ate our soup, we went through the Southern scene-setting small talk I could do in my sleep. Where do you come from? How long have your people been there? Where were they before? Where did *their* people come from? Mine had arrived in east Texas from South Carolina by way of Mississippi. Brent was aghast that I had no idea what part.

"We could be related," he said.

"I doubt it."

He looked at me and didn't laugh.

When our meal came, I picked up my fork.

"You can't eat Chinese food this good with a *fork*," Brent said, waving his chopsticks.

I thought probably I could, but I was curious to know how chopsticks worked, and it looked as if Brent knew. He did. He showed me what to do, slowly and patiently. He put the two sticks in the proper position in my hand and moved my thumb back and forth to demonstrate the pincer action that held the food in place. Each time I dropped a piece of fish or a clump of rice, he carefully showed me again.

We ate in silence for a while as I concentrated on working the chopsticks.

"You married?" he asked.

"No," I said. "You?"

He shrugged. "I was engaged once, but. . . . C'est la vie. Great-looking woman. Now, with the war and all, things are too complicated. You never settle down long enough to meet anyone. Maybe later. When it's all over."

"How'd you get to be regular Army?" I asked.

He glanced up from his rice and duck. "Applied and got accepted."

"No. I mean *why*? Is it something you always wanted to do?"

"Sure," he said. "White knight on a charger? Save the world? Why not?" His voice was loud, and he laughed.

I watched him eat for a minute.

"So what did you think of Colonel Fox's speech the other day?" I asked.

He glanced up again. "Terrific, wasn't it? Put everything into perspective. Why we're here. What we're trying to do. That's one reason I want to get out to the countryside. Things are clearer out there, from what I hear. Good guys fighting bad guys. Soldiers fighting soldiers.

"Here, nothing's what it seems to be. People smile and bow, call you 'Numbah one GI,' and throw grenades at you. It's too confusing. I can't handle that kind of stuff. Give me straight-out, upfront conflict any day. Me over here. Him over there. Let the best man win."

We paid our bill and walked along the street outside.

"Want to go down to Tu Do?" Brent asked. "Have a drink at least with some of the bar girls?"

"No, thanks," I said. "I'm pretty bushed. You go ahead, though. I'll be fine."

He thought for a minute. "No," he said. "That's all right. I'd better show you the way home."

As the weeks passed, we had breakfast together every morning, rode side by side on the bus to Headquarters, and usually hooked up for lunch. Sometimes, one or the other of us, or both, would go back to Headquarters after supper to work. Brent slipped off to Tu Do Street by himself from time to time, but all he said was that that's where he'd been. We didn't discuss it, and when we were out together, he came right home with me. He liked to go by the Officers' Club for a few drinks and a few pulls on the slot machines, and sometimes I'd go with him. Or to the bar downstairs in the BOQ for a drink or two.

A good many nights, though, after or instead of other activities, we were both in our room reading. I was surprised at how much Brent read. There were some shelves on the first floor where we could put books we'd finished and take ones we hadn't read. Brent plowed through them at the rate of two or three a week, far ahead of my own one-a-week pace. I realized those quiet, comfortable times together were not what I'd expected when I moved in with him.

Every evening before he went to bed, whether it was early or late, whether he was drunk or sober, Brent took a shower. His routine never varied. After he'd thrown his dirty shorts into the pile on the floor of his armoire, he would sling a towel over his shoulder, instead of wrapping it around his waist, and walk the length of the room from the windows into the bathroom. When he'd finished his shower, he reversed the process. Towel on his shoulder, he walked back to the armoire for a clean pair of shorts.

I very much enjoyed the view. The muscles all over his body were strong and pleasingly shaped. If he had worked out with weights, he was a master sculptor. If not, then nature was.

I made a habit of reading in bed instead of sitting up in a chair the way Brent did. I learned to hold my book just high enough that I could watch Brent under the bottom edge as he came and went. Long lovely penis as he came toward me. Firm white buttocks with a slight little bounce as he went. For those moments each evening, I was right where I wanted to be.

One Sunday we went to Saigon early in the afternoon. We walked around the zoo and stopped to watch the nervous little animals with unhappy eyes pace the limits of their concrete and steel cages. A bear with a heavy brown coat unsuited to that heat walked the length of his narrow space, his claws clicking each time they touched the floor. At the far end, he rose on his hind legs, breathed a quick snort through his nose, spun around, and returned to the near end, where he rose again. Down and back. Down and back. His pace never changed. The sound of his snort was always the same. Down and back. Down and back.

At dinner that night in Cholon, Brent couldn't stop talking and asking questions. His childhood. My childhood. His sisters. My brother. Mississippi. Texas. Family. Fishing. Mostly, he kept his eyes on his plate, and his voice was so low I had to strain to hear him.

"Are you glad you are who you are?" he asked. He didn't look up.

"I guess so," I said. "I never thought much about it."

"I'm not."

"You're joking!"

He looked up at me and back down.

"But all the guys think you're terrific," I said. "You're everybody's hero."

"Not everybody's," he said.

I wanted him to keep talking, but I had no idea which direction to go.

"Who doesn't think so?" I asked.

"Lots of people. They know I'm a fake."

I wished I could put my hand on his shoulder but didn't dare.

"A fake how?" I asked.

He laid his chopsticks down and stared at his plate.

"I created myself, Matt," he said. "I turned a skinny body into a strong one. And a basically quiet, shy kid into a loudmouth. Is that wrong, Matt?" He glanced at me. "To want to be something else? Something people can look up to?"

"Of course not, Brent," I said. "We all want to be the best we can be."

He looked back down. “The best,” he said. “I wonder.”

He picked up his chopsticks and started to eat again. He talked as he ate, quietly and without inflection.

“When I was a little kid, I loved music. The other kids hated piano lessons, but I begged my parents to let me take. My mother thought it was a good idea, and my father did too, till he saw how serious I was about it. ‘Don’t get carried away, son,’ he would say. ‘A little bit’s fine, but don’t let it detract from more important things.’

“I kept up my piano, though, long after all the other kids quit. And in high school I added trumpet so I could march in the band. That was a blow to my father, who wished I was playing on the team instead of in the halftime show. But he was good about it. Never complained.

“The end of my sophomore year, the boy who’d been drum major for two years was graduating. The band director, Mr. Perkins, asked if I’d consider trying out. ‘You’ve got a good sense of rhythm,’ he said. ‘You’re tall and nice-looking. I think you’d do just fine.’”

He’d stopped eating and was looking at the empty chair across from him.

“God, I was excited. Drum major! I couldn’t believe it. Out there in front of everybody leading the whole show. Maybe I *would* be good at it and end up being a band director myself. Or a conductor even. Why not?

“Chris, the kid who was graduating, agreed to give me some pointers. Twice a week after school he showed me what to do. ‘You’re good, Brent,’ he said. ‘Boy, you’re really good. I’ll bet you’re the one they pick.’

“One night after supper I was in my room studying when my dad came in. He sat on the edge of the bed.

“‘I’ve had some disappointing news, son,’ he said.

“‘What’s that?’ I asked.

“‘Marvin Jackson drove by the schoolyard this afternoon

and saw you prancing around with that Wheeler boy. Waving a big silver baton, Marvin said.'

"I waited.

"'Tell me it isn't so, son,' Dad said. 'Tell me you're not thinking of doing such a thing.'

"'It's nothing definite, Dad,' I said. 'They asked if I'd consider it, and I was just trying to find out if I was any good.'

"'Don't do this to me, Brent,' Dad said. 'Please. I'd never be able to hold my head up in this town again.' He wiped his brow. 'I've tried not to interfere in your life, son. And I don't remember asking you many favors. But I'm asking you now.'

"'I'm sorry,' I said. 'I wasn't thinking.'

"Dad got up, smiled at me, patted me on the shoulder, and went out."

I waited, but he didn't continue.

"So you told the director you couldn't try out," I said.

"Yes."

"And you quit the band?"

He looked up and nodded. He was drumming his chopsticks on the tabletop.

"Think you'll ever go back to your music?" I asked.

He stopped drumming.

"Maybe," he said. "In my next incarnation."

# 10

Through the large windows beside Brent's bed, we could see most of Tan Son Nhut—clusters of buildings up close, long runways, more buildings on the other side. We'd been given box seats, from which we had an unobstructed view of the dramas of attack and counterattack that interrupted many nights long after midnight. A barrage of rockets or mortar rounds always began it, often followed by groups of sappers infiltrating on the ground, trying to blow up a plane or an ammo dump or whatever they could find.

Sometimes we put pillows over our heads and tried to sleep. Other nights we sat and watched the show. First the blasts as the rounds began to hit. Orange balls of flame that ballooned up and subsided. Next the bright arcs of the flares, trailing sparks like a comet. Then the intermittent rattling of automatic rifle fire. The favorite targets all seemed to be on the far side of the huge airfield, which made it look more like a fireworks display than a life-threatening event.

One night, though, something woke me out of a sound sleep. Had the BOQ been shaken? I couldn't be sure. I sat up in bed. An explosion just outside lit up the room, and the building swayed.

Brent was leaning on the sill of one of the windows looking out. "My god!" he said. I went and knelt on the bed beside him. The warehouse next door was in flames. One group of men, shouting and waving, dragged hoses up and began spraying foam on the burning building. Another group, quieter and more intent, moved past the building firing automatic rifles as they went.

I heard the whistle of a round coming toward us. It exploded near the men with the hoses. Several of them fell to the ground. The shouting grew louder. Another long whistle. An explosion off to the left.

Brent put his arm around my shoulder. "Is this it, do you think?" he asked. "Is this where we get it?"

I slid my arm around his waist. "My god, it could be," I said. "Shouldn't we be doing something?"

"Yeah," he said. He reached up and turned my face toward him. He kissed me hard on the mouth. He pushed his own shorts down, then mine. He ran his big hand down my back and rested it on the curve of my buttocks. I shivered, put my arms around him, and pulled him close. We pressed against each other, breathing fast.

Another explosion shook the BOQ. Rifle fire just outside the window sputtered, stopped, sputtered once more. He kissed me again, eased me down onto the bed, and turned me over. I heard him spit and then felt him push into me from behind. I winced, and he stopped, but I pulled at his leg and he moved on in. That first sharp pain was a small price to pay for what followed.

Afterward, we lay side by side on Brent's bed, arms around each other, listening to the sounds fade off into the distance. "Guess they're going to miss us after all," he said.

"Guess so."

I stayed in his arms until his breathing became slow and regular and his hand slipped off my shoulder. I kissed him lightly on the forehead, stood up, pulled up my shorts, and went back to my bed.

The shower was running when I woke. It went off, and Brent walked into the room, drying his hair.

"Hi," I said.

"Morning." He kept drying and didn't look at me. He took a clean pair of shorts out of his armoire and pulled them on.

"So," I said, stretching. "Did you enjoy it as much as I did?"

"The mortars and stuff, you mean?" He stepped into his fatigue pants, still not looking at me. "Yeah. It was really exciting, wasn't it?"

"No," I said. "I meant the other."

He turned and looked at me steadily. "What other?"

I wrinkled my forehead, then gave two little nods. I got up and walked to the far window.

"Jesus, what a mess," I said. "We were lucky."

Brent came and stood beside me. "I'd say so, yes. Damn lucky. That depot next door's pretty well demolished."

"Wonder how many we lost?"

"Quite a few, I'll bet, from the look of things. Steve will know. I'll ask him when I see him this morning and tell you at lunch."

"Good," I said. "I'd be interested to hear."

I walked into the bathroom to pee and brush my teeth.

Brent stuck his head around the corner. "Meet you downstairs for breakfast?"

I nodded.

## 11

Not even a week later I ran into Brent on the stairs at Headquarters. "Great news, Matt!" he said, loudly. "I just heard. I'm gonna get to see this fucking war after all." He laughed.

"Oh?" I said.

"Colonel Dunhill got me reassigned. Combat intelligence for the 25th Division at Cu Chi. Isn't that terrific?"

"If you say so."

"Candy-ass!"

I chuckled. You know better than that, I thought.

"Our big attack wasn't enough for you, then?" I asked.

"You kidding? It only whetted my appetite." He laughed.

"How soon?" I asked.

"Three days. I'll hitch a ride with a convoy of choppers on Thursday. You up for Chinese food tonight? I won't be seeing many restaurants for a while, that's for sure."

The buildup had kept coming so fast that rooms were at a premium. On the day Brent left, another captain moved in. Craig Fuller, who had something to do with supply. I shifted over to the bed by the windows. He slept in the one by the door.

He had his own friends, a hard-drinking bunch of gamblers

who played poker, pool, and bridge for high stakes. He loved breezing in to tell me how much he'd won. I don't think he lost very often. He wore his shorts to and from the shower, and he never read a book that I was aware of. We had breakfast together a couple of times, when his buddies were hung over, I gathered, but that was about it.

## 12

The Sunday after Brent left, I went into Saigon by myself. I walked around the Botanical Gardens and sat on the grass near a bridge that spanned a pond full of floating lilies.

I had no way of sorting out what it all meant. If Brent had been willing to talk about it, maybe together we could have made some sense of it. Alone I was lost.

Did I love him? Probably, but I had no reference points for deciding one way or the other. I'd been fond of girls, sure. Dated them, necked with them, gone steady with them. But the emotions I'd felt for them resembled in no way what I now felt for Brent. How could they? Every girl I'd ever been close to had stayed outside where she belonged. Brent had become a part of me.

But did I love him? Nothing in my upbringing allowed for that possibility. As I'd grown up, I'd been taught that it was my duty to love God, love the United States of America, love my family, and love women. Those were the only choices I had.

The person who'd taught me the most about what a boy should be was my grandmother. She was a formidable woman who looked exactly the way a grandmother ought to look—matronly, well-cared-for, and eminently sensible. Her dresses and shoes, though elegant, tended toward maroons and navy blues. She combed her long hair out every evening and braided it into a tidy bun on the back of her neck every morning. And she never went out of the house, except to a picnic or to my grandfather's fishing cabin, without putting on a hat and a pair of gloves.

First and foremost, though, Grandmother was a Presbyterian. Her Scotch-Irish ancestors, of whom she was exceedingly proud, were all Presbyterians, and nothing could induce her to be anything else. Spending all those summers with her had acquainted me with her version of it. From the time I was old enough to sit still and look interested, I went with her to Sunday morning services, Sunday evening services, and Wednesday night prayer meetings as well. Since I loved Grandmother and wanted very much to please her, I tried hard to grasp the essentials of what was involved, but I never really succeeded.

I'd liked religion just fine when it was mostly singing pretty hymns and making little sheep out of cotton balls to stand up beside cut-out shepherds. Later on, it got to be more complicated.

A lot of it, I'd discovered through the years, had to do with people being bad. We were born that way, as part of some cosmic plan that either could or could not be changed. Whether the truth was one or the other, or both, was the central enigma I could never figure out. The way I'd gotten it, God knew everything. Of course. He put it all in motion and kept it running. Since He knew the past and the present, He must also know the future. And His knowing the future meant everything was already set, from as soon as He knew it. What was going to be was going to be, and our petty little human desires couldn't change that.

But—and here was the part that had confused me the most—it was still up to each of us to make the right decisions every minute of every day. To choose between the way of God and the way of the Devil.

The choice was there because, back when things were just getting started, God and the Devil had entered into some kind of bargain. God got to write the Bible, which everyone would recognize as the authoritative and unchallengeable blueprint for the way we were supposed to live. And God got to send His Son—the most wise and loving person ever born—down to Earth to show us that someone really could live that way, even if it wasn't quite fair since Jesus was half-holy. Then, to top it off, Jesus got to die this dramatic death, with earthquakes and thunder and veils in temples being rent in two, which turned out to be only temporary, since right away He got to come back to life and rise up off a mountaintop into the bosom of His Father.

This was powerful stuff. I hadn't thought about it much in recent years, after I'd gotten off on my own and had gone to church more out of habit than conviction. But if I'd been pressed to say what I thought about the matter, I would have had to admit that God had gotten the best of the bargain. Stacked the deck and dealt Himself an unbeatable hand. Life was beginning to show me that this wasn't so after all. The Devil, by getting to be in charge of everything that was any fun, had more than evened things up. Either the Devil was smart when he negotiated that deal or God wanted to make living a righteous life so hard only the truly faithful would succeed, but the fact was that the more enjoyable a thing was, the more of a sin it was likely to be. So much so, I now saw, that the most enjoyable thing I would ever do in my life was the absolutely most sinful of all.

No wonder Brent wouldn't talk about it. No wonder he left for Cu Chi as soon as he could. I was the oddball, for not being overcome by the guilt the whole force of my upbringing had tried to make sure I would feel.

# 13

Boots made every day a pleasure. He was smart and efficient and very funny. His humor could only be described as irreverent. He tiptoed along a thin line between what was allowed with an officer, and what was not. But within those limitations, pretty much everything and everyone was fair game.

His desk was on the far side of the room, facing mine. I liked looking up and seeing him there. He was of medium height and brawny, with blond hair cut so short it was just a hint of color across his scalp. His blond mustache was even harder to see. It made me think of a kid who'd gulped down a glass of milk and then wiped away most of the residue that had stuck to his upper lip. Boots was proud of that mustache, though, so I never mentioned it.

We worked hard, updating the maps and preparing special briefings, but we enjoyed ourselves, too. A couple of times a day we'd put our feet up on our desks, jungle boots plopped right on top, and smoke a cigarette together.

"So, Cap'm," he said one morning. "You hear about the deep shit the Big Red One got themselves into last week?"

"I don't even know what a Big Red One is."

"Jesus, sir! Not what. Who! The First Division. Up at Ben Cat."

"I *have* heard of them."

"Well, I should hope so. Want me to tell you?"

"Looks like you'd better. I've got a lot to learn."

He grinned.

"They had this assault planned for just at daylight. Big fleet of choppers. Couple of platoons. They'd heard there was a concentration of VC somewheres—maybe from us, who knows?—and they thought they'd go flush 'em out. Get 'em on the run and fly in a couple more platoons to finish 'em off.

That's what always happened before. But this time was a whole lot different."

"In what way?"

"The VC didn't run. Can you even believe it? Stood and fought. Shot down three choppers of the first assault. And when reinforcements got flown in, they shot down two more. Where'd they ever learn to do that?"

"Practice, I'd guess. Wouldn't you?"

"Yeah, but they've always just backed off when we went in with that much force. They're gonna start shooting us down, we're gonna have to do some rethinking."

He inhaled and blew a perfect smoke ring, one of his many talents. It drifted toward the ceiling, growing larger and fainter as it rose.

"How long've you been in-country, Boots?"

"Ten weeks tomorrow."

"Amazing. You must be a real quick learner."

"How's that, Cap'm?"

"Well. Here you are talking about what the VC have always done. And rethinking tactics."

"I been here before."

"My god. Like a whole tour?"

"Yessir. A whole tour."

"When?"

"'63-'64."

"And they made you come back two years later?"

"Wasn't a matter of 'making' me do anything, Cap'm. I volunteered." He took a long puff.

I stared at him.

"Something wrong with that, Cap'm?"

"No, of course not," I said. "It just surprises me is all. I mean, I'm wondering how hard it's going to be getting through *one* year, and here you are starting all over again. I admire your patriotism."

"It's not so much I'm patriotic, Cap'm, although I guess I am. I'd say it's more I'm realistic."

I shook my head. "Coming back to a place where people get killed is realistic?"

"For me? Sure it is." He looked at me steadily and blew another smoke ring. "I'm career Army, Cap'm, don't forget. Fighting wars is what armies do. So when there's one going on, that's where a bright, ambitious young sergeant needs to be."

"But. . . . Do you like it, Boots? Fighting wars?"

He narrowed his eyes. "Do I like it?" He shifted his feet, putting the left under the right for a while.

"I don't *love* it," he said, "the way some of the guys do. I don't think it's the greatest thing an adult man could spend his time doing. But there's a lot of satisfaction in it, yessir. You?"

"No, I don't like it. I think it's something that has to be done, I guess. Mostly because there's no one else in the world to do it. But. . . . I don't know."

"What, Cap'm?"

"I just. . . . I think what we're trying to do is right. Keep communism from spreading and give these people a chance to create a democracy for themselves. That part is fine. But I'm not so sure we know *how*."

"Welcome to Nam, Cap'm."

"But surely it wasn't like this when you were here before. Was it?"

"Worse, Cap'm. Far worse. Absolute frigging chaos. No one had a clue what the hell was going on. You think it's bad now? You shoulda seen it then. Diem was a turkey in a lotta ways, so they say. Cold as ice, no personality, and always favoring the Catholics over the Buddhists, of which there are a helluva lot more. But at least he managed to keep things together. Or was able to make it look like that's what he was doing. Once he got bumped off, though, it was a circus. Just a parade of incompetents, each one nuttier than the last. Pure free-for-all. Now that part I'm sure about, cause I saw it."

"You think we had a hand in it? Diem getting killed?"

He looked at me steadily. "Is the Pope Catholic?"

"But why? Didn't we know it would just get worse?"

"*Know*, Cap'm? You keep saying that. In this country, we don't *know* shit. We just keep ad libbing, doing the best we can. It's like. . . . It's like what's really happening just disappeared around a bend way off down the road, and we're huffing along trying to catch up. Soon as we get to that bend and think we're finally gonna get a good look at it, we catch a glimpse of its dust disappearing around the *next* bend. You see what I'm saying?"

"Perfectly."

"But that doesn't mean we oughta just give up. Just say, 'Aw, fuck,' and go on home. People here've gotten to depend on us. Staked their lives on our being around. We owe them something, don't we?"

"I guess," I said, rubbing the back of my neck. "It's just—"

"What, Cap'm?"

"Oh, I don't know." I laughed. "There I go again. What I mean is, you're right. I'm sure you're right. We just seem to be losing so many men, doing so much damage to everything, to not be getting anywhere."

"That's what you and me are here for, Cap'm. Sticking pieces of tape up on maps. We're trying to see if it's possible to get a grip on things. Help find a way to do something that'll work. I think we can do that."

"You do?"

"Fuckin' A. Don't you?"

I stubbed my cigarette out in the ashtray.

"Yeah, Boots. Yeah, I do."

## 14

I was on my way from Colonel Dunhill's office back to the secure room. All the desks in the big G-2 room were empty, and everyone was congregated by the windows on the east side. I went over but couldn't see out for all the bodies.

"What's up?" I asked Captain Osborne, one of the briefers.

"Concert time."

"What?"

"The CG's Monday morning band concert. Didn't you know?"

"Are you kidding? I had no idea."

"You should spend more time out here in the fresh air."

I pushed around beside him, and sure enough, a band was marching across the lawn toward us. Four abreast and eight deep. A thirty-two-piece band in fatigues and jungle boots.

"I don't believe it," I said.

"Well, there it is."

The sergeant out in front blew his whistle, and the band halted. He turned to face them, held up his hands, and whistled again. They began to play. "The Washington Post March." "When the Saints Go Marching In." "My Bonnie Lies Over the Ocean." "Abide With Me." "It's a Long Way to Tipperary." "My Blue Heaven." "When the Caissons Go Rolling Along." "Onward, Christian Soldiers." And, for a finale, "The Stars and Stripes Forever." Half an hour, almost to the minute.

The sergeant whistled, and the band did an about face. The sergeant did a left face, a right face, a right face, and a left face, ending up out in front of the band. He whistled, and they all marched away.

"Every Monday?" I asked.

"Every Monday," said Osborne. "0900 sharp."

"My god," I said.

## 15

Somehow I caught the eye of a major over in ordnance. When we'd meet from time to time on the stairs at Headquarters, he would beam at me. We could read each other's names over the pockets of our fatigues, so introductions weren't necessary.

"Captain Fairchild," he'd say, his eyes crinkling.

"Major Carlisle," I'd say.

Sometimes in the Officers' Mess, he would bring his tray over and we'd eat together.

"You know about my motorcycle, of course," he said one day at lunch.

"No. Should I?"

"Oh, dear," he said, the corners of his mouth turning down. "I thought I was famous."

"You probably are. It's just I'm sort of isolated most of the time."

"Right. In that secret room on the second floor. Must be exciting."

"Not really. Just a lot of details to keep up with."

"You're terribly modest. How becoming."

Uh-oh, I thought.

"So what about this motorcycle?" I asked.

"I bought it off a captain four months ago, and I'm crazy about it. I'd never ridden one before, but I find I have a natural flair for it."

"Good for you."

"You'll have to come riding with me sometime. It's great fun."

"But isn't it dangerous? You're like a moving target out there, seems to me."

"Dangerous? Maybe it is, but who cares? All I know is it's

very exciting, roaring down the streets. Scarf flying out behind. People jumping out of the way. I love it. I bet you would, too."

"I'll have to think about it."

He took a sip of coffee, and his eyes smiled at me over the rim of the cup.

One day after lunch, I wandered up to the roof of the BOQ. I'd been curious to find out how far you could see from up there.

As I stepped out of the doorway, I saw to my surprise that most of the roof was covered with men sunbathing. Plenty of others spent their lunch break around the pool downstairs, but they kept their suits on, in deference to the mama-sans and visiting nurses, no doubt. These men, more serious about their suntans, had nothing on at all.

Since no one is likely to work on an all-over tan unless he has a body worth showing, the expanse of bare fronts and backs was an erotic feast. A few of the more modest men facing up had draped a corner of a towel across their genitals, but all the backsides were in plain view. Rows and rows of them. I felt a tug in the crotch of my pants.

How long will I be able to enjoy this? I wondered. Pretty soon, someone's going to notice me staring. Sure enough, a man sat up and waved. It was Major Carlisle. He got up and walked over to me. He stood there, stark naked, chatting as casually as if we'd just bumped into each other in the hallway at Headquarters.

"Nice to see you, Captain Fairchild," he said. "What *is* your first name, by the way? We can't keep up this 'Major-Captain' routine forever."

"Matthew."

"Matthew," he said, smiling. "Mine's Frank."

I didn't know where to look. I couldn't let my eyes drift downward, but if I was too conscious about avoiding it, he'd know that's what I was trying not to do. Shit, I thought. I ended up dividing my attention between his face and the runways off in the distance.

"I'm buzzing into Saigon tonight to see some friends," he said. "Want to hop on the back of my cycle and go with me? You'd like my friends, Matthew. They're fun. A reporter and a man from the embassy."

"Thanks, Frank, but I really can't. Too much to do right now. I'll be pretty well tied up the rest of the week."

"In your secret little room?" He smiled knowingly. "I wonder what all goes on in there, just you and that *cute* sergeant of yours."

My heart started beating fast. Jesus, I thought. What message am I sending out that makes him think he can stand there, absolutely naked, and say things like that to me?

"We work, Major," I said. "Very hard."

His eyebrows flew up.

"*Maj*or?" he said. "I see. Well, *Cap*tain, if you should change your mind, you just let me know."

He turned to walk away. I saw that his carefully tanned buttocks were full and nicely rounded. Oh, god, I thought. He looked back over his shoulder in time to catch my glance. He narrowed his eyes and laughed.

# 16

Colonel Dunhill was greatly annoyed.

"I don't get it, Fairchild. We're losing planes like crazy. Two or three a night in some places. But it makes no fucking sense. Our men patrol a perimeter further out than the range of any weapons we know they've got. Mortars and standard rockets. That's always been good enough before, but not any more.

They have to've infiltrated a new weapon with greater range. But what?

"I want you to go up there. Dak To. Nha Trang. Wherever. Get everything you can on those attacks. Numbers of planes destroyed. Dates of attacks. See if you can find a frigging pattern. The ordnance people have been analyzing all the fragments they can find. See if they've come up with anything. We need to find out what weapon they're using and get an estimate of its range so airport security can alter its SOPs. Understand me?"

"Yes, sir."

"Your sergeant can handle the secure room while you're gone?"

"No problem, sir."

"Good. Then stay as long as you need to, but don't dawdle."

"No, sir."

"Ask the sergeant-major for anything you need. You'll have your own chopper and crew. Be ready by 1400."

"Yes, sir."

"This is important, Fairchild. Really important. Don't let me down."

"No, sir."

The chopper was a big Huey with a crew of six—a pilot, a copilot, a sergeant in charge of security, and three gunners. The sergeant was a tough Italian with what had to be a Long Island accent. He was curt and abrupt, sure he knew his job better than anyone else. He probably did. Everyone called him Sarge.

The pilot, a warrant officer called Ace, was tall, with light brown hair and freckles. His copilot, Dapper Dan, was a slender man whose fatigues had been starched and ironed so the crease looked like a knife blade. They stayed in the front of the chopper.

One gunner was a chubby wise guy called Meatball. He talked all the time. "I hope you've made out your will,

Captain," he said as I climbed aboard. "These crates have a life expectancy of about fifteen minutes."

"Shove it, Meatball," said a voice from the rear of the chopper.

"Sure thing, Sarge," said Meatball. "I don't know why they send along a security crew on these little jaunts. We'll all be dead by the time we hit the ground. The VC'll have to gather up little pieces of you and interrogate *them*."

"If you don't shove it, Meatball, I'm gonna make a bowtie outa your tongue."

"Right, Sarge. So the safest place, Captain, is the rear. When the rotors get shot off and you feel us heading down, move toward the. . . ."

"One more syllable, Meatball, and I'm throwing you out the door the second we're airborne."

"Gotcha, Sarge." He moved to the front of the chopper, where Ace and Dapper Dan were flipping switches and checking panels. "So, Ace," said Meatball. "Still nervous about your maiden voyage? No sweat. You have any questions about take-off procedures, you just check with me."

The second gunner was an art history major who'd been drafted two months after he graduated. His nickname, Horny, referred to his dark-rimmed glasses, he told me, not his sexual appetite.

The third gunner was a tall, broad, moon-faced cherub. He should have been singing in a choir, not lugging around a machinegun. His blond curls sat lightly on the top of his head. His cheeks were round and pink, and his eyes were a pale blue. They looked straight at you and seemed always to be smiling.

His nature matched his face. He was all sweetness, as if the sweetness that had filled him when he was a child had grown and expanded right along with his body, rather than shrinking and disappearing the way most people's did. Everyone called him Peaches.

We settled in and took off. Sitting inside the chopper was claustrophobic. It was hot and humid and everything shook and the constant thwap-thwap-thwap of the rotors was deafening. Outside, though, was astonishing beauty. The whole right side of the chopper was open, and the gunners took turns sitting in the open doorway, their heavy flak jackets snapped shut, aiming their huge machineguns at the tops of the trees. Sitting further inside, I could look past whoever was sitting there at the extraordinary colors and shapes speeding by below.

We flew to Nha Trang, Dak To, and Chu Lai, three airfields where planes had been hit in this mysterious way. At each place, local ordnance crews had gathered up as many fragments as they could find. Intelligence officers had talked with everyone who knew anything about the attacks and had written this information down.

I packed up all the fragments, each one wrapped individually and labelled, and put all the papers in a locked briefcase. Back in Nha Trang, the local S-2 provided me with a room off one of the hangars at the airfield. I put everything out on two big tables and called in the team of analysts I'd rounded up—an ordnance lieutenant colonel, a major and a captain from the Corps of Engineers, and a CIA man attached to the embassy in Saigon who was some kind of expert in Communist Bloc ballistics.

The four of them spent hours reading the reports, opening and closing reference books they'd brought along, and arguing, heatedly at times. They brought in four lamps with bright bulbs and examined every fragment under magnifying glasses. They held some of the tiniest fragments up with tweezers and passed them around. I sat and watched.

Late in the afternoon of the second day, they came across some fragments with heavy powder burns on them. The lieutenant colonel took them away with him and was gone for almost an hour. When he came back, he was smiling.

As they began to reach a conclusion, they got more and more excited.

"I think that's it," said the major. "That's what it's got to be. We in agreement?"

"Looks that way," said the CIA man. "But I have to say I'm surprised. I thought they were being more careful than that."

"It's a trade-off," said the lieutenant colonel. "Pure and simple. They've decided the extra firepower's worth the risk of blowing their cover."

"Maybe they thought we wouldn't be smart enough to figure it out," said the captain.

"They were almost right," said the CIA man. "Conjecture is one thing. Proof is quite another."

"And you agree we've got the proof we need?" asked the lieutenant colonel.

"Our agreeing makes it proof," said the CIA man. "Wouldn't you say?"

They all nodded and laughed.

The lieutenant colonel and the CIA man spent several hours explaining it all, very carefully, to me.

"You sure you understand this, Captain?" asked the lieutenant colonel. "All the technical stuff?"

"If I don't, sir," I said, "I know where to find you."

# 17

On the way back to Saigon, Peaches was manning the machinegun in the doorway. I leaned past his shoulder to try to get a look at the jungle canopy.

"Mind if I sit there a while?" I shouted at him. "It's beautiful down below."

He looked startled. His eyes shifted toward the back of the

chopper where the sergeant was sitting. "I'm not supposed to leave my post, sir," he yelled. "I've got to keep my gun trained on the ground. That's my orders."

The sergeant was watching us. "Could I sit by the door for just a minute?" I shouted at him. "I can't see very well from in here."

Sarge bit his lower lip and narrowed his eyes. "Not supposed to," he shouted. "Whole point of us being along is to keep you alive."

"But we're pretty far up, seems to me. There's no real danger, is there?"

"Always," he shouted. "There's never *not* any danger." He chewed on the side of his lip.

"Look," I yelled. "I know it's your responsibility, and I'm not trying to throw my weight around. I'd just like to see it for a minute, if I could."

"*Only* a minute," the sergeant yelled. "You stick close by him, Peaches."

Peaches unstrapped his safety belt and moved away. I sat down and hooked the belt around me. Peaches took off his helmet and sat next to me. His leg was against my thigh and his arm against my back. The feel of him was warm and comfortable.

The dark green treetops of the jungle suddenly gave way to rice fields, long rectangles contained within dams of raised earth. The water in the fields was a deep blue, and the leaves of the plants were a vivid chartreuse. Then the fields disappeared, and jungle canopy again stretched as far as I could see. Long narrow clearings cut through the vegetation in a number of places. I couldn't be sure which were roads and which were rivers. One was so straight I thought it had to be a road, but then I saw boats being poled along it and realized it was a canal. One bent and meandered so erratically I was sure it was a stream, until I saw the ox cart raising dust on the narrow road. The surest way to tell, I began to realize, was to look not at the shape of the clearing but to see if sunlight was glinting off of water.

Peaches tapped me on the shoulder. "I'd better get back to my post, sir," he said right in my ear.

We traded places, and I stayed close to him, looking out past his left shoulder. The rotors kept up their constant thwap-thwap-thwap, and the floor shook underneath me. I barely heard Peaches say something like "uunnngh." His hand dropped off the trigger of the machinegun, and he leaned heavily against the side of the door.

"Sarge," I yelled. "Sarge! You better get over here."

He came over, looked at Peaches's face, and said, "Shit!" He squeezed his eyes shut, pressed his lips together, and turned his face so I couldn't see it.

"Sarge?" I said.

"In a minute," he yelled. "*Sir.*"

I sat looking past Peaches's cheek at the tops of the trees rushing by beneath us.

"Meatball," the sergeant yelled just behind me. I jumped.

Meatball stood beside the sergeant.

"Do you believe that stupid fucker?" the sergeant yelled. "Never wanted to wear his fucking helmet. Stupid bastard. I *told* him. How many times I told him, Meatball?"

"Plenty of times, Sarge. He didn't like it, that's all. Said it made his head hurt."

"Well, his head's fucking well hurt now, the stupid bastard." The sergeant pressed his lips and turned his head toward the wall. He turned toward us again. "I should never've let the captain look out like that. Made Peaches think things was more all right than they was."

"Want me to move him back, Sarge?" Meatball shouted.

"We'll both do it," the sergeant yelled.

"May I help?" I asked.

"You may fucking *not*," the sergeant yelled. "*Sir*."

The sergeant laid his hand on Peaches's shoulder. It rested there like a caress. Suddenly he grabbed the shoulder, unsnapped the belt, and pulled Peaches away from the door. He and Meatball dragged the body to the back of the chopper.

"Horny," the sergeant yelled. "Take the gun."

Meatball unfolded a blanket and laid it over the body. The sergeant stood looking down at it for a long time.

## 18

At seven-thirty the next morning, I walked into Colonel Dunhill's office. He looked up from his desk. He cocked his head and stared.

"You got stubble on your chin, Captain."

"Yes, sir. I stayed up all night writing this report and haven't been back to the BOQ. I wanted you to see it right away."

He pulled at his mustache. "What's the matter? Something urgent?"

"It's Soviet rockets, sir. That's what's hitting our planes."

"Holy shit!" he said. He clapped his hands together. Then he narrowed his eyes. "You sure? *Soviet*?"

"Positive. It's all here. Fragments. Chemical analysis. There's no doubt at all, sir."

He whooped so loud it made me jump. "Then we got 'em, the bastards! Civil war, my ass. Internal insurrection, my ass. We goddam well knew it was communist aggression all the time, and now we can prove it. We *can* prove it, you say."

"Yes, sir. We can."

He pulled on his mustache. "So how come we didn't know this sooner? These attacks have been going on for weeks."

"Different people had different pieces, sir. No one could be sure."

"And now we are."

"Yes, sir."

"Holy shit!"

He stood and picked up the report lovingly. "You know what this is, Fairchild? My ticket to a star. Brigadier General Alfred Dunhill. Sound good?"

"Sounds terrific, sir."

"Soviet rockets." He shook his head and smiled. "Greater range than the stuff they've been using, then? Stuff they've been stealing from us?"

"Much greater."

"We know how much?"

"It's all in there, sir. Specifications. Ranges. Likely infiltration routes. I put in everything I could think of."

"Good work, Fairchild." He flipped through the report. "This'll put the fucking com-symps in their place. Tell us the Soviets are just interested bystanders. Bullshit. They're in it up to their eyeballs, and now we've *got* 'em."

I stood there waiting.

"Well, get the hell out so I can have the fun of reading it."

"Yes, sir." I turned to go.

"And, Fairchild. . . ."

I turned back.

"Shave your fucking face."

# 19

I heard the clicks of the combination on the door, and Boots came in grinning. "Well, well, Cap'm. You're sure the fair-haired boy around here these days. Everyone's peeing in their pants with pleasure over those Soviet rockets you found."

"I didn't find them, Boots. You know that. I talked to people who found them and just passed the word along."

"Don't be shy, Cap'm. It's your report, and the brass are all doing handsprings. Makes me look good right along with you. Just because I hang out in the room back here. 'Your captain really pulled one off, I hear,' the guys all say over at the NCO Club. They don't know *what*, of course, just that it's something big. 'Fuckin' A,' I say, and I sort of puff out my chest and bask in your reflected glory."

"Come off it, Boots. 'Hang out' here, bullshit. You taught me everything I know. You tell the guys I wouldn't be worth a damn without you."

His eyes widened. "Oh, they know *that*, Cap'm."

I laughed.

"Well, then," I said. "All's right with the world."

"I'm proud of you, though, Cap'm. Just between us."

"Thanks, Boots."

# 20

I'd written to Brent three times before a brief note came back. "This is what it's all about," he said. "The gooks are restless, and we're right in the thick of it. Fan-fucking-tastic."

Now, two weeks later, he'd written again.

"Want to try for R&R at the same time?" he said. "Iffy, but not impossible. Bangkok or Penang?"

"Penang, for sure," I wrote back. "Sounds quiet to me. I'll see what I can do on this end."

I sealed the letter, put it aside, and went back to looking

through that day's teletypes. I sat up. Wait a minute, I thought. We've heard nothing about Soviet rockets in any of the messages I've seen, and I'm supposed to be seeing them all. The only weapons they've talked about are the ones we already knew they had.

What if they aren't as gullible as we've been assuming they are? What if, never mind the enormous lengths we've gone to to keep them from knowing, they're aware that we're eavesdropping? What if they chatter on the air about what they want us to know and get their really important messages across some other way?

I'd have to ask Colonel Dunhill what he thought the next chance I got.

# 21

"Good fucking work, Fairchild," Colonel Dunhill boomed as I went in through his door. "That report on the Soviet rockets was top drawer."

"Thank you, sir."

"It's been a big help already in a couple of ways. In the first place, the security patrols now know how much further out to go and what they're looking for, so the loss of planes has eased off a good bit. But even more important than that, we've blasted that tired old frigging fable about a civil war. That crap about a so-called war of national liberation was always bullshit, but now. . . ." He grinned. "We've sent this new evidence to the Pentagon so they can *show* Congress it's naked communist aggression, pure and simple. I can't tell you how pleased I am, Captain. How pleased we all are."

"I'm glad, sir."

"Anything I can do to show my gratitude, you just let me know."

"There is one thing, sir. I don't know if it's possible. . . ."

"Name it."

"Well, a friend of mine is going on R&R soon, and I wondered if I could take mine early and go with him. It'd be more fun than my going. . . ."

"Consider it done. Just give the details to the sergeant-major."

I headed down the hall toward the secure room. Christ, I thought. I'd forgotten to mention my misgivings about the rockets. Well, no real rush. Some other time.

# 22

The morning we left, Brent flew by helicopter to Tan Son Nhut from Cu Chi, and I took a bus over from the BOQ.

When we met at the terminal, he smiled and patted me on the shoulder. We sat together on the plane and made small talk. Weather. Good to see you. Wonder if they'll feed us on the plane.

Our flight was short, just a couple of hours, not much further than from Saigon up to Hue. They served plenty of drinks but no food. We landed at an old British airfield on the mainland of Malaysia and took a taxi to a pier. From there we caught a ferry over to Penang. We could see the island almost as soon as we got under way. It was beautiful, low mountains rising out of the water, puffy clouds almost resting on their peaks. As we got nearer, the neat white buildings of George Town sparkled in the sunlight. Riding in a taxi from the ferry dock toward the center of town, we passed through narrow cobblestone streets lined with stucco walls. Branches covered with flowers crept over the walls from what must have been gardens inside.

We tried to think of the right words to describe such a place. Charming and quaint seemed too patronizing, but charming and quaint it was. And clean and lovely and tranquil. I was totally disoriented. People along the streets were going about their lives, smiling and chattering as if sudden death were not an immediate possibility. I felt as if I were watching it all from somewhere outside myself. Seeing myself move through a world that no longer made any sense.

Special Services had booked us into the Hotel International, a boxy modern building with no charm. Right on the busiest street in town. A smiling young bellboy showed us to our room on the sixth floor. "You want girls?" he asked. "I can get you best girls in town. Very healthy. You trust me!"

"Not today," said Brent. "Maybe later, okay?"

"Okay, GI," the bellboy said. Brent tipped him. The bellboy grinned and closed the door. Brent turned, grabbed me, pulled off my clothes and his, and led me toward one of the big twin beds. He'd brought a tube of vaseline, so when he pushed in, it didn't hurt like the other time. I could concentrate on how good he felt inside me. I hadn't known if this was going to be part of our trip or not, but I'd spent long nights hoping it would be. Like the other time, we never talked about it. We just did it. I didn't care.

Starting that afternoon, we explored the many wonders of Penang. Brent knew more than I would have imagined about Buddhism from his reading and could explain to me the significance of statues and carvings and even the roles of monks with shaved heads. One temple had an enormous reclining Buddha wearing a bright orange robe. Another was a haven for thousands of poisonous snakes, kept in a drugged state, the guidebook said, by powerful incense that never stopped burning.

High up on a hill was Kek Lok Si, Monastery of Supreme Bliss, a sprawling complex of stairways, temples, and gardens crowned by the awe-inspiring Ban Po Shu, the Pagoda of Ten Thousand Buddhas. We spent most of an afternoon up there, wandering around, reading our guidebook, staring down at the valley far below.

Off in one corner of the Hall of Kwan Yin was a magnificent dragon's head, carved from what looked like granite. Out of his wide gaping mouth dripped water from an underground spring. Many of those who passed by took a drink from the falling water—for good luck and good health, a monk told us.

"What do you think?" Brent asked.

"To hell with dysentery," I said. "Let's do it."

We dropped some coins in the offering box and each took a drink. The water tasted fresh and clean.

We walked past the Pool of Tortoises and up into the Hall of the Heavenly Kings. Around the walls of the main room hung enormous images of the Kings, guardians of the four corners of the earth. Their expressions were fierce, as they stamped with huge bare feet on the evil spirits they were there to guard against. Each one held his own symbol—the King of the East a sword, the King of the West a guitar, the King of the North a pearl and a snake, and the King of the South, incongruously, an umbrella. We both laughed.

"Look," said Brent. "He's the smart one."

"Practical, that's for sure," I said.

In the center of the room, in the eye of the storm of retribution swirling around him, sat a serene Laughing Buddha, known as the Merciful One. I looked up at the angry, snarling guardians and back at the gentle Buddha. I didn't know what to think.

One day Brent and I took a bus out of George Town to the beach area north of town. Along that coast, known as Batu Ferringhi, were the resorts where English colonials had vacationed and Malayans had patiently served them. The man behind the desk at our hotel recommended the Lone Pine, for the beauty of its beach and the quality of its food. We told the name to the bus driver and got off when he stopped and motioned to us.

The building was old and rambling and elegant. Out of another era. Flowering vines climbed the walls, and a wide green lawn under shady trees led down to the beach. On the lawn were small tables and white wicker chairs in which groups of people sat drinking tea and looking out at the water. A row of wide-open French doors led inside to a dining room, from which we could hear muted conversation and the clinking of glasses.

Everything was subdued, as if we were in an outdoor library. The waiters, dressed in crisp white, who walked in and out of the doors to the lawn, moved softly. A breeze barely lifted the leaves of the trees and vines.

"I feel like we ought to whisper," Brent said.

"Me, too."

"How about a swim before lunch?"

"Great."

Just to the left of the main entrance were two small vine-covered buildings. A large sign said "Changing Rooms." Two small signs said "Ladies" and "Gentlemen." Inside the gentlemen's room, along two walls, were booths with curtains across the doorways. Brent and I went into two of them and came out wearing identical navy blue bathing suits. We both laughed.

"New from the PX?" I asked.

"How'd you guess?"

"You look terrific," I said.

He winked.

We took towels borrowed from our hotel out of the satchels we'd brought along and put our clothes and shoes inside. As we walked to the beach, the sun felt good on our shoulders. We put down our satchels, spread our towels out on the soft powdery sand, and walked toward the water. Waves lapped against the shore, and the breeze was soft and soothing.

Inviting as the water looked, we walked in rather than running. Brent swam straight out to sea with what looked to me like perfect form. I'd always envied that ability in people who'd learned to swim properly. Head facing down in the water, two strong strokes, breathe to the side, head down, two strong strokes, breathe to the side. No matter how hard I tried, I could never master it. I'd always loved to swim, ever since I was a kid. But I had to be content with the strokes I'd taught myself, splashing along on my side or floating contentedly on my back. Brent swam a long way out, then came straight as an arrow, directly back to me.

"Want to walk down the beach to dry off?" I asked.

"Sure," he said. "Think our stuff'll be all right?"

"Who cares?"

He chuckled.

The beach curved around to the left, wide and more golden than white. It sloped up without dunes to the edge of rows of dark green trees, some palm, some a long-needled kind of pine. Under many of the trees were flowering bushes. All soft colors. Nothing vibrant.

The Strait of Malacca, clear and calm and turquoise blue, stretched out in front of us. Far offshore, a boat with large brown sails attached in a strange pattern to four masts moved majestically through the water.

"Wonder if that's a junk or a sampan," I said.

Brent looked at it.

"Junk," he said.

I stared at him. "You know, or you're just guessing?"

"I know."

"How?"

He squinted, just a little, and grinned with one side of his mouth. "You're surprised when I know stuff, aren't you?"

I hesitated. "Well. When it's something out of the ordinary, I guess I am."

He looked at me for a minute, then back at the boat.

"Junks are bigger than sampans," he said. "A sampan wouldn't have more than two masts. A junk could have as many as five. That boat has four. Simple."

"It's only simple if you know what you're talking about."

He continued to stare out across the water. "When I'm reading and I come across something I don't know, I like to look it up. Is that so unusual?"

"I would say so, yes. My guess is lots of people think about doing it, but not many do."

"And you think a career Army officer with a loud mouth is likely to be one of the ones that don't."

I didn't answer.

"Gotcha," he said.

We walked back toward the Lone Pine, to where we'd left our things. No one else was on the beach. Everyone seemed to be up under the trees drinking tea. With our towels placed side by side, Brent and I lay on our backs, our arms stretched out beside us, our eyes closed. The sun was just warm enough, soothing and caressing us rather than beating down and baking us. Brent shifted his hand so that his little finger barely touched mine. Every once in a while, he would move it, ever so slightly, up and down the side of mine.

"I wish we didn't have to go back," he said quietly.

"I know what you mean."

"Do you? I wonder."

"Why is that?"

He breathed in and out a couple of times before he answered.

"You haven't had to kill anybody yet, have you?"

"No. Have you?"

"Three."

"I've wondered, but. . . . I didn't know whether to ask."

I waited, but he didn't say any more.

"Want to talk about it?" I asked.

I felt him hesitating.

"I thought I wouldn't," he said. "I thought what I needed was time away from everything like that. Especially in a place as peaceful as this, I thought I wouldn't want to be reminded."

"But?"

"But I have the feeling now, for some reason, that I *need* to get it out. Maybe because it *is* so peaceful. Maybe that's just the right place to do it."

"You decide."

He was quiet for a while. Twice he rubbed his little finger against the side of mine.

"It was two weeks ago. Maybe a month after I'd arrived at the base north of Cu Chi. Mostly the duty's not a whole lot different from what it was in Saigon. I read a bunch of reports that come in. I prepare briefings. Same old stuff. It feels more immediate, though. At least there's that. And I get to talk to the patrol leaders sometimes, if they have anything unusual or significant to report. I like that. I like *them*. They're great guys.

"This day was just like most of the others. We were planning a chopper assault on a position to the northeast, and a bunch of patrols were out scouting, and I was in the HQ tent getting a briefing together on what we thought we'd find. All of a sudden, about the middle of the afternoon, there was shooting real close by. I grabbed a rifle and went out. A sergeant running by carrying an automatic rifle yelled, 'VC. Inside the perimeter. Eleven o'clock.' 'What the hell?' I thought. 'They don't attack in daylight.'

"I ran along behind him. As he cleared the supply tent, he spun around, dropped his rifle, and grabbed at his chest. Two more shots hit him. I watched them hit him. He fell face down on the ground.

"I ducked behind the supply tent, hit the ground, and peeked around the corner. VC in black pajamas were running toward me from the far side of the compound. I got my rifle in position and started firing. I was so nervous the first shots went high and wide. I shifted my aim, fired again, and a man fell. Just like that. I fired, he fell. He wasn't moving. So easy.

"I was exhilarated. I hate to say it now, but it's true. 'My god,' I thought. 'I've done it. I've killed him.' I tried to calm myself, aimed, and fired again. Nothing. Fired again. Nothing. Fired again, and another man fell. I was so wound up I let out a little yell.

"And I thought—honest to god, Matt—I thought, 'Ride 'em, cowboy!' Isn't that the stupidest goddam thing you ever heard? 'Ride 'em, cowboy.'

"Then, all of a sudden, a VC ran around the far corner of the supply tent, heading right toward me. He glanced at the ground, saw me, and stopped. It took him off guard. He was so surprised he almost smiled. He was very young, just a kid. I shot him in the face.

"It must have been because I was looking at his mouth that I aimed there. I wouldn't have done it otherwise. Shot him in the face, I mean. Somewhere else, but not in the face."

He was quiet for a while.

"I heard more shots from our guys on my right and off to my left. The other VC started falling back. Good thing, too, because I couldn't have done another thing. Not then. It was seeing him up so close, you know? Looking right in his eyes. I could've done the other thing all day, shooting the ones far off. Like popping those little ducks off a wire at the county fair. You pop 'em, they fall down. Like 'Cowboys and Indians' when we were kids. Only thing is, these guys don't get back up when it's time for supper.

"Well.

"The shooting faded off into the distance, and I just lay

there and shook. I felt terrible that I'd shot that kid. And I felt even more terrible that it was bothering me so much.

"'You wimp,' I thought. 'You fucking wimp. Can't even do what you came over here to do without sniveling about it.' I kept wishing I'd joined the Air Force. I could drop bombs all day and all night, since I wouldn't have to watch them explode. See the people flying in bloody pieces through the air. Yep, I told myself, I shoulda been a pilot."

He stopped talking, and I didn't have the least idea what to say.

"I'm all right now, though," he said in a minute. "Pretty much. I can do it again, I'm sure of that." He took a deep breath. "I just wish I didn't have to."

I put my hand on top of his. He squeezed it hard.

## 23

Every afternoon before dinner, we'd go back to the hotel, close the drapes, turn on a small lamp, take off our clothes, and lie on one of the beds. We never talked about it. We just assumed that's what we would do.

Brent would turn me over, push his way in, thrust a few times, not many, tighten his hands on my sides while he breathed hard, pull out, and flop on his back with his eyes closed. Letting me look at his naked body while I stroked myself was as much as he seemed able to give me in return. But it was fine with me. I felt a powerful emotion—for him, for the way he looked lying there, and for what it was we were doing. It seemed like more than enough to me.

# 24

Our last night in Penang, we went to an Indian restaurant we'd walked by a couple of times. A huge array of food filled tables along two sides of the room, and we went back and forth serving ourselves. Everything was hot and delicious. We recognized most of the curries—chicken, lamb, shrimp, which they called prawn—but not much else. We ate it all anyway, including bananas between courses to cool down our mouths.

The meal took nearly two hours. When we'd finished, we walked along the wide street that ran by the edge of the water. We came to a big, ornate white building, so decorated with columns and cupolas and finials it looked like a gigantic wedding cake. Across from it was a circular park that jutted out into the water. The street was illuminated with wonderful old gaslights, but the grassy area was dark. Just offshore were maybe thirty boats, some large, mostly small, swaying at their moorings. Dim lights twinkled here and there among the boats.

We walked across the grass toward a large tree with thick roots sticking up above the ground. We sat on the grass between two of the roots and leaned back against the smooth bark of the trunk. Brent put his arm around my shoulder and pulled me toward him. I slid down a little so my head could rest in the space where his chest and arm and shoulder came together.

A slight breeze off the water brought with it the sound of voices, most of them quiet and unhurried. Occasionally someone shouted and was answered by a shout, but most of what I heard was a low murmur. Torches flickered on several of the small sampans. Was that safe? I wondered idly, but I didn't really care. I leaned against Brent, rested my hand on his chest, and watched the boats lifting and settling ever so slightly. No one came our way, so there was no need to move away from Brent, as I would surely have done.

A large junk with five masts, but sails up on only two, threaded its way among the other boats and glided to a stop. Was it tying up to something out there or dropping an anchor? I couldn't tell. Muffled voices drifted over to us as a great many men, working by lanternlight, lowered the last of the sails and secured them. A rowboat appeared beside the junk. It filled with men and went toward the shore over to our right. One man rowed it back out, sat while it filled again, and rowed it in. Two men left on board squatted beside a lantern near the front of the boat.

The wind picked up. The gentle sound of water lapping against the seawall became a louder, more insistent slap. Along with the wind came a hypnotic smell. Sweet. Not as heavy as gardenia but like it. Spicier, though. What was it? I wondered. I was sure Brent would know, but I wasn't about to ask. That small bit of knowledge wasn't worth breaking the powerful bond of silence between us.

The boats were now rocking back and forth, back and forth, as rougher waves went by. Something metallic hit rhythmically against something wooden. Ding. Ding-ding-ding. Ding-ding. Ding-ding-ding. I couldn't see any stars. No moon either, so I guessed there must be clouds high up. A light flared on the deck of the junk. The two men squatting there had lit cigarettes. Through the clear air I watched the two orange glows as they inhaled.

Brent's arm slipped off my shoulder, and I heard his steady breathing. I tilted my watch until I could see the hands. One-thirty. I sat up and looked at Brent's face. His eyes opened a little, drooped, opened again.

"Sleepy?" I asked.

He stretched his arms. "A little, I guess."

"We could curl up here for a while. No curfew, you know."

He smiled and yawned. "Maybe we better head back. It's starting to feel a little damp."

I stood and held out my hand. Brent took it and pulled himself up. He brushed off the back of his pants, stretched again, and reached for my hand. He held it as we walked across the grass. When we neared the lights of the street, he let it go.

We walked to the hotel without talking, brushed our teeth, lay with our arms around each other, and went quietly to sleep.

# 25

For the first time, the secure room seemed claustrophobic. I missed the breezes and the bright blue sky. And Brent. But the last week's lists of coordinates, which Boots had diligently ripped off the teletype machine, were stacked in order on the corner of my desk. Boots got out his pocketknife and rolls of colored tape, and we went to work.

A few minutes later, we heard the clicking of the combination, and Colonel Dunhill came bursting in. "Fairchild," he said. "Thank god." His voice was too loud for the small space, and it hurt my ears. "I've been kicking myself for letting you go."

"Why is that, sir?"

"We've got frigging Congressmen coming, that's why. Day after tomorrow. MACV says it's got to where General Westmoreland's had to wade through the VIPs—don't it break your heart?—so they're shipping these two over to us. I want you to brief them back here, Fairchild. Pull out all the stops. God, the secrecy and the fancy lock and knowing they're seeing stuff nobody else gets to see. They'll fucking eat it up."

"But. . . . day after tomorrow?"

"Yeah. Pisser, ain't it? Considering."

"Jesus, sir. Morning or afternoon?"

"Morning. Ten hundred."

"Oh, shit," I said. "Well. It'll be tight, but we'll be ready."

"Good man. That's what I like to hear. Oh, and. . . . Check with me as you go along, Fairchild. Let me know how things are going. I don't have to impress on you how goddam important this is."

"No, sir. You don't."

He went out and pushed the heavy door shut with a thud and a click. I looked at Boots. He was grinning.

"Hot stuff, Cap'm," he said.

"Sizzling. Shit. I hope you haven't made any plans for the next forty-eight hours."

"I have, Cap'm, but they're history."

Boots went to sign a jeep out of the motor pool, and we headed straight for the MACV compound in Cholon. The sergeant-major called ahead to say we were coming. And why. The magic word "Congress" opened every door in the place. After we'd talked with Air Force and Marine Corps intelligence for an hour and a half, a CIA man came in with charts and graphs and lists of statistics.

Back at Headquarters, Boots started filling in outlines on some vu-graph slides. I checked with Colonel Dunhill and then got busy reading and writing. Boots and I skipped lunch, took a break for supper, and stuck colored tape on wall maps till after midnight. I told Boots to go get some sleep and stayed up typing till nearly three. The driver on duty downstairs took me to the BOQ.

I ate breakfast at six and was back in the secure room by six-thirty. Boots was already there, hard at work on his slides. I showed him the information that had to go on them, and he got out his colored cellophane and exacto knife. I kept typing. We'd stop every once in a while and stick tape on the maps, both of us determined to catch up. The Congressmen wouldn't know the difference, but we would. I looked in on Colonel Dunhill every couple of hours to tell him everything was going just fine.

No lunch again and a quick supper. Around seven, I took the finished text into Colonel Dunhill's office.

"Would you like to read this over, sir?" I asked.

"Looks thick. How long is it?"

"Thirty pages. I figure forty-five minutes, with graphics and tapdancing and all. Long enough to seem substantive without getting them squirming in their seats."

"Good man." He looked at his watch. "Damn," he said. "I'm due at the club for drinks. You really think I need to see this?"

"Not as far as I'm concerned, sir. I'll use the same format as the briefing we gave that WAC general last month."

He nodded. "Tour of the maps and then a slide show?"

"Yes, sir. But much more elaborate on the slides."

"Lots of body counts? They love body counts these days."

"Yes, sir. I've put them in everywhere I could."

"Well, then. I'll head on over to the club and leave you to it. Just don't disappoint me, hear?"

"Would I dare?"

He laughed.

While Boots finished the last of the vu-graph slides, I memorized the text. Numbers, dates, unit names, over and over and over in my head. Around ten, we started rehearsing. Me with my collapsible metal pointer moving past the wall maps, Boots by the light switch. I turn on the vu-graph, Boots flicks out the lights. The first slide appears in the blank space on the wall between the maps of North Vietnam and southern China. I point and talk, Boots changes slides. I turn on the lights, Boots turns off the vu-graph. Again and again till we get it right.

I practice a technique I learned watching Brent in action. The other briefers always raised their voices and *stressed the words* to emphasize important points. Not Brent. He would pause. . . . lower his voice. . . . and make the point slowly and deliberately. It worked like a charm. Never saw it fail. The critical thing, though, was the timing. Too long a pause, and the listeners might think you'd forgotten what you'd intended to say. Too short, and the effect was diluted. Boots suggested I try counting beats.

At quarter of four, we decided we'd done all we could do and headed for bed. The driver dropped me off first, then took Boots on home. We were back by a little after six, starched and polished to a fare-thee-well. I read off the latest list of coordinates, and Boots stuck up the last little bits of colored tape. We checked to be sure the slides were in order, Boots flipped the vu-graph on and off a couple of times, and I went to tell Colonel Dunhill we were ready. Then Boots and I sat and smoked and waited.

Just after eleven, we heard the lock begin to click.

"Typical," Boots whispered.

Colonel Dunhill held the door while two men walked in. He closed the door behind them with a sturdy-sounding thump.

One man was tall and round with a large red nose. The other was thin and gray. Both were wearing green fatigues and heavy black combat boots. It was all I could do to keep my eyes from rolling upward.

"Gentlemen," said Colonel Dunhill in that loud voice that echoed off the walls. "This is Captain Fairchild." He didn't say their names. I guessed I was supposed to know.

They shook my hand.

"We're honored to have you here," I said.

"No, sir," the big one said, his voice a shade louder than Colonel Dunhill's. "The honor is ours. You fighting men have our highest respect and our undying gratitude."

"You do indeed," said the thin one, not to be outdone. "We

can't tell you how impressed we've been at the splendid effort you fine young men are making over here in our behalf."

"Thank you, gentlemen," I said. "It means a lot to us to hear you say that. May I introduce my assistant, Sergeant Anderson?"

They nodded perfunctorily in his direction.

"If you'll be seated, please," I said, "we'll begin." They sat in the three heavily padded swivel chairs, borrowed from the CG, we'd lined up in the center of the room.

I explained the setup of the maps—four of a very large scale for the various sections of South Vietnam, five of a smaller scale for North Vietnam, Laos, Cambodia, Thailand, and southern China. I told how the information we used was gathered and impressed on them how extraordinarily secret it all was, both the information itself and how we managed to get it. Their faces reflected the proper amount of awe and respect.

Seemingly at random—but of course not a bit of it—I picked a couple of North Vietnamese and a couple of Viet Cong units, showed the paths of colored dots their movements had created, and told what we thought those movements meant. I quoted a few messages we had intercepted and showed where they had originated. I paid special attention to the large number of colored dots all along the Ho Chi Minh Trail from North Vietnam down through Laos and Cambodia.

I turned the vu-graph on. Boots turned the overhead lights off and went to sit beside the vu-graph. Using a series of slides and my little pointer, I took us, blow-by-blow, through two recent operations.

"Just last month," I said, "the 325C North Vietnamese Division crossed the Demilitarized Zone from North Vietnam into South Vietnam. I'd like to show you how their engagement with U.S. forces came about, how we responded, and . . ." pause, two, three, four ". . . the unfortunate result."

I described for them Operation Hardwood. How a squad of

Marines on routine patrol ran into elements of the 325C. How they called in reinforcements, but found the enemy so well entrenched it took us nearly two weeks to dislodge them. Slide after slide showed enemy advances, U.S. counterattacks, locations of air strikes, strafings by helicopter gunships, and artillery bombardments. A brightly colored chart showed numbers of all these activities and 1,027 enemy killed. The final slide showed the routes the NVA took as they retreated across the DMZ and the positions on this side of it where our forces came to a reluctant halt.

Next I talked about Operation Junction Falls, a massive thrust by twenty-two U.S. battalions into War Zone C northwest of Saigon. I told how troops from the 503d Airborne Brigade dropped from the sky in the first airborne assault of the war. I showed how they hooked up with ground forces flown in by more than 250 helicopters to set up a variation on search-and-destroy maneuvers called "cordon-and-sweep." Once the paratroopers and elements of the 1st and 4th Infantry Divisions had formed a huge horseshoe, the cordon, units of the 25th Infantry Division and the 11th Armored Cavalry began sweeping north through dense jungle in an attempt to trap the 9th Viet Cong Division in between.

My pointer followed the paths of giant bulldozers and Rome plows as they tore through the thick vegetation. A chart on another slide showed the thousands of artillery shells fired, the tons of bombs dropped, the 861 VC killed. A final series of slides showed the sweeping force moving steadily toward the blocking force in place to the north.

"But," I said quietly, "as the two forces came ever closer, those Viet Cong, several thousand strong, who had survived the bombs and the artillery and the earlier assaults turned suddenly toward the west and . . ." pause, two, three, four ". . . escaped across the border into Cambodia."

Pause, two, three, four, five. Lights on. Vu-graph off.

"Any questions, gentlemen?"

They both stared at the now-blank wall. The big one opened his mouth, closed it, shook his head, and looked up at me.

"Well, sir," he said. "That was most impressive, Captain. Most impressive and informative."

"It was indeed," said the thin one. "Clearest picture of the war effort we've had so far. Wouldn't you say?" He turned toward the big one.

"I certainly would say that. I certainly would. Clearest picture by far. But I'm mightily troubled by something I picked up from what you were saying here, Captain. It seems to me that in both those operations, we were within a gnat's eyebrow of finishing off those bastards when they up and skedaddled across some border or other. Am I right? Is that what happened?"

"That is correct, sir."

"And," said the thin one, "they are able not only to escape certain defeat from our forces, but after they get across there, to sit in that sanctuary, safe and sound, licking their wounds and regrouping. Yes?"

Pause, two, three. "Absolutely, sir. *And* bring in reinforcements and new supplies of weapons and ammunition. Yes, sir."

"But, Christ, man," said the big one. "That makes not a particle of sense to me. You fight a battle, you fight it to win. Aren't there rules of combat that allow for hot pursuit?"

"Not in this war, sir. I'm afraid not."

"But why the hell not?" asked the thin one.

"These are international borders, sir. With other sovereign countries. And we're not, at this moment, in a state of war with either Laos or Cambodia."

"But we sure as hell are with North Vietnam," said the thin one, "declared or not. If they're able to come barging across a demilitarized zone with the sole intent of killing our men, I don't see why we can't follow them right back across once we've licked them. Keep after them till we've crushed them once and for all."

"Well, sir . . ." pause, two, three, four, five, six, seven " . . . I'm afraid that's a political decision. Not a military one."

The two men looked at each other. The big one rose first and held out his hand to me. I shook it.

"Damn fine job, Captain," he said. "We can't tell you how much we appreciate all this."

"Not at all, sir," I said. "My pleasure."

The thin one shook my hand heartily.

"Yes, indeed," he said. "I feel like we've finally gotten a look at what's really going on here. What we're really up against. We read so much garbage in the papers and see such sensationalized crap on the TV. What we'd hoped to do by coming here in person was to get the real lowdown. From the people, like you, who are in a position to know. So thank you again, Captain Fairchild. It's been most enlightening. Most enlightening."

"We're the ones who are grateful to you, sir," I said. "To both of you. For taking the time, and for having the interest, to find out for yourselves."

Colonel Dunhill was standing by the door smiling broadly.

"You're to be congratulated, Colonel," said the big one. "Splendid young officer you've got here. Absolutely first-rate."

"Thank you, sir," said Colonel Dunhill, still smiling. "One of the things I do best is pick good men to have around me."

He clicked open the big steel door and stood aside as the two men went out. He turned, winked at me, and closed the door behind him. Boots and I started rearranging the furniture.

About twenty minutes later, Colonel Dunhill came roaring back in.

"Fucking brilliant, Fairchild," he said, grinning. He patted me hard on the shoulder. "I've gotta hand it to you. That was fucking brilliant. Those bozos think they've discovered the dangers of cross-border sanctuaries all by themselves." He laughed and shook his head. "You sly bastard. When I realized what you were up to, I couldn't frigging *believe* it."

He punched my arm with his fist. "If we'd gone at it head-on and tried to convince them ourselves, we'd probably have succeeded, god willing. But *this* way. Christ! It's their own private *crusade*! Shit, they'll go right back and huddle with their cronies at Defense, and we'll be bombing Laos and Cambodia this time next month. You wait and see."

He laughed again. "Take the afternoon off, you sly bastard," he said. "Go lie by the pool."

# 26

Jeremy, Captain Collins, who worked in counterintelligence, lived down the hall from me in the BOQ. After Brent left, he and I did some things together, some drinks, some lunches, some trips to Saigon.

One Sunday afternoon, we wandered around the city for a while, ending up at the Botanical Gardens. As we rounded a bend in the pathway, I saw two ARVN soldiers coming toward us holding hands.

"Would you look at that?" said Jeremy. "Makes my stomach turn over."

We stopped. The two soldiers passed us, deep in conversation, not acknowledging our presence. I looked at Jeremy's face. His narrowed eyes followed them as they walked away. His lips were pressed tight together, and the ends were turned down.

"No wonder they have such a screwed-up army," he said. "It's full of goddam queers."

I knew I should just say nothing, but my tongue got away from me.

"What makes you say that?" I asked.

He whirled around and stared at me. "Didn't you see them? Holding hands like a couple of sweethearts? Jesus! Goddam queers. Makes my skin crawl."

Just keep quiet, you fool, I thought.

"My guess is they're not," I said. "If they were, they'd be keeping it a secret. I'll bet they're just friends."

He looked at me, eyes still narrow. "Where'd you ever get such a hare-brained idea as that? You a student of Oriental sexual practices?"

I laughed. "Hardly. But I've spent a good bit of time in Mexico, and the toughest guys there all walk everywhere with their arms around each other. Because they're friends."

"You think that's supposed to prove something?" he asked. "Goddam Mexicans. Goddam gooks. It's all the same. It's all cultures that don't have the slightest clue about what's right and what's wrong."

More likely, I thought, it's that when men feel certain enough of their masculinity, they aren't afraid to show affection. But at least I had sense enough not to say *that*.

# 27

When I'd first arrived, I'd had some vague idea that the Vietnamese, deep in their hearts, were probably pretty much like us. Only shorter, poorer, less sophisticated. The more I moved among them, however, the less certain of that I was. I began to wonder if the differences weren't far more fundamental.

Their language was strange to my ear. Lilting in a high-pitched, sing-song sort of way, but too jarring to be musical. Sometimes it seemed almost like a parody. Like a second-rate American comedian trying his damndest to sound Oriental. Still, I wished I could speak it. Or at least understand it. Then I would have known what people were saying as they passed on the streets or squatted in that funny flatfooted way beside the curbs, chewing betel nuts and spitting the black juice with expert aim out into the street. I could have overheard what the mama-sans chattered about so energetically in the hallways of the BOQ, where they seemed forever to be cleaning our boots, folding our underwear, and ironing our shirts. Most of them looked up and smiled and bobbed their heads, the strangers on the street and the mama-sans in the hallway, but we made no real connection. Our smiles acknowledged that the other existed, but added not one particle of human understanding.

Even though I couldn't listen, I could watch. Intently. Every chance I got. I was struck by the fact that the women of a certain age and class were universally attractive, but the men, of all ages and classes, were not. Young girls from families of comfortable means glided along the sidewalks in an aura of self-contained loveliness. Their features were regular and perfectly proportioned. Their hair, black and shiny, hung down their backs to their waists.

Long silk pajama pants, white or black, almost covered their tiny high-heeled sandals. Over these pants, they wore a long-sleeved dress, called an *au dai*, of clear and vivid colors. The top fit snugly over small but shapely breasts. The bottom of the dress, as long as the pants, was split to the waist so that flowing panels in front and back waved gracefully as they moved along.

They never seemed to be walking but rather to be transporting themselves forward by an act of will that involved nothing so mundane as placing feet in front of each other. They looked like a breed of exotic bird. As soft as doves, as serene as swans, as sure of their own splendor as lyre birds. They appeared to be unconcerned with the effect they created, unaware of everything, especially the fact that their existence reversed the natural order of things.

The men who walked those same sidewalks were more like the female birds of most species. Small, brown, unadorned. Their features were plain, their lips too plump or too thin, their noses too short or too long. They were, like hard-working pea-hens, functional not ornamental.

One of the busboys at the Golden Dragon was a startling exception. I saw him the first night Brent and I went there, off in a corner of the room clearing dishes from a table. As I watched, he turned our way. He was the most beautiful man I'd ever seen. Throughout the evening, I kept glancing over whenever I saw him come out of the kitchen. His short body nicely filled his white shirt and tight black pants, and he moved with the unconscious grace of the women in their *au dai*'s.

Each time we ate there, I looked for him, and usually he was somewhere around. Watching him move across the room was comforting to me. After Brent left, I didn't go into town for a while. Didn't think of it, really. Then one night, not long after I got back from Penang, I was feeling antsy. I tried to find someone to go with me, but Donnie was headed for a poker game and Jeremy had a date with a nurse. I ended up going alone. After walking around Saigon for a while and sitting in the park watching the people go by, I thought of trying some-place new for dinner. When it came to deciding which one, though, I found that was more than I wanted to deal with. I took a cyclo over to the Golden Dragon.

I had finished my soup and was waiting for my meal when I saw him come out of the kitchen. With the freedom granted to those who eat alone, who have nowhere definite to focus their attention, I just watched him. He moved from table to table, carried a heavy tray into the kitchen, came out, moved from table to table. The next time he came in, he looked directly at me. He smiled. I smiled back.

The waiter brought my meal, and I forced myself to concentrate on it. I was handling chopsticks with ease by then and was proud of my dexterity.

"You enjoy this meal?"

I looked up. He was smiling down at me, a dish in one hand and a glass in the other. He was even more beautiful up close.

"Yes," I said. "It's great."

"You do not come for many weeks."

The comment startled me.

"No," I said. "I've been busy."

He nodded. "Your friend soldier does not come this night?"

"He's been transferred."

"Ah, yes," he said. "So many soldiers come and go. If you will excuse, I must take these for washing. We may talk again?"

"Please," I said.

He worked for a while on my side of the room, then on the other. As I was drinking my coffee, he appeared again at my side.

"When you finish your eating," he asked, "do you. . . . mmm. . . . remain in Cholon for some whiles?"

"I hadn't thought about it," I said. "But yes, I could."

"My work end until nine o'clock. If you stay for then, we may talk a little?"

"I'd like that very much."

His smile sent my heart completely out of rhythm.

"I must go out from back door," he said. "You know of it?"

"I'll find it."

"You promise?"

"I promise."

"Nine o'clock."

"I'll be there."

He looked at me for a second or two and went to clear a nearby table.

I paid my bill and walked outside. Seven-forty-five. I had more than an hour to kill. I started down the sidewalk. What was this? What was happening? I couldn't imagine. The thought of him made my heart pound, but surely he wasn't interested in me in that way. Or was he? Probably he was taking English lessons and just wanted someone to practice with. We would talk a while, I would help him pronounce words and correct his grammar, and that would be it.

I had a moment of panic. He was Vietnamese, so there was no way I could trust him. Everyone said so. The ones who smiled the most and were the friendliest were the most likely to be Viet Cong spies.

The minute the ugly word popped into my head, it lodged itself there and wouldn't go away. Spies. That was the worst thing about this place. Anyone might be a spy. You couldn't tell who was who. Who was your friend, and who wanted to do you in. Maybe the same person was one on one day and the other the next. All of them—friend and foe alike—could move in and out of a society we blundering Americans could barely understand.

So which was this young man? As I walked, I thought of him growing up in a village somewhere to the south. His looks would have caused a stir from the time he was a baby. Everyone would have waited for him to start looking ordinary like the other little boys, but he never did. When he reached adolescence, the war was heating up. The Viet Cong infiltrated his village and started sending the young men out into the jungle. First to train, then to fight. They were killed, and more had to be sent. The Viet Cong cadre saw the young men as an unending supply of soldiers, to be trained, then lost, then replaced.

But this one young man was too precious a commodity to

be wasted like that. He was a jewel for whom a special role was ordained. Among the American soldiers, there would surely be some who would find this young man appealing. Maybe a married man who could convince himself that sleeping with another man was less of a betrayal. Or a man like me who could say no to every whore on Tu Do Street but would find this young man irresistible.

And they knew who we were, make no mistake about that. Who were the officers and where we worked. We could wear civvies to town all we wanted, they still knew who we were. The mama-sans on the base, after they scrubbed our toilets and ironed our fatigues, could tell the cyclo drivers just outside the gate, who, as they roared around the city, could stop off anywhere and tell the VC local coordinator, who could take the information out to VC headquarters. There, in that mammoth compound of tunnels and underground rooms were sure to be cabinets full of files. One for each intelligence officer, the most intriguing targets of all. In among the F's, I was sure, was a file on me, with a picture taken as I walked along a Saigon street and a full report on the fact that I had slept with no women since I had arrived.

Our enemies were primitive in some ways, that was true. They lived underground and transported supplies and weapons on the backs of thousands of little men trotting along jungle trails in sandals made of old tires. And all our planes and bombs and defoliants and napalm couldn't stop them. Barely even slowed them down. They just kept running back and forth like swarms of obedient ants, sure of their purpose.

We smiled at all this living in tunnels and shuffling around on old tires. We thought it meant they were naive and maybe a little stupid. But we were wrong. They were neither. I'd been there long enough to be certain of that. They were sophisticated and very, very smart. Smart enough to know that an intelligence officer named Matthew Fairchild, who worked in a sealed-off room and ate at the Golden Dragon, would be unable to resist a beautiful young Vietnamese busboy, would go with him wherever he wanted to go, would do whatever he wanted to do, eagerly posing for the secret pictures that would ruin him.

That's what this was all about. The most beautiful young man in Vietnam was about to trap the most gullible. What I had to do, right now, was find a cyclo, head back to the base, and forget all this foolishness.

If I was so eager to fuck, I could fuck all the women in Saigon. All the women in Vietnam, for that matter, old or young, willing or unwilling. I could set one of them up in an apartment and screw only her. Or I could screw a different one every night for a month. Or I could gather five of them in a room and screw them one after another until my strength ran out. I could stick my dick into any female orifice within a two-hundred-mile radius, and my superiors would smile and nod. What I couldn't do was meet that lovely young man. Walk by the river and practice his English, if that's what he wanted. Or go somewhere and hold him in my arms, if, by some miracle, he wanted that.

It's shit, I thought. All a big fat pile of shit.

At nine o'clock, I was standing on the corner looking off toward the river. A soft touch on my arm made me jump.

"You keep your promise," he said. "I am glad."

He was smiling, and his white shirt glowed under the streetlight.

"My name is Nhan."

"Mine's Matthew."

"Mah-tyew?"

"Matt, if you like."

"Oh, no. Mah-tyew is more grand. Yes?"

I laughed.

"Good," he said, nodding. "You *can* be happy."

"You thought I couldn't?"

"I thought maybe not. I have never seen you so. We will walk this way?"

"Sure. How often have you seen me?"

"Many times. With your friend soldier. He talk. You listen and never smile. You watch me when I work and never smile."

He touched my arm, and I stopped at the edge of a curb. A jeep roared by. We crossed the street.

"Many American soldiers come to Golden Dragon to eat. They seem to me. . . . mmmmm. . . . not interest. You I see, and I think myself, 'Him. I like to know him.'"

"But why?"

He looked up at me and wrinkled his forehead.

"You have a funny way you think, Yankee GIs. Always why, why, why. I do not understand. You leave no place for what *is*. I see you, and my heart smile. This is a thing that *is*. What do I care for *why*?"

And I'd almost sneaked away back to the base. To hell with rational thinking. Tonight, let *why* take care of itself.

He touched my arm again.

"In this building have apartment a friend of me. Will we go there?"

An alarm went off in my head. A friend's apartment? Not even his own? What a perfect setup. Gullible old Matthew being led to the slaughter.

"If you are afraid, we can just walk," he said. "I will like to be with you even so."

I looked at his face. He was standing calmly, waiting for me to decide. Oh, my god, I thought.

"I *am* afraid," I said. "But I want to go with you."

He smiled. "Good, Mah-tyew. Take a risk . . . mmm . . . you say 'take a risk'?"

"Yes."

"Take a risk is sometimes how to be alive."

He turned and led the way up dark stairs to the third floor. He took a key out of his pocket and opened a door. He flipped a switch. Even with the light on, the room was dark. In one corner was a small bed with a brightly colored spread on it. Pillows of other bright colors filled the corner. A smiling Buddha sat in a niche by the windows, which were covered by heavy drapes. One window was open a bit, letting in a breeze that moved the drapes from time to time and a constant noise from the street below.

Nhan closed the door behind him and turned the lock.

"My friend is clerk of hotel. He work for nighttime. My home with mother and grandmother is far away. Other side of Saigon. Some nights I go there. Some nights I work too hard and feel tired I sleep here. This is good friend to me, you think?"

I nodded.

"You like a something to drink?"

"No," I said. "Not really."

He walked over and put one hand on each side of my face. He pulled my head toward him and kissed my mouth, very softly. He moved back and looked up into my eyes.

"I think this when I see you watch me tonight," he said. "I think you not mind to kiss me."

I leaned down and brushed his lips again. I put my arms around him, and he pressed close against me.

He moved away, lit three large candles and a stick of incense, and switched off the overhead light. He stood beside me and slowly unbuttoned my shirt, kissing me lightly each time he undid a button. When he got to the last one, he slipped my shirt off, tossed it onto a chair, and kissed my chest. I unbuttoned his shirt the same way, the slowness and the incense making it seem like a dream. The skin of his chest was smooth and brown. Soft. Nothing I'd ever touched had felt so good.

He stepped out of his shoes and pulled off his socks. I did

the same. He unbuckled my belt, unzipped my pants, and pulled them off. I did the same with his. He moved away and turned toward the bed, looking at me over his shoulder. He pushed the back of his shorts down, very slowly, letting the lovely mounds appear a fraction of an inch at a time. He faced me and slid the front down just as slowly. His penis was full and hard and snapped up as soon as he pushed past the tip. He stepped out of his shorts and threw them on the chair.

"Now you," he said.

I did what he had done. Slowly the back. Slowly the front. Shorts on the chair.

We stood and looked at each other for a minute. He walked over to the bed, moved most of the pillows, lay on his back, and stretched his arms toward me.

I was unprepared for the overwhelming eroticism of leisurely touching. He brushed his hands softly across every inch of me, and I brushed every part of him. He sighed with pleasure. It was a kind of getting acquainted far deeper than talk. Through that touching, I came to know him well. He gave, the better to receive. His touches guided mine. Gentle strokes on the insides of my thighs let me know he would enjoy that, too. Gentle kisses up and around my penis taught me how to please him there.

He guessed my wants by listening to my sighs and the pace of my breathing, by responding to the tightening of my hands on his shoulders. I wasn't sure how I knew that's what he was doing, but I did. And knowing it, I began to listen to his breathing and feel the guidance in his hands.

The pace of everything, touching and breathing, increased from slow to insistent. When it came time to thrust, he guided me into him as he lay on his back, his legs across my shoulders.

Oh, yes, I thought. This is the way. I can see your face. I can watch you stroke yourself. I can bend down to kiss you. Oh, yes. Yes.

I exploded inside him, and a second later, he exploded onto

his chest. We wrapped our arms around each other as tightly as we could and lay there, panting. As we calmed, he nestled beside me, his head resting on my chest. I rubbed my hand up and down the smooth skin of his back.

After a while, he sat up and looked down at me, smiling. "Will we talk now?" he asked.

I felt uneasy. "About what?"

"Many things. What you think and what you do."

"You're interested in what I do?"

"Surely I am. I have seen all that is outside of you. Where you are soft and where you are hard. How you look down there. That your arm is strong. Is very nice to see this. But I know nothing of what is your life."

"Such as?"

"One thing of course I wonder, is what part you make in this war."

"Why do you want to know that?"

He wrinkled his forehead. "Some soldiers go to jungles to shoot. Some drive a truck through the streets. You do not?"

"No."

"So I wonder in myself what it is you do."

"I sit at a desk in a big building."

He giggled. "A *desk*? You make a war with a *desk*? I want to know how you do that."

"Why?"

He stopped smiling. His face was angry. "Why? Why? Why? Is that all you know to say? Take off your clothes and lie here is not all I wish of you. I wish to know what person you are. Is this seem. . . . mmm. . . . seem strange to you? You have not a wonder of what person *I* am?"

"Of course I do."

"So! Just so! You to wonder is OK. No problem. Me to wonder mean you say 'why?' Your mind is not like mine, Mahtyew. It go to places I do not understand."

"I'm sorry," I said.

He hit his fist on one of the pillows. "Do not be sorry. Sorry is only useless. It is. . . . mmmmm. . . . a thing I hear you GI say. Mmm. Waste of time! Sorry is only waste of time. To do, to learn, to talk with a friend is a worth. Feel sorry is a useless. You do not know this, Mah-tyew?"

"No. I guess not."

"Mmmmm. I think I must play your game. I must ask why it is, whatever I say, you ask me 'why'?"

I looked at him. His eyes were direct and unwavering.

"Because I'm afraid," I said.

"*Afraid*?" He shook his head. "You say this is so before we come up stairs. You are afraid here with me?"

"Yes."

"Of what are you afraid? Of make love with a man?"

"Partly."

"And partly what more?"

"I'd rather not say."

"Oh, yes, I see. Afraid when you touch me because I am so funny color! He is so dark, poor Nhan. He will make me dirty."

"Never!"

"'Never,' you say? I see this in faces of other GIs. They move when they pass us on streets so they will not touch us. *Our* streets in *our* city, and they will not touch us."

I pulled him down beside me and held him close.

"Some of them may feel that, but I certainly don't. I think you're beautiful. I love your color and your size and your shape."

He moved my arm and sat up again.

"Then it was some other thing. The other part you were afraid."

I looked away. He waited. I looked back at him.

"I was afraid you would betray me," I said. "Tell someone

we were in bed together. Let them take pictures of us like this so they could make me tell them things they wanted to know."

For long, painful minutes, he looked down at me. His eyes were sad.

"You are strange man, Mah-tyew." He continued to look straight at me. "You know this river of Cholon where poorest people live? That river is full of waste from their bodies and old food from their tables and fish that float upside down because they cannot live in such a water. Your mind is like that river, Mah-tyew. Full of things that rot and smell bad."

He sat still for a few minutes, just looking at me. I didn't move.

"Next time when you are alone," he said, "play your game of 'why' with yourself. Ask yourself why ugliness fill your head so full it cannot know who is good and who is not."

I felt tears running down my cheeks and onto my neck. He bent down and kissed the corner of each eye.

"I am glad you cry," he said. "It tell to me you are some good after all. That what I thought was in you may be there even so."

I pulled him down beside me again. He put his arms around me and kissed the side of my neck.

"Please help me," I said.

"Yes, I will. If I can."

I raised up on my elbow and looked into his eyes.

"Captain Matthew Fairchild," I said. "Serial number 05416280. Army Intelligence. Assigned to Headquarters, U.S. Army Vietnam. Tan Son Nhut Air Base. My job is to figure out where enemy troops are and where they may be going."

His eyes crinkled. "'Enemy,'" he said. "Funny word." He put his hand on my cheek. "Thank you, Mah-tyew. I will never say these things to any person."

I looked at my watch. Eleven-thirty.

"I have to go," I said.

"I wish not."

"I wish not, too." I kissed him, and he smiled at me.

"You feel better now?" he asked.

"You don't know how much."

"Good. We will do this again?"

"If you want us to."

"*If*? Dead fish in your brain, Mah-tyew. What do you think this is meaning? That I would do all this with you, say all these things, and wish you would not come back?"

"I thought maybe I had offended you."

"'Offended.' I am not sure of this word. If it mean make feel sad, yes. You did. If it mean make too much angry to see again, no. No, no. I do not understand what dark streets your mind go down, Mah-tyew, but I see in you a person of. . . . of a worth. And. . . ." He shrugged. "To touch you is excitement for me and to lie by your arm make me content. These are not things that come for a man each day. You think?"

"I think."

He smiled.

"Then come again. Maybe you begin to see a more kindly way Vietnam people. All of us are not 'enemy,' you know. Some are just people."

"Maybe so. But not you. You're extraordinary."

"What is this?"

"Splendid. Marvelous. Wonderful."

He giggled. "Oh, yes. 'Wonderful' I know. I think not so much of that I am, but inside I feel happy that you may think so."

"Then I still make your heart smile a little?"

He leaned over and kissed me, slow and soft and comfortable.

"If it smile more, it will jump outside."

After I had dressed and he was standing beside me at the door, I said, "Look. I have a crazy schedule. I don't ever know when I'll be able to come into town. I have to travel around, and sometimes things come up. . . ."

He put two fingers on my mouth.

"Please you will not worry. I work every night but only Monday. I will make no plan for after until I see if you come or no. If you come, we will not talk there but I will meet you here in this place. Is this plan good?"

I nodded.

"You know how to find this place?"

"Yes."

"In this way, no one will see us talk in restaurant. No one will see us walk on streets. Then those who wish to harm you cannot do so by me."

I held him close and wanted never to leave.

# 28

"We've gotta get a handle on this fucking war, Fairchild," said Colonel Dunhill. "Somehow. We're pouring the men in, finally. We're whipping the sons-of-bitches every time we get close enough to try. We're bombing the goddam supply bases in Cambodia. And what happens? We end up further behind than we were when we started. I know we can do better than that. Fuck! We sure as hell better, or it's gonna be one long, frustrating frigging war."

He pulled at the ends of his mustache. "I want you to get your ass out there. Spend some time in the field with guys who've been in combat. Ask them what it's like. What it is that goes so fucking wrong."

"I have a feeling, sir, if I ask them, they'll tell me. Warts and all. Is that what you want to hear?"

"Goddam right. The frigging wartier the better. Our asses

are on the line here, Fairchild. Yours, mine, the CGs, all the way up. We're trained to *know* this stuff, for god's sake. We got the fanciest fucking technology the world has ever seen, and these runty little dipshits in pajamas are running us ragged. You get yourself out there and find out why."

"Got any places in mind, sir?"

"Yeah. The sergeant-major's been in touch with some folks he knows. He says you'll get a better picture if you spread yourself around. I figure two places—somewhere down in the Delta, then up around Chu Lai."

"How long can I take?"

"Not long. I don't like you being away from here more than a couple of days. Don't forget those frigging Congressmen who crept up on us."

"Not likely, sir."

"So. Is a day in each place enough?"

"I'll make it be, sir."

"Good man. That's what I like to hear. Get all the coordinates up to date, whip up a sort of comprehensive summary of all the latest stuff so I can give the CG a special briefing, and be ready to leave by noon tomorrow. That way you'll be back by the end of the week."

"Yes, sir."

"And be sure the sergeant-major knows exactly where you'll be. If I need you, I want to be able to haul your ass right back in."

# 29

I went first to the Delta, to a base camp near Can Tho. I flew over in a chopper with a crew whom I made no attempt to get to know. The pilots flew, the sergeant gave orders, two gunners took turns keeping watch through the open doorway, and I sat strapped to an inside seat, not even thinking of looking out.

The sergeant-major had done his job well, as usual, and everything went smoothly. I talked with a couple of lieutenants about organizing patrols and the logistics of helicopter assaults. I talked with some sergeants about the difficulty of integrating new arrivals into smoothly functioning units and the frustration of rarely being able to choose when a fight would take place. I had a surprisingly good supper with the officers—hot, flown in by chopper—and went back for more.

I was feeling discouraged. Nothing I'd heard so far was anything new or revealing or even very helpful. Well. I'd been through the chiefs. It was time to try the Indians.

One of the lieutenants had picked out three grunts, the most experienced in his platoon. They were waiting for me in a tent, sitting on stools around a table lit by a lantern hooked up to a generator. The lieutenant introduced us and left us alone. They were a corporal named Ortega, called Taco, and two PFCs, Beanie and Wireless. They were nervous at first, but I tried to explain what I was after.

"No one knows better than you that we've never fought a war like this before," I said. "All the brass are having a hard time getting a handle on it. They're used to fighting an enemy they can see, not one that leaves boobytraps lying around and disappears every time we get within five miles of him.

"We need every bit of information we can get on what it's like for you guys out there humping around in the jungle. It doesn't do any of us any good if the brass decide to do something any one of you could tell them hasn't got a chance in hell of succeeding."

They all nodded.

"You're the ones who know. Not me. And not the men I work for. You. So if you can try to tell me what you've learned, just shoot the breeze and say whatever comes into your mind, maybe we can come up with something that'll make things better for you. Easier for you. And help us start winning this war, if we can. Does that make any sense to you?"

They looked at each other.

"Yes, sir," said Taco. "It does."

"So tell me," I said.

They looked at each other again. Beanie cleared his throat. I waited.

"It's the boonies, sir," said Wireless, a thin, nervous man who spoke so softly I had to lean forward to hear him. "The jungle, or whatever you call that shitass kind of vegetation. Nobody hasn't been there could ever understand what a creepy goddam place it is." He had a circle of rattan he kept pulling through his hands. He stared at the table and didn't look up. "They got a hundred ways to kill you out there, Captain. All of 'em awful. The ordinary ways are bad enough. You stick your head up, and somebody shoots you. OK. It's bad, uh course. Your buddy's dead, and you're sorry. But it seems. . . . It seems fair somehow, you know what I'm saying? I mean, he stuck his head up, like he oughtn't've done, and he got it shot off. Fair enough.

"But *this*! Shit! You don't know where to put your hand or where to walk. Things blow up all around you, or the ground just ain't there no more."

"They got stakes, Captain, rip right through your boots," said Beanie. "Or fly up and poke your eyes out. They're so painful you scream your guts out. You scream and scream, and it doesn't do one damn bit of good. You get to thinking it's the dead guys that're the lucky ones after all."

"It's not just the VC, neither," said Taco. "The jungle's trying to kill you, too. All by itself. You ever see elephant grass, Captain?"

I shook my head.

"It's the worst stuff God ever put on this earth. It gets to be tall, like way over your head. And tough. So tough you can hardly hack your way through it. And the edges are so sharp you can't believe it. Sharper than the sharpest razor blade you ever saw."

He held out the backs of his hands. They were covered with tiny scars.

"Every place you put your hands you get a cut. Every fucking place. You walk through it two feet you're bleeding from every piece of skin's not covered up. And we don't walk no two feet, Captain. We walk fucking miles. Every day we walk fucking miles, and the goddam *plants* are chewing us up. Never mind no Charlie trying to get at you. The fucking *plants* are eating you alive."

"And what blood they don't get," said Beanie, "the frigging mosquitoes suck out. Big as goddam model airplanes. They buzz around and bite every goddam place they can get at. You got both hands on your rifle, for Christ sake. You can't go swatting at 'em like you were on a goddam picnic. So they just chew away."

"I hate the leeches most of all," said Wireless, just above a whisper. "They latch onto your balls and suck the blood right out of 'em. All the time you're walking along, they're sitting there, hitching a ride on your balls sucking the blood right out of 'em. Just getting fatter and uglier while they fill themselves up with your blood."

"That's what makes it so frigging creepy," said Beanie. "Everything's after your blood. Plants and insects and leeches. All trying to get at your blood."

"Trying, hell," said Taco. "They damn well succeed. You leave more out in the boonies than you bring back with you, shot up or not."

They were silent, all looking down at the table. I waited.

"Still," said Beanie, "it's Charlie makes it the worst. Sets up all those boobytraps all over the goddam place. I mean, how the fuck does he do it? We can barely hack our way through with a meat cleaver, but he slips himself in, wires up the cleverest, most invisible fucking boobytraps you ever seen, and slips right out again without the tiniest fucking trace. I mean, how the fuck does he *do* it?"

"However he does it," said Taco, "we can't *move* without checking every inch of ground. Every leaf. Every blade of grass. Shit! All the time you're thinking you're about to get it, and you don't have any fucking idea from where. It eats at you, Captain, you know? Your nerves get so twisted up and stay so tight all the time you can't ever get no relief. Never mind even *thinking* about getting a good night's sleep. What's that?"

They all laughed.

"You wake up just as tired as when you went to sleep, and you *know* you got a day ahead is gonna need some real sharp wits. And you know that's the one frigging thing you got the least of."

"That's it," said Wireless. "That's the thing really gets you down in the end. You're always so frigging tired. You never get to sleep. Not really. You always got half a eye open and a ear cocked for the slightest sound. Just in case. It fucking wears you down, Captain. It does."

"You know why?" said Beanie. "Cause what we don't get is any fucking kind of routine. You can't count on anything. Not fucking *any*thing. We get hit at night. Then another night. And another night. 'Charlie always attacks at night,' we say, nodding at each other. 'Fucking cowards. Scared to show their ugly slanty-eyed faces in the daytime.' They hit us another night. And another night. 'Yeah,' we say. 'Fucking cowards.'

"Then they hit us with everything they got at high fucking noon. Rip through the camp. Blow up the vehicles and the ammo dump. Fade away before we know which way they're headed. So we up the guards, day *and* night. For nothing.

Nothing happens. We ease up. Then a night attack. And another night. And another. I tell you, Captain, you could lose your fucking marbles, if you had any left to lose."

"I hate 'em," said Wireless, louder this time. "Sometimes I think that's what it is gets us through all this shit. Having somebody to hate." He pulled his rattan circle around and around in his hands. "The thing about it is, it's gotta be some*body* you hate. Not some*thing*. That don't work. It's gotta be some*body*. You can't hate leeches or mosquitoes or goddamn blades of elephant grass. Not the way I'm talking about. They're just being what the fuck they are and doing the only things they know how to do. Nope. For hate to really do you some good, it's gotta be aimed at somebody's got the possibility of doing something else but's decided to do the things make you hate him."

"Wireless is right," said Beanie. "What keeps us going, what makes us able to get out there and hump through those shitty frigging jungles day after day, is hating the goddam VC. Pure and simple unadulterated hate. Never mind Ho Chi Minh or fucking North Vietnamese regulars or any that shit. They're off somewheres else. Charlie's like our own private enemy. Squatty little slant-eyed bastards in fucking *pajamas* trying their damndest to waste us. You know what I'm saying?"

I nodded.

"Every buddy gets blown off, you hate Charlie more. 'Fucking bastards,' you yell. 'How could they do this?' Course you know damn well how they could. Same way you do it to their buddies every chance you get. But you ask it anyhow. 'Fucking bastards. How could they do this to Rodriguez? He was a helluva good guy, and they just blew him away.' 'We'll get 'em,' says somebody. 'Fuckin' A, we'll get 'em,' you say back. And when you do, you shoot their dead bodies all full of holes. To make you feel better, you're thinking, and when it doesn't, you hack off a finger or an ear and carry it around in your pack. You feel of it sometimes and you grin to yourself. 'One less fucking bastard out there prowling around. I got the proof of it right here.'

"Hate, you see, Captain. It's a powerful thing. And once you turn it on, you got a helluva job turning it off."

No one spoke for a long time.

"It's the sneakiness makes me hate 'em the most," said Wireless. "The way you never see 'em. They don't fight the way they're supposed to, see? That's the thing. They wait for you to go by and then shoot you in the back. 'Bout as un-American as you can get."

He crushed the rattan circle into a ball and squeezed it. His knuckles were white.

"When you just get here and go out on your first patrol, you think trouble's in front of you, where you're headed. Don't take you long to find out it's everywhere. *Every* fucking where. You come to a village and nobody's there. Not a fucking soul. You search all the way through it, lose three guys to a mine hidden in a jar of rice, move on out carrying your dead buddies, and thirty seconds later the bastards are right back there in their village laughing at us. Fucking *laughing* at us, Captain. You know what they're thinking. Big stupid asshole gorillas is what they think we are. Three men dead just so we could pass through their shitass village and not change a fucking thing. You see what I'm saying, Captain?"

"Yes," I said.

"We patrol all over the frigging place, and nothing changes. We *don't* patrol, and nothing changes. We get orders to do this or do that, and we think 'Yeah. Yeah. Sure. Big fucking deal. It ain't gonna change a thing.' So why do we go out? Why do we keep doing such a dumb-ass thing that don't accomplish shit? Because we hate Charlie. And going out means we got a chance to kill him. Like he killed Doughboy and the Ranger and Sammy-pie and Trader Vic."

"Hate's an easy emotion to live with, Captain," said Beanie. "You'd be surprised. It's not like some of the others that have to be tended to. It takes care of itself. Feeds itself, if you know what I mean. All you have to do is give it a place to live and do what it tells you to do.

"And here's the great part. What it wants you to do and what your CO orders you to do are exactly the same frigging thing. Kill the bastards before they kill you. Beautiful. Just beautiful."

"But, you know," said Taco, "I hate 'em all right. But I respect 'em, too. I can't help it. I mean, look what all we throw at 'em, and they just keep on a-coming. Right into our frigging camps. Shit! You wouldn't catch *me* crawling into no VC camp in the middle of the goddam night. Think how big your balls gotta be to do something that fucking brave."

"You're thinking of that sapper last week," said Beanie.

"Yeah," said Taco.

"What's that?" I asked.

"Well," said Taco. "Last—what was it? Thursday?"

"Coulda been," said Beanie.

"Whatever," said Taco. "Real late at night, these three sappers come crawling in through the concertina wire on the perimeter. *Through* it, I'm saying. You ever look real close at concertina wire, Captain?"

"No."

"It's got these thousands of little bitty razor blades all over it. Sharper than elephant grass even. Shit, you walk within three feet of it, you got a cut on your hand. And these guys come inching their way in through all—what?—six, seven feet of it. They was all the way inside and headed for the trucks, maybe, or the supply tent, when one of the guys on guard duty just happened to spot them. He killed one and thinks he wounded another, but those other two just disappeared. Back out through the concertina somewheres, we reckoned.

"We was all awake then, because of the shooting and all, but nobody saw them go. Scary. Like ghosts. A couple of us pulled the dead one over to the light. And you shoulda seen him. He was wearing just this G-string kind of thing, so his clothes wouldn't snag on the wire, we figured. But the thing was, it was his skin that got snagged. Hundreds of slices with little drops of blood oozing out. Jesus! Can you even imagine how frigging painful that must of been? But he just kept on a-coming. How much do you have to care about something to be willing to give yourself that much frigging pain? You gotta respect somebody willing to go through all that."

"Christ," said Beanie. "You got to wonder why. Why the fuck would he do something like that?"

"Maybe 'why' isn't the question," I said.

"How's that?" asked Taco.

"Nothing," I said. "Just thinking out loud."

# 30

Next morning a different chopper crew flew me up to a base camp northwest of Chu Lai, stopping at Nha Trang on the way to refuel. The sky was clear when we landed at the camp, but the ground was wet. It looked as if it had been wet for a long time. Puddles of orange-red water sat in a sea of mud. Boards nailed crosswise on upright planks created walkways that went off in all directions. The air was hot and heavy, full of the moisture the sun was pulling up from the muck around us.

Once again, I sat first with some of the officers and then with some of the sergeants. They talked about tactics and weaponry and the need for better coordination all around. Again I asked to see some of the grunts. The commander of C Company suggested his second platoon and sent me over that way. The platoon leader, a Lieutenant Morehead, didn't think much of my plan.

"I can tell you whatever you need to know, sir," he said. "I keep up with what all's happening in my platoon, and I debrief every patrol as soon as it gets back in. There's nothing goes on around here I don't know about."

"Of course, Lieutenant," I said. "I appreciate that, and the last thing I'd want to do is undermine any of your authority. But this is the best chance the top brass is likely to get to hear what the guys who do the fighting really think. I certainly don't know what that is, neither does the CG, and, to be fair, neither do you."

He glanced up sharply.

"When you talk to them," I said, "they've got to be worried about looking good in your eyes, so they might think they need to hold things back. I'm just a jerk from Headquarters they've never seen before and probably won't ever see again. I'm not going to be using any names, so they can tell me whatever they want. I've got to hope that'll be closer to the truth of what's really going on than anyone at Headquarters usually gets to hear. Does that make any sense to you?"

He shook his head but said, "Yes, sir. I guess maybe it does."

"You're welcome to come along, of course, and listen to all of it, if you like. But I expect you have plenty of other things you need to be doing."

He stared at me for a second or two. "As a matter of fact, I do," he said. "Just let me know what you find out, if you could, sir. I don't like to feel I'm not in charge here."

"You're in charge all right, Lieutenant. I have a hell of a lot of admiration for you guys out here making life-and-death decisions morning, noon, and night, while some of the rest of us sit around with our thumbs up our asses trying to figure out what to do next."

He smiled, for the first time. "I couldn't have put it better myself, Captain. Make yourself at home and talk to anyone you like who's not on duty."

"Thanks," I said.

He nodded curtly and walked away.

I headed over toward what seemed to be the mess tent. Two young men were sitting on wooden boxes near the back edge of a wide walkway. They had no shirts on so I couldn't tell their names or ranks, but neither one could have been more than twenty. Both were barefooted. The bigger one was cleaning his rifle, and the other was rubbing powder between his toes. They glanced up as I came closer.

"As you were," I said before they could get up. "This is a hell of a place for formalities."

They grinned at each other.

"Mind if I sit with you and talk a while?" I asked.

"What would you do if we said no?" asked the big one, a black man with about a two-day growth of beard and huge arms.

"Oh. Probably sit down and talk a while."

He winked at the red-haired man, whose ribs showed through his slender chest and whose pale face was pocked with old acne scars.

"In that case," said the big man, putting down his rifle, "we're glad to have ya. Aren't we, Creeper?"

"Thrilled," said the other. "Pull up a mud hole and join us."

I sat on the wooden walkway across from them.

"My name's Matthew Fairchild." I stuck out my hand. The big man shook it.

"Arthur Tolson," he said. "But everybody calls me Chowhound, for reasons you may be able to guess. This here's Creeper."

The other man shook my hand.

"Jacob Fleming," he said.

"Where do you hang out, Captain?" asked Chowhound.

"USARV Headquarters. Saigon."

"Intelligence, I see."

"Yes."

"You sit behind a desk?"

"Most days, yes."

"Fucking life of Riley."

"It has its moments."

"We don't care much for REMFs around here, Captain. You gotta know that." He squinted at me questioningly.

"Yeah," I said. "Rear-echelon motherfuckers. I know the term, and I know what you mean by it. But I'll tell you something. I got my assignment the same way you did, by pure accident. Don't get me wrong, I'm damn glad to have it, but I didn't do any maneuvering to get it. I wouldn't have known how. Fair enough?"

Chowhound looked at Creeper.

"Fair enough," he said.

"The way I figure it," I said, "we all end up trying to do our best, whatever it is they've asked us to do. Right now, what they've asked me to do is talk to as many guys like you as I can. Ones who really know what it's like out there. The more you can tell me, the better chance there is I might be able to do all of us, including you, some good.

"And even if I can't, what have you lost by spending some time shooting the shit?"

The two men looked at each other again. Chowhound raised his eyebrows once and looked back at me.

"Not a thing, Captain, come to think of it." He reached into the pocket of his fatigue jacket lying on the walkway. He took out a cigarette, offered the pack to Creeper and me, lit them all, and leaned back against the side of the tent.

"So, you're slumming around up here trying to make sense of this fucking mess?"

"Something like that."

"Well, by sheer dumbass luck, you've come to the exact right place, isn't that right, Creeper? We can solve it all for you in ten seconds. The truth is there's no sense to be made of it because there isn't any in it to begin with."

He took a puff and looked off past my shoulder.

"You know what I think about a lot, Captain? You'll tell yourself what a shithead moron I am, but this is the god's honest truth." He stopped. "You really interested in what I think, or you just playing around with us?"

"I'm really interested."

"Well, then. I keep remembering something from history class in high school. Some asshole Indian, either laughing his guts out or flying in outer space smoking mushrooms, tells these Spanish explorers all about these seven cities made out of gold. The Spaniards buy it, lock, stock, and barrel. Those crazyass fuckers gallop around the wilderness for fucking *years* looking for these cities that are gonna make 'em rich. What they keep running into is these beatup, dusty old adobe pueblos, but do they stop and say, 'Now, hold it. Maybe there isn't any such thing as these seven cities of gold'? They do not. They say, 'We just haven't looked hard enough in the right places,' and they go galloping off again. They're so frigging sure what they're after is out there someplace that most of 'em get themselves pumped full of arrows or just shrivel up and die looking for those cities that were never there."

He looked straight at me.

"Same here, Captain. Everybody first gets here starts out saying 'What's it all about? What're we all fighting for?' The smart ones, us grunts who get the picture in about a day and a half, stop looking and stop asking. It's the same fucking thing, Captain. No cities of gold out in the wilderness. No sense to this frigging war. Same same. You want to drive yourself crazy looking for it, be my guest."

"So how the hell do you do it?" I asked. "How do you keep going out there day after day if you think there's no sense to any of it?"

"Cause we're here," said Creeper. "Cause our buddies are here. And cause the fucking VC'll kill us all if we don't kill them first. How we got here gets to where it don't make no nevermind. Only thing matters is getting out. You, and as many of your buddies as you can get out with you."

"Creeper's right, Captain," said Chowhound. "Politics is for politicians. And high-blown theories are for pointy-heads never saw a jungle in their lives. They stand around looking at maps rubbing their chins and going 'Mmmm-hmmm' while we hump through the goddam boonies getting our asses blown off. Their big concern is world fucking domination. Ours is a whole lot more basic. Being alive when the next day rolls around."

"You're saying the brass over here don't have a clear picture of what's really going on?"

"I'm saying the brass any fucking where don't have a clear picture of anything but their own assholes, which is where they keep their heads most of the fucking time. Far as I'm concerned, the whole idea of war went straight downhill the minute the man deciding it was time to go off fighting stopped being the one riding at the head of the frigging column. Any time it gets where you can fucking well send off raw meat like Creeper and me to do your dirty business, reality's gonna take a goddam hike."

He stubbed his cigarette out on the side of the box he was sitting on.

"What's the worst thing about being here, would you say?" I asked, putting mine out too.

They looked at each other.

"Easy," said Creeper. "This fucking rain. Once it starts, it don't stop for six fucking months. Well. Some mornings, like today, it may ease off and give us a fucking break. But that's just like a teaser. Like it's up there saying, 'You think you're gonna have a chance to dry out, don't you, you poor motherfucking slob? Come halfway round the world with your prissy ideas about being dry and comfortable. You think it's been bad already? You ain't seen nothin' yet.' And sure enough, all we get is a few hours of relief now and then, and sure as shit the fucking stuff starts all over again."

I looked up at the sky. Big purple-gray clouds were moving in from the southeast.

"It's like the worst torture you ever heard of," said Chowhound. "It fucking rains and rains and rains and rains and rains. Christ! I been wet before. We all have. You get caught in a storm, and you run back to your nice warm house and change into nice warm clothes and hang the wet stuff up over the stove to dry. Here? Good fucking luck! You take off sopping wet socks and put on ones still damp from yesterday. You cram 'em down into your poor old boots that's just as wet as when you took 'em off. And out you go.

"Christ! It grinds down your nerves till there's nothing left of 'em. There's just the raw ends out flapping in the breeze, so tender anything touches 'em you want to scream. The next drop that starts to fall, you want to scream, 'Just stop fucking raining! You hear me? Just fucking stop! Give us a frigging *chance*!' But it doesn't stop. It just rains harder. So what happens is you get the idea the more you scream, the harder it's gonna come down. So we get mad at each other. 'Don't scream, you asshole,' we say. 'Can't you see you're just making it worse?' Christ!"

"And," said Creeper, "it ain't like it's gonna rain the next couple days and let up. It's six fucking, ever-loving, shit-eating *months*. Like now, we're only halfway through. How we gonna make it to the fall?"

He stared at me. I had to look away. The difference between our lives and theirs had never been so clear to me. For us, the rain was just a nuisance that meant we had to wear ponchos as we ran from the bus to the Headquarters building.

"It's your feet get the worst of it," said Chowhound. "Poor fuckers. Days like today you can get 'em out in the air, try to get 'em moving toward drying out. But it's a hopeless fucking battle. Pretty soon you gotta cram 'em back in those damp socks and down into those moldy old boots. Right away the mildew starts eating away again. First they get soft and puckered. Then they get all green and nasty-looking. Finally—god, here's the worst part—pieces of 'em start falling off in hunks. You pull your foot out of your sock, and part of it stays in there. Shit!"

He shook his head and looked away.

"And the smell," said Creeper. "Worse than anything you ever imagined. Kids always tease each other about smelly feet, but nothing you ever smelled before comes close to this. Like a rotten carcass only it's still hooked up to your live body. Sounds stupid to say it in a hellhole like this, but it's embarrassing. You feel like fucking *apologizing* for your feet."

"Remember Angie?" said Chowhound.

Creeper nodded.

"Who's that?" I asked.

"A good guy," said Creeper. "A real good guy. Sort of too tender like for this asshole place."

"What made you think of him?" I asked.

"We bunked right by each other. Me and Angie and Chowhound. One night we was getting ready for bed, and we heard Angie crying. 'What's up?' I said. 'I'm sorry, you guys,' he said. 'I know my feet stink real bad, but I can't help it.' 'We know that,' I said. 'Course you can't help it.' 'But it stinks so awful,' he said. 'I can't stand it myself, so how can you?' Chowhound come over and put his arm around Angie, but Angie wouldn't stop crying. 'They stink so bad,' he said. 'I'm rotting all away.'"

The two of them sat silent, staring at the walkway.

"Is he better now?" I asked.

Chowhound looked up sharply.

"Depends on your point of view," he said. "Two weeks ago, out on patrol, he stepped on a mine. Blew both his legs off at the knees. He bled to death while we waited for a medevac."

He looked back down at the walkway. I couldn't think of a question that wasn't intrusive.

"Problem is," said Creeper, "we gotta keep on going out. We got no choice. Charlie loves the monsoons. We figure he knows how much we hate 'em, so he picks the worst weather to step up his action. Don't seem to bother him a bit."

"Well, no wonder," said Chowhound. "It's his fucking jungles and his fucking monsoons. He *oughta* be used to 'em."

"Used to 'em or not," said Creeper, "he pushes us hard this time of year, so we always gotta be out in that shit. Patrolling. Poking around checking on what he's up to. But it's hell, I can tell you. It's bad enough when the sun's out and you can see. But when you're walking around out there and it's dark and gloomy, you can't believe how scared you can be. It's fucking terror every second of the way. You look at every leaf for a sign of a tripwire, but you can't quite make anything out. You look at every inch of ground to see if it's been tampered with. If a mine's under there, or a fucking pit full of punji stakes. But the rain messes up the signs. You can't really tell, so you look harder. It's hell, Captain. Pure living hell. Not once while you're out there can you let your guard down. Or you're dead. Or a buddy's dead."

"That's it," said Chowhound. "You asked what's the worst thing, Captain? It's not the rain. That just *seems* like the worst. What's really the worst is trying to keep all your buddies alive, and knowing there's no chance in hell you're gonna succeed. Even more than for yourself, you're scared for your buddies. Cause you love 'em. That may sound faggy to you, Captain, but it's the god's honest truth. You love those guys more than you ever thought you could love anybody on god's green earth. They're part of you, you know what I'm saying? They're going through just what you're going through. And they're looking out for you just like you're looking out for them. And you hate the thought that something you could do might get one of 'em hurt. Or killed, god forbid. That would be the terriblest thing of all. Much worse than dying yourself. Fucking up in some way that got a buddy killed. And you being still alive to remember it."

"When I was up at Pleiku," said Creeper, "before I got transferred here, a guy in my squad, Thumper, was on guard duty up there." He was twirling a splinter he'd pulled off the walkway round and round between his thumb and forefinger. He looked at it as he spoke. "We'd all been out the whole day on patrol, but after supper, somebody had to go right on guard duty. Had to. No choice. Everbody was dog tired. Thumper was just the one got picked. He caught himself nodding a couple times, but he just couldn't keep his head up straight, is what he told us. He nods, jerks up awake, nods again, like that. Then while he's nodding, he hears somebody coming towards him. Christ, right at him. He's scared shitless, so he fires. Not just once. Seven or eight times.

"'Jesus, Thumper,' says this voice. 'It's me, Corky.' It was the guy coming to replace him. A good buddy of his. A guy he really cared about. He'd gotten himself all twisted around while he was nodding. Thought inside the perimeter was outside and vice versa. So Thumper runs over, but Corky's hurt bad. 'Jesus, Thumper,' Corky says. 'Didn't you know it was me?' The medics got right to him, but there wasn't much they could do. He was all shot up. I mean, that close a range and all.

"We all sort of gathered around, not really believing it. One buddy is bleeding to death right there in front of us, and another is running up to everbody saying, 'I didn't know. You gotta believe me. I didn't know.' Well, the guys at the inquiry did believe him. 'Justifiable,' they said. 'Extenuating circumstances.'

"Try telling that to Thumper. First, he talked about it all the time. He'd grab people by the arm and go over every fucking detail, over and over and over. This went on for days. Then he stopped talking altogether. He just sat down and started rocking. Wouldn't say another word. Just stared and rocked and stared and rocked. Poor bastard. That's the most awful thing I can think of. Killing your own buddy."

"What happened to him?" I asked.

"They took him away somewheres. To try and help him, they said. As if anything could."

# 31

I worked all the next day on my report, gave it to the sergeant-major about seven, showered, changed, and headed straight for the Golden Dragon. I saw Nhan working but said nothing to him. I was waiting on the landing outside the apartment shortly after nine when he came running up the stairs, his key already in his hand. He leaned his umbrella against the bannister where I'd hung my poncho.

After we had made love, more feverishly than before, I lay beside him running my fingers through his soft, blue-black hair. I put my arms around him and held him tight. He kissed me gently on the lips and sat up. I lay on my back looking at him.

"Something bothers you," he said.

"Yes."

"It helps to say what it is?"

I hesitated. "I don't know. . . . Maybe. I've just spent two days talking to people about hating and killing, and it's upset me a lot. I'll tell you about it, sure, if you'd like to hear. I don't want you to feel left out of anything."

He put his hand on my mouth.

"Hating and killing I know too much already."

"Good. I'd much rather talk about you."

"Me?" He giggled. "What of me is interest to you?"

"Everything. Tell me about your name. It's beautiful."

"Was thought of by my grandmother, who is poet, to name me this. Is . . . How can I say to you? In Confucius teaching, are five virtues a person must . . . mmm . . . must work hard to have. One is *nhan*. Mean love of all persons. But special kind of love. Not one person to one person, but . . . mmmmm . . . sympathy love. Love that make you understand joy and sadness that come in life to each person."

He looked up.

"You know of this I speak?"

"Yes. We say compassion."

He smiled. "Such big word. Com. . . . Say again."

"Compassion."

"Com-pash-shun. Is me?"

I laughed.

"For sure is you. It's a perfect name. Either your grandmother was psychic, or you've managed somehow to grow up to fit your name."

"What is psy-chic?"

"Able to see the future."

"Is my grandmother, yes! She see very clear the past *and* future."

"And what's the rest of your name?"

"Tran Le Nhan. Family name first. Person name last."

"What do the others mean?"

He smiled.

"Names of emperors, both, who create peaceful and just

society from thousand years ago. I am proud to have their name."

I was startled. "A thousand years ago? You had emperors a thousand years ago?"

He pressed his lips together and narrowed his eyes. "You know nothing of our history, Mah-tyew?"

I shook my head.

He sat straight up and stared at me. "I know Plymouth Mayflower. Thomas Jefferson. We hold this truth to be self-evident. Emancipation Proclamation. I know all these things, and you know nothing of Au Lac, Dinh Bo Linh, Tran Hung Dao, Gia Long? These are only. . . . mmm. . . . funny names to you?"

"Yes."

"When your Christopher Columbus sail into unknown sea and find America, emperors of my people have already rule for two thousand years. Do your leaders, your great generals, know of this?"

"I doubt it."

He nodded, and his eyes were sad.

"You come so far, from other side of this world, to tell us how to rule our land, and you know *nothing* of what go before? This is a. . . . mmmmm. . . ." He hit his head with the palm of his hand. "What is, think you are so much important you have no care of other persons?"

"Arrogance?"

"Hmmmm! This is arrogance too big to think of. Can you explain me how such a thing can be?"

"No. I can't."

"And *you*, Mah-tyew? You in who I think I see some trying to understand. You had no thought to read of this before you come?"

"No," I said. "Will you tell me?"

He looked at me steadily. "Do you want to know because

it. . . . mmm. . . . because it matter to you, or because I am angry?"

"Both."

He laughed. "You are honest, Mah-tyew. I am glad for this. Yes, I will tell you."

I pulled him down beside me. He curled up in the angle of my arm and talked quietly, just below my ear.

"Vietnam people come from north. Not China, no! We are not same as China. No, no. These people, our ancestors, come from somewhere else and say they will live near where is now Hanoi. They come long before time of your Christ. They clear land. They plant rice. They build cities and palaces. In these palaces live emperors call Hung."

I loved the sound of his voice. The soft tickle of his breath on the side of my neck.

"Once these people make happy place, China emperor find he is hungry to take it for himself. Armies come, too strong for us. We lose. Hundreds of years, Chinese rule. Through Vietnam emperor, yes. But still they rule, not us. Sometimes rule is kind. Sometimes is cruel. But either one, kind or cruel, we feel the same. We want them to go so we can rule for us.

"Many times we fight. Many times we lose. Heroes from these fights we still honor today. But Chinese stay and stay. Vietnam can grow rice, can go out to fish, can write poems. But we cannot be happy because Chinese are here. No good. We want our own emperor to say what happen to us. So thousand years ago, we fight, and miracle happen!"

He sat up, his eyes sparkling.

"What you think? Chinese lose and go away! First we have great dynasty of Ly emperors, hundreds of years. Then great dynasty of Tran emperors, hundreds of years. Happy time for Vietnam. Artists make art. Poets make fine poems. Builders make palaces big and beautiful.

"Then, terrible thing." He frowned. "Mongol army from

Kublai Khan beat everyone. Go everywhere, beat everyone. Oh, yes? Not here!" He smiled. "Vietnam army and Tran Hung Dao, genius leader, stop them here and send them home. Much celebration. But, sad for us, only short. Chinese come again. Can you believe? They come again! This time they rule so bad. They steal all of Vietnam books and take to China. They force Vietnam people dress like Chinese, make hair like Chinese, study only Chinese books. Even, they say, we are no more Vietnam. We are province of China, Giao Chau. Terrible time, Mah-tyew, for my poor country."

He stared at the bed.

"But!" He threw back his head. "Just when time is most terrible come greatest hero, Le Loi. Oh, such great man. He lose, he fight. He lose, he fight. Each time, more people go to mountains to be where he is. Fight for him. When ten years go by, Le Loi win. Yes! Chinese go. Vietnam is free again. His name when he rule is Le Thai To, and he is good father to Vietnam people. With him is. . . . mmm. . . . is justice and food for all."

He stopped and sat shaking his head.

"And then?" I asked.

"Then. Ah, well. We think no one can be so terrible as Chinese. We are wrong. Next come worst of all. French." He said the word harshly. "But this you surely know."

"I knew they came, but I didn't know they were bad."

"Oh, yes. French rule here, so bad. Too long they rule so bad. Then is big war. Japanese come. French come back. Viet Minh win from them. Americans come. Who is strongest rule here. No thought for what is wishes of poor small Vietnam. Sad little country, my Vietnam. Always war. Always some big country come to tell us how to live."

He stared off somewhere past the top of my head.

"That's an amazing story," I said. "I had no idea."

He looked down at me. "Is better you know."

"Much better."

"Because I think to know story of these people is. . . . mmmmm. . . . is help you see they are more than cyclo driver or dishwasher or mama-san clean your toilet. These are proud people, Mah-tyew. We have poems. We have art. We have music. This way you see us now, poor and weak and dirty, is not only way we can be. Is way so many years of bad rule have make us."

I was about to say I was sorry for having been so unaware, but I remembered in time not to. Instead, I said, "Thank you for telling me all this. It does make me see things much differently."

"Is much in each life, even the most small," he said. "Each life of each person is big story, very important to that one person."

"And to those who care about him."

He smiled and bent over and kissed me.

"So what about your life?" I asked. "What's your story?"

He stopped smiling, and his eyes were sad again.

"Is not so grand as what I just say."

"But very important to me."

He put his hand on my cheek and looked at me. He nodded and rested his hand on my chest.

"I was born in Hue, where rule old emperors. My father was very smart man. He work. . . . he *worked* in library build many years ago by emperors. Big and beautiful, people say to me. Here were all important books of Vietnam history and culture since Chinese steal early ones. Place my father loved. When I was small child, was. . . . mmm. . . . was trying for revolution in Hue. Communists wanting to take charge there. They lose, but while they fight, library is all destroyed. Such a sadness. So many books. So much story of Vietnam all gone.

"We move to Saigon—my father, my mother, the mother of my father, my sister, I. My father work in library of university.

But is not the same. Can never be same as great library of emperors in Hue. My father come to be sick, and he die. Doctor say cholera, but my grandmother say no. Say his heart is so heavy it break.

"My mother then must earn food for us. She has already many years of school so she can be professor for university. My sister, three years more than me, has husband and two small childs. I live with my mother and my grandmother. I must help them to earn food, so I carry dishes for Chinese restaurant. Chinese! Is this a story? All these times, they force their rule on my poor country. All these times, we fight and make them go. Now I carry dirty dishes to their kitchen. This is all I can find for me to do. If this is not so sad, I could smile."

I looked up at him, and he looked down at me. The curves of his bare chest and arms, smooth and a deep warm brown, were so appealing I felt a stirring between my legs.

He glanced at my erection and laughed.

"So," he said, grinning. "History lesson excite you so much?"

"I think maybe it's the teacher."

He laughed again and fell over on top of me.

## 32

A report was lying open on Colonel Dunhill's desk. "Well, Fairchild," he said. "Looks like you've done it again."

"Thank you, sir."

"Almost."

"Sir?"

"The parts about what the men are facing out there are good. Damn good. Gives those of us back here out of it all a real feeling of what it's like to poke around in jungles and slog through rice paddies. Really vivid. On the whole, what you've got here's fine."

"But?"

"But your usual good judgment let you down a couple of times."

"Like where, sir?"

"Well, like all this fucking complaining. All this belly-aching about no sleep and wet feet. Come on, Fairchild! Soldiers are born complainers. Been at it since the first tribe of cavemen jumped the bunch across the valley. It fucking goes with the territory. I'll put you not knowing that down to youth and inexperience."

He pulled at his mustache. I waited.

"It's what we call goldbricking, Fairchild. Guys sitting around figuring out ways to get out of doing what they're ordered to do. And no fucking wonder. You gotta hand it to them for trying. Hell. What they're being asked to do is go out and maybe get themselves killed, for Christ sake. Very few of us just get on out there without some goddam prodding. Some heroes and some psychopaths, maybe, but everyone else needs a bit of a frigging push. And that's what military discipline's all about—breaking down a man's natural tendency to resist and making obeying an order fucking automatic. You see what I'm saying?"

I nodded.

"We drill those guys in basic till they're a well-oiled machine. Smooth as can be. They hear an order, they fucking well obey it. Automatic. Then they get to the real war, and it's not so frigging easy. They see poor bastards getting killed all around them, and they think, 'Fuck. The next one might be me.' So what do they do? They sit around thinking up reasons not to be out there where the fucking danger is. A few night attacks, and they say, 'Aw, please, Lieutenant. I'm too tired.' A little rain, and they say, 'I can't go out on patrol, Sarge. My boots are wet.'

"Come on, Fairchild. Use your fucking common sense. Wherever a war is, whatever the physical conditions, it's bound to be unpleasant. And the smartest of the guys are damn well going to seize on whatever they can find to keep them out of danger and excuse their own fucking mistakes. Which brings me to your most flagrant misjudgment of all."

He flipped through the report to the end.

"Here."

He tapped his finger on the page.

"This part about the sentry who killed his friend. Now that's really strong stuff. Makes a great story. But that's not the kind of thing I can send in to the CG. Not by a long damn shot. Or on up to MACV, for Christ sake. I mean, one incident of a guy too fucking confused to know which end is up? Just a frigging aberration. One we all regret, of course, but an aberration all the same. We can't go having people think our men over here are so out of it they're going around fucking *killing* each other. Now can we?"

I said nothing.

"Can we, Fairchild?"

"No, sir. I guess we can't."

"Not only is the thinking misguided, but the implications could damn well have serious repercussions. Let's face it. If a soldier gets so fucking screwed up he shoots one of his own buddies, well, that's his lookout. I don't say the circumstances weren't extenuating and he should be punished. Necessarily. It would all depend. But he sure as hell shouldn't be excused of all responsibility."

"He felt his responsibility all right, sir. I'm sure of that."

"Maybe. Maybe. But your version of the story leaves that a little vague. Makes it sound like the way his unit was running things contributed to what was, in fact, just an unfortunate fucking accident. And there's no way I'm going to pass that kind of unfounded rationalizing along to the CG."

He closed the report.

"Take this back and give it a good reworking."

He stared at me hard.

"We don't need a lot of fucking hearsay from some disgruntled soldiers who have no way of understanding the demands of leadership. What all's required to fight a war, especially one as frigging off-the-wall as this one.

"Our responsibility here, Fairchild, and down at MACV, is to look at the big fucking picture. We need to have some of the little-picture aspects pointed out to us from time to time, sure. The feel of the jungle and the dangers of goddam boobytraps and such. The things you've described so well. Of course we do. That's why I asked you to write this up for us in the first place. It helps make it all seem more real to those of us back here. Gives us a handle on why things are so different this time around.

"But it's still our responsibility to fit these littler things into the rest of the goddam picture. Our overall objectives here. What it is we're trying to do and how we've decided it can best be done. You see what I'm driving at?"

"I understand what you're saying, yes, sir."

He tossed the report across the desk toward me.

"Take out all that emotional crap and concentrate on the real military stuff. Patrolling. Chopper assaults. The need for better coordination. Stuff we can use."

"Yes, sir. Whatever you say."

As I turned to leave, I saw rain slashing against his office windows. Snug, I thought. We're very snug here.

# 33

The secure room became a haven for me. Most nights when I went back, Boots wasn't there. Only if we had something important, a briefing to be prepared on short notice or a great many troop locations to get posted, did I ask him to work for a while after supper. Usually, he'd go off drinking or to see his girlfriend, and I'd sit there with every intention of reading reports, jotting down my conclusions, and deciding what to put in Colonel Dunhill's daily briefing for the CG.

When I was in the room alone, I switched the music on the big tape player I'd bought at the PX from pop to classical. From The Mamas and The Papas to Bach or Chopin. I'd only begun to learn about classical music while I was in Washington, and I found myself buying every new tape the PX got in stock. I always intended to work, but often, when the music was especially beautiful, I'd stop reading or writing and lean back with my eyes closed, letting my thoughts drift.

Late one night, listening to Mozart, I discovered something extraordinary: the interior of my own mind. It was as unexpected as it was sudden. I have no idea what the moment itself was like. I only know that before, I was not aware. Afterward, I was. Aware of what? Of myself *as* a self, I guess. That I was the self doing the thinking and the remembering.

My mind had functioned perfectly well all along. I could hold conversations, study and memorize, recall someone's name when I saw his face. And, when I'd been alone, I'd had a fairly constant flow of memories and random thoughts, the way I assumed everyone did. But they just moved through my head of their own accord. I'd been observant enough and curious about the events that were going on around me. I'd just never given much thought to what they might mean.

Suddenly it was different. I was the thinker. I was the

rememberer. I was both the little boy in the memory and the man in whose head the memory resided. The two were connected, and I was connected to them. How did it feel to be me back then? I could try to sort it out. How did it feel to be me now? I could probe around and see if that was something I knew. It was exhilarating. And scary.

The music was a help. No, it was more than that. It was almost as if it was the music that was taking me to the places in my mind where these thoughts had lain hidden. Or, if hidden is too active a concept, had lain unlooked-for. Because I had never realized that it was possible to look.

The clearest, and in a way the most painful, result of all this was that there was no going back. I could never again regain that blithe indifference. That moral certainty based primarily on inattention. Once I'd become aware in that way, I could never be completely unaware again. I could try to ignore the messages, try to just drift the way I'd done for so long. But the part of myself that had been jolted awake wouldn't let me get away with that for long.

Come on, I'd say to myself. Who do you think you're kidding? And I'd know that I was the "I" doing the saying, the "myself" I was saying it to, and the "you" who'd been trying to do the kidding. All of them. I began to feel there was no place left to hide.

And sometimes I wanted to. Very much.

Every once in a while, when the memories were too painful or the connections too unflattering, I'd wish for those earlier, more obtuse times. They would seem to have been easier. Less demanding. Safer. But, more often than not, those feelings would pass, and I'd be glad again to be in touch with all of me, not just the surface.

# 34

One night at the apartment, lying in bed, Nhan said, "I talk of you sometimes to my mother, and she say she will like to know you."

"Oh?" I said.

"She meet some Americans, before and now, but no soldiers. She say she will like to talk some. Is okay, Mah-tyew?"

I was pleased and excited. "Of course it's okay. When?"

"She think for dinner Monday, the night I have no work. At Vietnam restaurant in Saigon. Is good idea?"

"Just tell me where."

Nhan and I met outside the restaurant, went in, and sat at a table near the center of the small room. I was watching the door when a slender, elegant woman wearing a dark blue *ao dai* walked in.

"My mother," said Nhan. We both stood up.

Her bearing was erect and, the thought occurred to me, regal. She greeted the man behind the cash register with a slight nod and walked toward us. She was small, but her presence filled the room.

She smiled at Nhan, placed her hands together, and bowed in his direction. He bowed in hers.

"My good friend Mah-tyew," he said. "My mother."

She bowed her head toward me, and I bowed back. I pulled out her chair for her, and she looked up at me quickly and smiled.

I was drawn to her instantly. Her face, though striking, was less beautiful than Nhan's, more lived-in. Her smile was warm but a bit remote. Not ingratiating like an American smile. More serene and self-contained. It was not meant to make me like her, it told me. I would have to decide that for myself. It was the outer demonstration of an inner sense of assurance, I decided. Well, why not? To be such a woman, a person of dignity and intelligence, and the mother of such a son? She had good reason to smile in just that way.

"It is kind of you to spend this time with me," she said. "I am grateful."

"Oh, no," I said. "The gratitude is all mine."

She looked at me steadily. "You are gracious."

"And honest, I hope."

"I hope so, too. Well. There are so many things to talk about. So many things to tell you about our country. Nhan says you have an interest." She ended with a slight rising inflection.

"Yes. Very much so. Mostly because he created it, not because I was wise enough to have it myself."

She nodded. "However it comes, it is a good thing. So we will talk. And if you become bored, you must promise to tell me. Otherwise, I will just keep on talking."

I laughed. "I promise, but I think it's going to be a long time before that happens."

Her smile was warmer, less remote.

The man from the cash register was standing beside her.

"Shall I order for us?" she asked.

"Please," I said.

She turned to the man and spoke in lilting Vietnamese. He walked toward the kitchen.

"What shall we talk of first?" she asked.

"You," I said.

She laughed. I saw that Nhan was smiling.

"First," I said, "and I don't mean to be impertinent, but how is it you speak English so perfectly?"

"You are generous," she said. "Languages have been a specialty of mine for many years, along with history. At first I learned them in order to read the history in the original texts. Then I began to teach them as well."

"Them?"

"English, French, Chinese, Japanese, and Hindi. These I read and teach. Some Italian, and a few words of Dutch. Enough to get by."

"My god," I said. "I've never known anyone who spoke so many."

She narrowed her eyes and tilted her head. "It is a great aid toward understanding."

The man put a plate of small dumplings in front of each of us. She and Nhan picked one up with their fingers. I did the same.

"Nhan told me you are a professor at the university," I said. "You teach languages?"

"English mostly, because it is what everyone wants to learn. But history is my love, and I teach several courses of that."

"Ancient or modern?"

She looked at me steadily. "You are shrewd, Matthew. I am pleased. More ancient than modern as a rule, these days. Ancient is patriotic. Modern can be. . . . complicated."

"She have been in trouble for this," said Nhan. "She will not. . . . What is. . . . ?" He said a word in Vietnamese.

"Back down," she said.

"She will not back down when government say she must. Is strong woman, my mother."

She smiled.

"I believe it," I said. "Then you're not a supporter of the current regime?"

"How could I be? They have their own interests at heart, not those of Vietnam."

"And what are Vietnam's interests?"

"To be left alone to find its own way."

"That doesn't seem likely to happen anytime soon."

"Sad to say, it does not."

"So which side do you think is closer to being right, the North or the South?"

She looked away, drummed one finger on the tablecloth, and looked back at me.

"It seems to be evading the question to say neither, but I must say it."

"I see."

"And what do *you* think of Vietnam, Matthew?"

I hesitated a moment before answering. "I think it would be beautiful, if we weren't always blowing it up."

"And the people?"

"I think they would probably be happy and productive, if our two sides weren't pulling them in so many different directions."

She nodded. "You have seen correctly. I am glad for that. And what do you think is your government's objective here?"

"To stop a communist aggression from taking over a country that could otherwise be free."

"Mmmmm," she said. "And do you personally believe that this is a worthwhile goal? Or that it is truly what is happening here?"

I looked at her eyes, but I couldn't read anything in them. "I want to be honest with you, but because of. . . . everything, I feel some reluctance. I feel a need to be cautious. I felt that way at first with Nhan, but I learned to trust him. Or decided to, I guess is more accurate. I would like to trust you, too, because of him, but I find I am hesitant."

Her eyes changed slightly. There was more warmth in them.

"You are looking for certainty in an uncertain world, my young friend," she said. "And you are not going to find it. It is a matter of loss or gain, not certainty. If we can be honest with each other in even the smallest way, we will have gained. Will good or harm come from it? We cannot know. We must make our small decisions as we go along, based on what we can see and what we feel. But I do know this: if we do not share our thoughts, harm is sure to be the result."

I nodded. "I believe you're right."

"I wish very much for you to know what this country is truly like," she said. "What has happened to its people. I cannot know what the result of this will be, but I know in my heart that without knowledge and understanding, decisions cannot be humane. They are made for other reasons, and people suffer."

Her gaze, though friendly, was intense. I was grateful when the man set bowls of soup in front of us. It gave me a little more time.

"The answer to your question," I said after tasting the soup, "is that I came here convinced that my government's goals here were entirely correct. And generous. And humane. I want to continue to believe that, and, for the most part, I do. But the more I see, the harder that is."

"Thank you, Matthew," she said, nodding. "This is a fair answer. Let me tell you some things, and then leave you to make your own decisions. What would you most like to know?"

"Nhan has told me some about your history. The emperors and the Chinese. But I've been wondering, how did you get from there to here?"

She put down her porcelain spoon and thought for a minute. "You will not like my answer. But I have to say that what you see now, the confusion and the scrambling for position, is the result of hundreds of years of European influence. Of greed and total unconcern with the people who live here."

"You're right. I'm *not* sure I like that answer. Tell me why you think that."

"All of you—Portuguese, French, Americans—came here believing that we, the Vietnamese, had no knowledge worth listening to. No experience worth taking the time to explore. So much has to do with what you came here expecting to accomplish. To conquer and to take, not to listen and understand. You from the West had the great ideal—progress. We were poor, backward people who revered the past and would have to run to catch up."

"And the Vietnamese, I assume, saw things differently?"

"Very much so. When those from the West first came here, we thought they were barbarians, with no idea of the proper way of doing things. We have not—forgive me for saying this to you—we have not much altered that view. Will it be inhospitable of me to tell you why?"

"Maybe, but I'd be grateful if you'd tell me anyway."

Her head jerked a little, and she looked over at Nhan, then back at me. "My son has said you have a sympathy unusual among your people. I begin to believe he may be right."

Nhan moved his leg under the table and brushed his knee against mine. I smiled at him.

"If you will be patient, I will go far back," she said. "To the 1600s, when our country was divided, as now, with the Trinh ruling in the North and the Nguyen ruling in the South. In those years, the Portuguese came to our shores seeking outposts for their trade. Their interest was not in us, of course, but in rich and powerful China. We were merely a convenient place to stop off on their way further north. In our history, you see, it is always China."

She sipped a spoonful of soup, talked a while, took another sip, talked some more. I liked watching her face. Her smile was the same as Nhan's, and her eyes sparkled the way his did when he was excited. I glanced over at Nhan. He was watching her as intently as I was.

The Portuguese, she was telling me, realized that it would be to their advantage to take a side in the bitter feud between the Nguyen and the Trinh. Since they'd set up their first outpost near what is now Danang, they took the side of the Nguyen. They brought to the Nguyen heavy guns and shiploads of ammunition. The Nguyen were delighted to have these arms, which made their power more equal to the more numerous Trinh.

In exchange, she explained, the Nguyen allowed the Portuguese to create a center for their trading on Vietnamese soil. But it quickly became apparent that the Portuguese had no intention of adhering to the laws and customs of Vietnam.

"These Portuguese," she said with indignation, as if it had happened last month, "wanted to act exactly as they had at home. They wanted to ignore our laws, violate our customs, and cheat our people. The Nguyen said, 'But no, you must obey. When you are in our country, you must do as our laws and customs require. When you are elsewhere, live as you choose. But here, have respect for our ways.'"

The Portuguese were unwilling to bend. So much so that when the Nguyen remained adamant, the Portuguese gathered up their arms, loaded their supplies onto their ships, and sailed away.

Next came the Dutch, who, she said, cared just as little about the customs of the Vietnamese and were even more cruel. The feud was still going on, and the Dutch decided to take the side of the Trinh and help them impose their will on the people of the south. When the Dutch sailed their fleet against the Nguyen, however, the Nguyen repelled them, damaging their fleet and making them very angry.

"And what did these Dutch do?" she asked, sitting up very straight. "Did they tend their wounds and repair their ships and sail again against the forces of the Nguyen? To see if this time they could beat them fairly? They did not. In their anger, they sailed far to the south to where the shores were not well protected. They landed there, took from the villages every person they could find, and, one by one, cut off their heads.

"I ask you now, young Matthew, is this the act of a civilized people?"

I shook my head.

"Even so," she said. "It is not. And what did this bizarre act gain for them? Nothing. Before many years had passed, they too had gathered themselves onto their ships and sailed away.

"From these experiences, which you may be sure we have not forgotten, we have learned two important things. We have learned that the men of the West and their ways are strange to us. Though we may try to understand these men, they do not try to understand us. And the second thing, perhaps the most important thing we have ever learned, is the value of patience. Even more powerful than all the guns and planes ever made is the ability to wait.

"We suffer. Sometimes we suffer much. But we endure. We remember our past, we hold up our heads, and we endure. Once again, even now, we will wait, and in time your people, too, will be gone."

The man took away our empty soup bowls.

"But surely the Europeans must have brought you *something* of value," I said.

"If they had come to share, we might have found a value together. But since they came to impose their will, we saw no value in it. Oh, not all of us. Some saw quickly the advantage in cooperating, and they and their families have become rich. But most of us, no. We have watched with resentment and wished that all of these foreigners would go away."

"I thought I heard you say earlier that progress is not something your people have looked kindly on. This surprises me. I've grown up believing that progress was the whole purpose of civilization."

She nodded.

"Yes, I can believe that. But it has been, you see, *your* concept of progress and *your* idea of what makes civilization worthwhile. We have our own ideas, developed over thousands of years. They served us well, until those from the West came here to tell us otherwise."

The man put plates of noodles with shrimp and what looked like pieces of squid in them in front of each of us. Nhan's mother smiled, ever so slightly, when I picked up my chopsticks. She and Nhan picked up theirs, and we all tasted it. I took a piece of squid first.

"Delicious," I said.

She nodded. I had the feeling I'd passed some kind of test.

"All who have come to our country from the West," she said, "have talked of this need for progress. Their kind of progress. They have talked of us as being stuck in the past. With great enthusiasm they have attacked the old Confucian order. It looked too much toward what had been, they said, and allowed no movement toward what must come.

"I have thought of this at great length, and I remain unconvinced. What are the things, I ask myself, that this progress has brought us? Science and technology. Two things the Confucian teaching did not include. Yes, this is true, I say. But are we better off? Let us look."

Nhan turned to me and raised his eyebrows. I rubbed my knee against his and smiled at him. Don't worry, I thought. I want to hear all of this. He nodded as if he'd heard me say it, picked up a clump of rice with his chopsticks, put it in his mouth, and looked back at his mother.

In the past, she was saying, the rulers of Vietnam, the emperors and the mandarins, were careful to make sure that each village man had his own plot of land on which to grow his rice. He either owned it himself or was loaned it by his village. No man was allowed to gather together large parcels of land. When times were hard and crops failed, the taxes each man owed to the emperor were lowered to what he could pay and still feed his family. When rain was more regular and floods less severe and rice was plentiful once again, the taxes would be raised. In this way, emperor and villager prospered or only made do together.

Under no circumstances, she said, was a man's land taken from him to pay his debts. This would never have been allowed. The man's land was his livelihood, both what fed his family and what made him a man of value, to himself, to his village, and to his country.

"Why, you of the West may say, was this our way?" she asked. "Because at the foundation of everything—home, family, village, love of emperor, religion—was a deep and abiding sense of how we, the Vietnamese, saw the world. We valued order and continuity and our ties to those who had gone before and those who would come after. It may have seemed to be a slow-moving and unchanging world, but each person, each man, woman, and child, had a place there."

"What about technology, though?" I asked. "You brushed past it awfully fast. Isn't it true that it can make lives a whole lot easier?"

She looked at me steadily for a minute. "That depends on what we choose to think 'easier' means. Does it mean a life that is more productive, less harsh? If so, there are things we have added to our lives that have done this for us. Chinese technology of dikes and canals, to keep the rivers of the north from destroying our fields, this we were grateful to learn. Use of the buffalo for plowing our fields, this we were glad to know as a way of making it less hard on a man to prepare his land. But did we need more than this? Did we need highways and ports and factories? I wonder.

"I can only tell you what happened when the French brought their progress to us and told us we would accept it whether we liked the gift or not.

"Our farmers had always owned and worked small pieces of land. Only so much as a man and his family could cultivate themselves. It was theirs, they had pride in it, and they made it blossom. The French believed a different thing. They believed in a piece of progress called 'efficiency.' A plot of land should not be allowed to produce only enough. It must be made to produce all that could be imagined in the mind of man. More, and always more, was the cry of their progress.

"And so, you might think, the result of this efficiency and increased production would be more food and prosperity for everyone. But no. The idea behind forcing the land to give forth all it could was to increase the wealth of the Frenchmen who thought of the idea, not the Vietnamese who worked the land.

"Small plots were less efficient than bigger plots. One man walking behind his buffalo took more time than many men with many buffalo. Our rulers had worked to keep farms small, so that many could own them. The French worked to make them large, so that the few could grow rich.

"It was a simple matter of mathematics, which we Vietnamese were not too backward to work out. The amount of land remains the same. The number of people continues to grow. If the size of the farms becomes larger, the number of those who can own them becomes smaller, and the number of those who own no land at all grows ever and ever greater.

"And how did this happen? How did small farmers lose their land?" She frowned. "By the Frenchmen's 'progressive' way of ruling and their 'progressive' administration of justice, both very different from our old ways stuck in the past.

"Under the French, when times were hard and less rice grew, taxes went up, not down. Suddenly, we were told, these taxes could not be paid in rice as before, but only in money. To find money, a farmer had to go to the lenders, who charged him dearly for the privilege of borrowing. You cannot pay your taxes? You cannot repay the lender? So sorry. We will take your land.

"In not many years, the few French who bothered to come here and the Vietnamese who had seen the value of collaborating with them had become wealthy beyond their dreams, and thousands, more thousands every year, became poor, with no land, no way to feed their families, and no place in the world. This made them—unprogressive people that they were—angry and resentful.

"Was the world only good, then, in this past for which we have so much reverence? Of course it was not. We had good rulers and bad, mandarins who were just and others who were greedy. But we have been better off—less unhappy, if you prefer—when they have been our own rulers and our own mandarins.

"What the French saw as static and unchanging, we saw as ancient and enduring. They believed we needed to uproot ourselves and move rapidly into a modern world of commerce and manufacture. We believed we needed to hold on to our ties to the past and not forget the accumulated wisdom of our ancestors."

She had eaten only a few bites as she talked, while Nhan and I had finished ours. She put her chopsticks down on her plate.

"All of history is complex," she said. "One reason, young Matthew, that I love it so much. What people have done and why and what has been the result is an intricate story not always easy to decipher. But there is one piece of it that seems to me to be simple. Who knows best how to be Vietnamese? The Chinese? The French? The Americans? I believe it might be the Vietnamese."

"But which?" I asked. "Those of the North or those of the South?"

She waved her hand. "As I told you before, it is neither! You see our dilemma? Neither. This is the curse of being small and powerless. We are seldom left alone to work out our own destiny. The rulers we have now in the South are the leftovers of the corrupt French. They have gone against our religious traditions and become Catholics. They have gone against our social traditions and become wealthy landowners at the expense of their own people.

"In the past, our social order was thus: emperor, scholar, farmer, worker, merchant, and, at the bottom, soldier. We have always believed that those who used their minds and those who worked with the soil were of more value than those who traded things made by others or those who wanted to fight. Here now, in the South, you see the result of your progress. When the force of tradition loses its power, the force of arms has nothing to control it, and the soldier, the man of arms, rises to the top. Because he can and because no one else can stop him. Not because he is wise or virtuous or compassionate."

"He has strength, but he lacks *nhan*," I said.

She smiled broadly. Nhan laughed.

"Bravo, Matthew," she said. "The leaders here in the South lack *nhan*. A grievous fault. And the rulers of the North? Them I detest."

"Why?" I asked.

She looked away.

"Because of her brother," Nhan said.

"What happened?" I asked.

She continued to stare at the wall.

"If it's something you'd rather not discuss. . . ."

She looked at me. I had the feeling she was deciding whether I was worthy of hearing this. Finally she nodded.

"My older brother Kim was an extraordinary man. Very handsome, like Nhan. Always a good student, but more important, always concerned about his family and his country. The future of Vietnam. He hated the French, more even than the rest of us. He made our mother tell over and over the story of her grandfather, a mandarin in the court of the Emperor Minh Mang who refused to serve the French conquerors.

"Kim loved history, too. Our history. When he was young and played with other boys, they must be Chinese invaders and he was Tran Hung Dao, the brave general who drove them from our land. As he grew older, he loved to organize—history clubs, debating clubs. The French began to know of him, and their security men began to watch him. But he was clever. He would not antagonize them. In public, he would say, with wide innocent eyes, 'I speak only of the past. Of glories that are gone and are no more.' In private, he worked with other young men to drive the foreign invaders from our country.

"First it was the French. Then, when war reached us, it was the Japanese. Toward the end of the war came the Americans. Kim worked with and against them all. He smiled and maneuvered and conspired, playing this one against that one. That one against this.

"'Be careful, beloved brother,' I would say. So many times I said it. 'These men do cruel things to those who stand in their way.' He would laugh and kiss my nose. 'Do not worry, little sister,' he would say. 'I am the buzzing fly. I buzz around their heads to annoy them, to see if they will react. They wave their hands, I move away, then buzz again. If they try to smash me, I fly very fast and am gone before the blow can land. Is this not the way of the buzzing fly?'

"'Yes, beloved brother,' I would say. 'It is the way.'

"'Then I am safe,' he would say, 'am I not?'"

She stared at the wall as she talked. Nhan pressed his knee against mine.

Her brother, she said, went from Hue to the university in Hanoi. His family was very proud. Not many did well enough to be chosen for the university in those days, but Kim was determined. He studied hard and off he went. He heard of secret organizations—the Communists, the Nationalists, the Buddhists—all working to make sure that when the war ended, the French would not regain control. That Vietnam would at last be free.

Since Kim had such a love of his country, she explained, he moved toward the Nationalist groups. He studied, he organized, he made speeches, he huddled in dark rooms to conspire. It was a glorious time for him. He came home full of talk about the way things would be when the war was over.

"Always there was open and secret," she said, still staring at the wall. "Public and private. Openly in public, he arranged visits to historic places. Sites of battles or temples or ruins of old castles. Groups of students would ride their bicycles to the spot and listen to fervent talks about what had occurred there hundreds or even thousands of years ago. How the Trung sisters threw out the Chinese army. Or Tran Hung Dao, Kim's childhood hero, or Le Loi. The trips filled them all with pride. They saw themselves, especially Kim, as the modern descendants of those ancient heroes. The ones on whom the responsibility had now fallen. They were part of the uninterrupted stream of Vietnamese history, from the oldest of times to that very day. The patriotism of these young people and the uneasiness of the French who spied on them grew in equal measure.

"Privately in secret, Kim attended meetings at which hidden arms and hoped-for revolts were discussed. He met there partisans of the Viet Minh, of course. He believed in their desire for freedom, but was skeptical of the depth of their love for Vietnam. They were looking to a power further north—always the curse of Vietnam in the past. Kim saw clearly, though, that the Nationalists could use the help of the Viet Minh. They were well organized and received money as well as training from their patrons in Russia. They could be useful. After all, the struggle required every person and every piaster that came its way."

She picked up her chopsticks, took a small bite, but had a hard time chewing it. She put the chopsticks down again, stared at her plate, and continued.

She told how, through the years, the Nationalists and the Viet Minh had fought among themselves, had even killed each other in ambushes and direct attacks. But, when the time came, Kim had believed, the two factions would join together for the good of Vietnam, and the Nationalists would prevail. They, after all, were the true inheritors of the mantle of Tran Hung

Dao, of Le Loi. They would be the ones who would lead Vietnam to freedom.

First Germany surrendered. Then Japan. Kim and his friends were ecstatic. It was only a matter of time. France, soundly defeated for a second time by Germany, would not dare to reassert its claims in Indochina, they believed. The pathetic Vichy government was gone. The Japanese were gone. America, the vanquisher of them all, the torch of freedom to the world, would help create an independent Vietnam. In a short time, the Nationalists would *be* the government of Vietnam.

She looked up at me, smiled slightly, and shook her head.

"Ah, no," she said. "Kim and his friends were idealistic. But Ho Chi Minh and *his* friends were pragmatic. While the Nationalists dreamed and made pretty speeches, the Viet Minh recruited, organized, put their people into key positions. Ho worked secretly with American intelligence, the OSS, giving them important information to use against the Japanese. And, actions that touched many hearts, he helped rescue American pilots shot down by the Japanese. He prepared his way with care and much cleverness.

"Thus, when Ho, to fill the vacuum created by the end of the war, established the Provisional Government of the Democratic Republic of Vietnam, with himself as President, no one else had the power to oppose him. The Americans, the only ones who could have changed things, looked on instead with approval. So, Kim and his friends thought, we must work with Ho Chi Minh to achieve our goal of independent government. Later, we can take control ourselves.

"Toward the end of 1945, when Nhan was a baby, Ho Chi Minh declared that elections for an assembly would be held in just three weeks. 'A trick,' cried many of the Nationalists. 'They are organized, we are not. How can we compete?'

"'If you will join with me in these elections,' said Ho, 'I will set aside so many seats in the assembly for Nationalist candidates.' 'Ah,' said Kim and his idealistic friends. 'You see?'"

She looked back down at her plate.

"Kim ran for one of those seats and was elected with many votes. He came home glowing with pride. To our mother, he said, 'You have lived to see it, beloved mother. Your son will help govern a free Vietnam.'

"Nothing shook his optimism. Not even when the Chinese allowed their troops in the north of Vietnam to be replaced with those of the French. It was a bitter blow, the French in control again, but Kim and his friends believed it was only temporary. One brief detour on the way to true independence. After all, there was a National Assembly, and Kim sat in it as a representative of his people."

Her voice had begun to waver. She sat for a minute with her eyes closed, breathing deeply, before she continued.

As time went by, she said, her brother saw his illusions die in the face of realities even he could not deny. Viet Minh forces in the northern provinces attacked the Nationalist forces, and many of Kim's allies were killed. When the Assembly met, the Viet Minh were always in control. They set the agenda, passed what they wished, adjourned without allowing others to speak. Kim grew more and more discouraged. He knew the Nationalists must do something to turn the tide. The question was, what?

Word came that Ho Chi Minh would be going to Paris to discuss the future of Vietnamese-French relations. With him would go his strong right hand, Pham Van Dong, along with some of the Nationalist leaders, as a show of unity. With two of the three most important Viet Minh leaders out of the country, this would be the time for Kim and his friends to rally support to themselves. They would rescue the floundering Nationalist cause.

But, she said, they underestimated the cunning of the man left in charge of the government, Vo Nguyen Giap, commander of the Army and the police. As soon as the others had left the country, Giap began his attack on Ho's opposition. The Chinese troops were gone, and the French, believing the Viet Minh to be the strongest of the contending groups, were happy to let them have their way. Giap's troops smashed their way into Nationalist headquarters in Hanoi, arrested everyone in sight, and burned all the files. The timing was brilliant. If all went well and the opposition was crushed, Ho Chi Minh would return with all power in his hands. If anything did *not* go well, Giap would be responsible and Ho could remain the kind paternal leader. All went well, however, and many Nationalists were arrested, intimidated, or killed.

I saw that Nhan was watching me watch his mother. I wanted not to be unfeeling, but I couldn't take my eyes off her face.

"When Ho returned," she said softly, "in the autumn of 1946, he called for a meeting of the National Assembly. Of all the Nationalist members who had been elected, more than half were nowhere to be seen. Armed guards stood around the meeting room, and the other Nationalists sat meekly by. Kim rose to be recognized. 'Where are my compatriots?' he asked in a loud voice. 'They are not here.'

"His friends tried to silence him, to pull him down into his seat. But he threw off their hands. 'I demand to know,' he said, 'where are my compatriots? We are all members of this Assembly, elected by the people. We are the government of Vietnam. We all together, not you alone. I demand to know, where are my friends?'

"'Oh,' said one of the leaders, 'they have been arrested. They were common criminals, and they have been arrested.'

"'Criminals?' said Kim. 'My honorable friends? Criminals? Then show me the charges. Show me the proof of their guilt.'

"'We have no time for these petty matters,' said the man in charge. 'We have important affairs to attend to.'

"'But I demand. . . . ,' said Kim.

"'Sit down and be quiet,' said the man.

"No one else objected, and Kim sat down.

"He had buzzed and buzzed that day, my beloved brother, but he had forgotten to dart away. When the session ended, he was not there. Someone, some of his friends, must have seen them take him away, but no one could remember. Fear blinded their eyes.

"But we knew where they took him. They made sure we knew, so that fear would quiet our tongues. They took him to the edge of town, to where they could dig a deep hole. And they buried him alive."

She looked at the wall, back at the table, back at the wall.

"I wake up in the night, even now, sweating and screaming, thinking of him at the bottom of that hole. Tied up, I have no doubt, so he could not move. But with his eyes uncovered so he could watch as they threw the dirt down over him. I think of his last moments, as the weight of the earth presses on him. My own breath grows short as I feel his lungs straining for the last of the air around him. I feel his heart break with the knowledge that he has failed. He has failed himself, his friends, his family, his people. He believed he could bring peace and freedom to the land he loved. But he could not."

She sat for a minute, then rose and said, "If you will excuse me please, I must go. I have been glad to talk with you, young Matthew, but I must go."

Nhan and I stood up.

"The bill for this meal will be sent to me," she said.

"No, please," I said. "Let me. . . ."

She turned to me and raised her hand. "You have been my guest, and I am grateful to you for coming."

"Thank you," I said.

She bowed her head, just a bit, toward me and then more deeply toward Nhan.

"My son is fond of you," she said, looking directly into my eyes. "Treat him well."

It was not a request.

# 35

When it came time for Major Sinclair to go home, the other officers organized a party for him. I was not so much asked as told I should be there.

The meeting room on the first floor of a small hotel downtown was crowded when I walked in. The air was already smoky, and some of the men had been drinking for a long time. Maybe a dozen young Vietnamese waiters carried trays of food around the room and kept drink glasses always filled. If Nhan had been among them, I would have left.

I had a much better time than I'd expected. Captain Thorne, the new office clown, had an unending supply of jokes. Most of them I'd never heard, and I found myself laughing as hard as the rest. Thorne didn't just tell his jokes, he acted them out—wiggling his eyebrows, screwing up his mouth, waving his hands. He was especially fond of faggot jokes, and I laughed at them too.

Sometime after eight, two of the waiters cleared the food off a large table at the far end of the room. Chuck Thorne jumped up on the table and held out his arms.

"Could I have your attention please, sirs and otherwise?" he said. "We got something really special lined up for the major's farewell. We want to be sure he remembers the best part of being in this godforsaken place. I haven't been here long enough to speak from experience about the gruesome parts of this war—the mortar attacks and the getting shot at and the watching people die.

"But I've had a taste of the sweet part—forgetting all those other things in the arms of a soft and gentle woman. And I can tell you this, from my vast and varied experience, there aren't any sweeter or softer women in the world than the ones we got here. So before he flies off home, we want to remind the major of that fact.

"Here to entertain us all is the very beautiful Miss Fortunes of War! Give her a big hand everybody."

A lovely young girl with long black hair walked through a door and over to the table and stepped onto a wooden box turned upside down beside it. Chuck gave her his hand and helped her step onto the table. Whistles and applause filled the room.

She stood there, looking down, waiting. She wore a white T-shirt, bright red panties, and blue shoes with very high heels. From a tape recorder in the corner came the sound of Elvis singing "Love Me Tender." As she began to dance, slowly and languidly, I saw the waiters leave the room.

She moved from one end of the table to the other, raising her arms and turning from time to time but never looking up. After a while, she reached for the bottom of her T-shirt and pulled it over her head. Her breasts were full and round and rode high on her chest. The men whistled and cheered their appreciation. She moved around a while longer, covering her breasts with the T-shirt and then taking it away. She stopped near the center of the table, dropped the T-shirt, and slowly pushed the red panties down to her ankles and stepped out of them. She stood still for a minute, looking down at the table. She bowed her head briefly, turned, stepped onto the wooden box, and left the room. Someone turned off the tape recorder.

I looked around. The other men were applauding and whistling, all except Major Sinclair. His face was flushed, and his lips were tight. He was as angry as I was.

If you felt that way, you hypocrite, I thought, why didn't you stop it?

Then I realized. He wasn't the biggest hypocrite there. Not by a long shot.

Afterward, at the apartment, Nhan looked wonderful in the candlelight, and touching his skin excited me the way it always did. But nothing—not looking at him lying naked beside me, not feeling his hands on me, not wishing with all my strength—nothing could make me hard.

"Is all right," Nhan said, snuggling into the curve of my arm. "Is good to just lie together sometimes, you think so?"

"I think so."

He kissed my chest and sighed contentedly. I should have told him about the major's party, but I was afraid. I thought of the waiters who'd left the room. Telling Nhan might raise a barrier between us, and I didn't want that. But *not* telling him was raising a barrier, too, maybe a stronger one. I couldn't win either way. I decided not telling him was safer.

"I am wondering, Mah-tyew," he said. "Was talking with my mother . . . . mmm. . . . unhappy time for you?"

"No!" I said. I pulled him tight against me. "Not at all. I loved meeting her. I thought she was terrific."

"You are sure? She is not shy to say what she think. She do not make you. . . . offended?"

"No. Well, a little. But mostly she made me think."

"About what?"

"You. Your family. She said her grandfather was a mandarin?"

"Grandfather of her mother, yes. Very high mandarin. In court of Emperor Minh Mang."

"So your family is of the nobility?"

"What is this?"

"Of royal blood. Like the emperor."

"Oh, no. Tran is name of many Vietnam people. From respect for old emperor, may be. No, no. Parents of this man were farmers. In small village. In that time, a man get to be mandarin because of his mind, not because his family is important."

"How do you mean, his mind?"

"Were examinations. All over Vietnam. Young men who know the most go to national examination. Literature and philosophy. Confucius thought. Those who do best go to be mandarin. Is Confucius way."

"I never heard of such a thing," I said. "Are you sure?"

He laughed. "Because you have not heard of this is not reason it cannot be so. I am very sure. Family could be of importance, yes, if it mean they have money to pay best teachers. Young man do not have to work in rice fields so has time for study. But position of family do not decide. No. What young man know in his head decide. Grandfather of my grandmother is very smart man. He do best in examination of all young men in Vietnam. He go not to province to be in government there. He go to Hue to be in court of Emperor Minh Mang."

"My god," I said.

"He rise far, this man. To side of Emperor. He help this Emperor rule wisely and well, and he have much respect. 'Study hard,' he tell all his children, my grandmother say. 'Study and remember. See how far learning have take us?' They tell their children and their children, and my mother tell me."

"So you studied, too?"

"Oh, yes. In university of Saigon, but. . . . These days are different. Mind is not so much important now. Is strength and money."

"But surely your family is still important?"

He laughed. "To some, yes, who remember old ways. To people who make decisions, no. Is all turn top to bottom. Happen already for this mandarin very long ago."

"How?"

"When Minh Mang die, this man stay at court. Help next emperors, Thieu Tri and Tu Duc. They are less wise men and less just rulers, but this man do what he can to help them keep away the French. No use. French come anyway, and soon they say they make the rules. This man say no. He is Vietnam man. Proud. He will not bow to French. If Minh Mang is alive, maybe he can say this. But Tu Duc is weak ruler. This man must leave the court. He go to Emperor's library to be man of the mind. He think. He write. But he can no more help Emperor say what will be done."

"Sad." I shook my head. "So did you study long enough to get a degree?"

"Yes. I finish two years ago."

"How old are you, then?"

"Twenty-four."

"But. . . . How is it you're not in the Army? Aren't most men your age being drafted?"

"Surely they are, but my grandmother pay."

"She *what*?"

"In this country, is possible to pay to not be in army. If you know the . . . . mmm. . . . right persons and if you give them so much money."

I was horrified. "You're telling me you *bought* your way out of serving your country?"

He gave me a patient look that irritated me.

"The side streets your mind go down are forever fascination to me, Mah-tyew."

"Don't give me any of your philosophical crap. Just answer the question. Are you saying your grandmother bought your way out of the army? Yes or no."

"Yes."

"So you're willing to let other young men die in your place, just because your family has money and theirs don't?"

"Yes or no is what you want?"

I nodded.

"Yes."

He sat looking at me.

"And how do you justify that?"

"Does this mean explain the reason?"

I ground my teeth together.

"Yes, of course it means explain the reason."

"First you say, 'don't give crap,' which I understand very well. Then you say, 'justify,' which I do not understand. All I ask you is, shall I tell what I believe of this or no?"

I exhaled slowly.

"Yes, Nhan. Tell me what you believe."

"Inside your question are many other questions. Do I fail to love my country because I do not rush to die for it? No, Mah-tyew. I love my country deep inside me. I love what it have been and what it may someday be. I do not love the men who now control it. They are happy to destroy it for their own small purposes.

"You hear about our history. We are tiny country, and always there is big, strong country want to tell us what to do. If our history mean anything, it mean that time work for us. In time, someone come who say what we believe. If such a person come in my life, I fight and die for him, yes. If he do not, I fight and die for no one."

He sat looking at me for a minute.

"I have only this one life, Mah-tyew. Many of your people say we of Vietnam do not put value on any one life, but with this as with many things, they see through crooked eyes. We love our life as much as anyone. Some Buddhists say one life do not matter. Say it is only place of suffering to which I come back again and again until I am wise enough to escape from it. But I do not think this way. I love this life. I love color of the sky when sun rise up. I love mists that sit on side of mountains. I love wind that move through fields of rice. I love strong curve of muscles in your arm. I want to see these things as long as I can."

His eyes were so intense I had to look away.

"I do not control if I live or die, Mah-tyew. I may die

tomorrow. *You* may die tomorrow. What I do control, in my small way, is do I choose to go where I most surely may die. If I think there is good in this, if my death and this good are. . . ." He moved his hands side by side, touched them several times, and raised his eyebrows.

"Connected," I said.

He nodded. "If this is so, this 'connected,' I will go to fight, yes, and be glad. But I do not see it so. Not now. Not here. If I die, I am only one more of thousands pile up in ditch, and nothing have change because I am gone. Rulers here will still be corrupt. And you Americans will still not care what happen to us, only that your place in this world stay strong. My death is then for nothing. Change nothing, Mah-tyew. You like to ask, 'for why?' Ask it of this.

"You curl your lip when you speak of money from my family that mean I do not go away and die. Because of me, my family have money no more. We once have very much, but as years pass by it go away. My grandmother give all that is left so I will not go to be in army. I do not ask her to. She decide and she do it. Now she have her house, and that is all. My mother earn not enough to feed us, so I take away dishes in restaurant own by Chinese.

"You think I enjoy this? In my family was mandarin in court of emperors. My grandmother is poet with much respect. My father work long time ago at great library in Hue. And I? I clean messy tables use by loud men who drink too much and go to sleep with women who could be my sister. My grandmother did not buy for me some life of happiness and chance to do things worth while. She buy for me only life I have, and I make from it what I can."

Once again, as on the first night we met, I had been crying for a long time, unable to move to brush away the tears. Nhan leaned over and kissed the corners of both eyes.

"You do not understand what have been my life, Mah-tyew.

I have been in middle of war every day I can remember. For me it is not a. . . . mmmmm. A. . . ." He shook his head. "I cannot remember how to say. Is a thing you hold in your mind but do not see in front of you."

"An abstraction?"

"Yes. For me, war is not abstraction, way it is for those in your country before they come here. They have had blessing of peace at home and war only far off in lands of someone else. For us it is opposite—always war here and peace what we hear of somewhere else.

"Is my thought that when peace have surround you, you can believe war is glorious thing. A. . . . mmmmm. Wait. I can find it." He closed his eyes for a second. "A ideal! A ideal of braveness and sacrifice that is part of what it mean to be a man. I see too often that no, war is ugly and cruel. And I do not need it to tell me if I am a man or no.

"Those in this world who are big and strong can march around and talk of glory and honor. We who are small and weak must try to stay alive. If we can."

He wiped my cheeks with the back of his hand.

"So, Mah-tyew. When I see that war is ugly and cruel and lead not to peace forever but only to next war. . . . When I see that reasons men say they have war are like morning mist. . . . When I see that those who ask me to fight are little dolls who dance on strings pulled by men who do not even like me, am I to put my life in danger for what I do not believe?

"To myself I say the answer is no. To my grandmother, who have more reasons than most others to love this small country and wish it to make its own way in this world, the answer is also no. We give them what they want and are happy to have, so much money. I keep something that, only for knowing you, has not much joy in it. . . . my life. If this is not a bargain worth making in your eyes, it seem so in mine."

I pulled him close to me and held him as tightly as I could.

# 36

Dvorak was a composer I'd heard very little about. But in a way I couldn't really put my finger on, I came to know him through his music. Although he had traveled and explored new worlds—that much was clear—he had either always known, or had come to know, that the roots of his passionate romanticism lay in his own past.

I put down the report I was pretending to read, leaned back, and felt the waves of intensity in his music washing over me. He was restless, looking for something, reaching out. I could tell by listening, though, that his seeking had a purpose. That wherever his wandering might take him, his sense of where he came from was the solid foundation on which he stood. Like Nhan and Nhan's mother. All three of them seemed to have put the pieces of their world into some kind of coherent order. I knew for a fact that I had not. Had never tried. I wondered if it was too late.

Three things I'd been intrigued by in college were history, anthropology, and mythology. It occurred to me that my childhood—anyone's childhood—was a strange and wonderful combination of all three. Could I work my way back and see if sorting out the past was something I could manage? It was worth a try.

I kept thinking about Nhan and his mother. What was it about them that struck such a resonant chord in me? Probably their sense of being connected to their world. Their bond with the present that came from a willingness to confront the past. Well, maybe that's what a life is, after all, I thought, a series of connections. Experiences and decisions and beliefs all moving in and out of each other, over and around, to form an intricate web. Most of us have a vague idea, as we go along, that something's being woven, but we can't see what the pattern is until much later, when we've moved on past and some event or recollection causes us to turn and look back at it.

We may sense, in our most intuitive moments, that there are things in that web we ought to be trying to understand, but, as with so much else, we leave it to others to do the explaining. Well, I thought, this is nothing new. It's been going on for thousands of years. Someone with a special kind of vision would look back, catch sight of something important, and tell those around him what it was he thought he saw. The rest of the clan, freed of the necessity of having to look for themselves, sat in the firelight and listened and nodded. In time, groups of these stories became tales, tales with special power and insight became myths, and myths that explained the way the world worked became cosmologies. To know the cosmology was to understand creation. Where we came from and why we are here.

The most elaborate of these cosmologies, the ones I'd studied with such fascination, are works of art. On the surface, they tell how the Earth rides on the back of a turtle, how the blood of warriors captured in battle nourishes the sun and gives it strength to rise again each morning, how gods and goddesses on a mountaintop work out their rivalries and jealousies in the lives of men. But, in reality, the thing they are telling is what it means to be a Hindu or a Maya or a Greek.

It occurred to me, in a flash of insight, that I'd grown up with a cosmology, too. It was a good deal less grand but no less fervently believed. It told what it meant to be a Texan in the middle years of the twentieth century. But what was its aim? What were we young men just embarking on life being taught to do? Three things came immediately to mind: we were to love God, love our country, and protect our women. Stand between them and anything that might bruise their delicate natures. We learned to open doors—of stores and cars and houses—for them. We learned that it was all right to let our minds wander when they chattered on, so long as we smiled and nodded every so often. We learned to praise their cooking and their child-raising skills and to always tell them how pretty they looked.

These were important lessons, as important in that world as making the sun rise, and the more diligent among us had learned them well. Everything had gone along smoothly, so far as I could remember. No one complained, least of all the women. What lay beneath their cheerful compliance was a mystery it had never occurred to me to explore. Now, though, I could see it clearly. It was the church. Both the institution and the building where we gathered so many times throughout the week. Sunday morning sermons set out the guidelines, and observing the pious before and after services and at church suppers showed how those guidelines could be acted out from day to day.

I felt myself nodding as I remembered the way religion had lain at the center of everyone's life, even the most irreverent. The drinkers, the cussers, the businessmen who cut corners Monday through Saturday all showed up at church on Sunday morning. There they sat among us as we learned about the three figures who, for us Presbyterians, shared center stage. First, there was God, stern, demanding, requiring eyes for eyes and teeth for teeth, fond of shouting "Thou shalt" and "Thou shalt not" from high up in the sky. Then there was Jesus, the Lamb of God, a vaguely effeminate, long-haired, doe-eyed, soft-hearted man who loved fishermen, little children, and prostitutes willing to reform. Finally, there was the Holy Ghost, who usually looked like a white dove but who could also talk to you if you stayed still and quiet long enough, giving you tips on how to live a clean and virtuous life.

We were taught that all three were of equal importance, but I'd never seen how that could be so. God got to carry the terrible swift sword and Jesus got to be the most lovable. All the

Holy Ghost got to do was whisper in your ear when you cheated on an exam and needed comfort. It had seemed unequal to me, but I learned not to ask too many questions.

Prayer was big. People prayed before every meal, at the beginning of every meeting, over the loudspeaker every morning at school, and at the start of every sporting event. Men prayed that their businesses would do well, women prayed that their children wouldn't disappoint them, and athletes prayed that they would make a strike, a basket, or a home run. Sports prayers had a special code. When they were said out loud, the one praying would always say, "And may the best man win," but it was understood by all that God was surely paying enough attention to know who that was supposed to be.

In this lineup, I suddenly realized, the Virgin Mary was nowhere to be seen. Well. She'd been the property of the Papist Catholics, one or two of whom insisted on living in most Texas towns, where they were not made to feel welcome and were certainly not invited into the better homes. This, of course, didn't count all the Mexicans around, who were inscrutable in so many ways that being Catholic was something you just expected of them anyway. And there were more obvious reasons for not inviting *them*.

Understanding flickered around the edges of my mind. Good old Protestant Texas men, I could see, had preferred to worship their women in other ways. By courting them and marrying them, by giving them a home and children and financial security, and by making all their important decisions for them. This sequence of events had allowed the men to be as attentive as was necessary in the earlier stages, progressively less so later on.

Yes. The sexes had conspired together to produce a certain kind of woman—loyal, of a sunny disposition, and willing to make meals as tasty and homes as comfortable as was humanly possible. Looking back now, I could see that things were almost exactly the opposite of what I'd thought they were: the women had been tough and resilient, and the men had been mostly afraid.

What the women did, they did well. Meals got cooked, children got raised, and tranquility reigned. Voices were seldom raised, harsh words were rarely exchanged, and a calm surface was universally admired.

Why, I wondered, was this so important to the men who came and went? Well, of course. These homes were their secure rooms, their refuges from the harshness of the rest of the world. They counted on having these peaceful havens to return to, because their lives outside them were so precarious. Promotions didn't come through, jobs were lost, and businesses failed. People they counted on let them down, and ideas they thought were surefire just didn't pan out. The world was a scary place, and one way of feeling safe in it was knowing where to place the blame. Disappointment, failure, unhappiness that wouldn't go away—the things a man wished for and couldn't seem to make happen—all this had to be the fault of someone else. Some alien who didn't, or wouldn't, belong. Disrupting the quiet order of things was such a grave offense that hate, otherwise frowned upon, was an appropriate response.

And who were these offenders? Niggers, Mexicans, and Jews, I remembered, were high up on the list, but people knew enough good ones here and there, ones that were hard-working and decent and accommodating, that they were generally acknowledged to be not *all* bad. The pinnacle of pure hatred was reserved for a more odious trio about whom nothing good could be said—atheists, communists, and queers. By the time I'd come along, they'd been lumped together for so many years it seemed unlikely a person could be one without being all three.

The more these painful but illuminating memories began to

fall into place, the more excited I became. I realized that connections, once again, were the key. If a man loved God, it followed that he loved his country and the institution of womanhood. That's the way things were meant to be. If he didn't love women, inconceivable but apparently it happened, he very likely didn't love his country either, and he sure as hell had no business thinking he could love God.

Religion and patriotism. In that time and place, I remembered oh so well, the two could not be separated. Each molded and shaped the other so thoroughly that neither could exist alone. America, after all, was God's own chosen land. History and geography proved that. God had created a beautiful, perfect place, full of wide open spaces and natural resources in abundance. But He, in His wisdom, had kept it hidden until men with just the right blend of independence, industriousness, and devotion were ready to claim it.

And claim it they certainly had—and subdued it and turned it to the purposes for which it had always been intended. So pleased was God that He promised to watch over and bless the endeavors of these His chosen men. Just as they looked after and guided and protected the weak and the helpless—women, children, and the inhabitants of other, less favored lands—so He would look after and guide and protect them.

But these blessings, like everything good in this world, came at a price. God required that every man prove his devotion. In times of peace, prayer and regular churchgoing were usually enough. But when enemies threatened, each man lucky enough to have been born in this blessed land had to be willing to do what was necessary to keep it safe. It was his duty—my duty—to go off and die, without hesitation, without regret, and, if necessary, without understanding just what the threat might be.

The only way a boy could grow up in such a world and retain his sanity was to believe everything and question nothing. I'd become a master of both.

# 37

Around that time, I heard from Brent. He'd sent a couple of cards since we were together, but this was the first letter.

"Penang was great, of course," he said. "I want to be sure you understand that. But being back has been so hard for me I wonder if going off to places like that is really such a good idea. To be here, then suddenly there, then suddenly here again is too much of a psychological jolt for a guy like me.

"When you see the same kind of life day after day, however bizarre and unreal it may be, you start to get used to it. You figure out what you have to do to get from day to day, and that's what you do. And, if you're lucky, you also manage to stay alive.

"Seeing civilization again—quiet streets, flowers, people going peacefully about their daily lives—throws all your coping mechanisms out of whack. You have to get back to where you were before, to not seeing or not caring, whichever works best, but it's much harder the second time around. The first time you're excited in a goofy kind of way. It's all new. And if it's scary or weird, well, it's a war, for god's sake. What did you expect? The second time, though, it's not new. It's the same, only worse than you remembered.

"This sounds gloomier than I'd intended, and probably isn't a good picture of how things really are. I'm fine, the work is always interesting, and I'm glad I'm here. Truly I am. It's not whether to be here or not that's the problem. I've settled that. It's how to get through it from day to day.

"You may be able to guess from this that we've had a rough couple of weeks. Charlie's obviously figured a lot of things out, and we're paying the price. He's shooting down many more choppers than before, and he's getting really good at ambushes. He sets a decoy force, we engage, they put up a little bit of a fight and then run. Our guys think, 'Runty little cowards. We've got them now,' and they go off after them. Pow! Right into the most carefully laid-out ambush you ever saw. It's my job to keep things like that from happening. Tell the platoon leaders and company commanders what to expect. I try. God knows I try. But they get out there in the excitement of the moment and think they know better.

"Trouble is these guys are all so green. Two reasons. First, the life expectancy of a raw new lieutenant is about forty-five minutes. Just long enough to get out where things are happening they don't know yet how to handle. That's not a criticism, don't get me wrong. They're good guys, and they do their best. They just don't know.

"The grunts are much better. They figure it out fast, because they arrive here knowing this is something they've never done before, so they damn well better listen to their buddies. And they do. They respect the experience of those who've been around awhile, so they listen and they benefit.

"It's exactly the opposite with some of the officers. Not all, thank god. Some. They think they've got to hit the ground knowing all there is to know. They're in command from the second they walk out in front of those troops, and they damn well better show it. What was all that high-priced, high-powered infantry training all about if not to prepare them for this very moment? They stagger around thinking a he-man image is what it takes to pull it off. Poor bastards. It's enough to break your heart.

"They listen to me eagerly enough about locations and strengths of enemy units. That's what I'm here for, to tell them where Charlie is and what he's likely to be up to and where he may be going. Fine. But tactics? Cautions about things I've seen go wrong? Not on your life. I'm a staff officer. They're command officers. I should tend to my business and let them tend to theirs. But god damn it, Matt. Helping them stay alive *is* my business, and I feel some real heavy guilt when I fail at that. Which I've been doing with unsettling regularity these recent weeks.

"Funny thing is, though, the ones I feel the sorriest for are the grunts. They all seem to have these built-in bullshit detectors. They scope out who's who and what's what real fast. Which means they end up being torn apart. They know when they're being told to do something that's a real bad idea, but all their training has taught them they've got to do it anyway. An order is an order. Sometimes it's following the order that gets them killed. Sometimes it's the indecision. Either way, it's all the luck of the draw. If they happen to get an officer who actually knows what's what—or knows enough to do some listening—their chances of survival shoot way up. They've won that roll of the dice.

"Which brings me right to the second problem. The system is rigged against letting officers get enough experience to keep themselves and their men alive. We've got lots of officers moving through the pipeline and only so many command slots. This is the only war we've got and the only opportunity those men may have to punch their command tickets. Without it, their chances of climbing very far up the ladder are about nil. Is that fair to them? Of course not. What's the solution? Rotate them in and out as fast as seems reasonable to whoever is doing the rotating. This means that the officers who live through the early months—and therefore, you assume, are doing something right—get transferred out just when they're getting to where they really *know* some important things. And who takes their place? Another babe in the woods with his newly punched ticket right there at the top of his personnel file. Hell of a way to run a war, if you ask me. But no one's asking.

"Sorry to load so much off on you like this, but it's been building up, and you're the only one in the world I could ever say all this to. Now that I've let off so much steam, I figure I can go back to playing along. And I'll be all right. I'll just keep on doing what I have to do, like everybody else.

"Well, Matt. What I remember most about Penang is afternoon naps. When I tell you I miss them very much, you'll know what I mean."

# 38

I sat alone in the secure room thinking about what Brent had called the "bizarre and unreal" world in which we found ourselves. I was struggling, almost every day now, not only to find a way to live in it but also to help others understand it. I was managing one all right but failing royally at the other.

They were asking too much of me, I was sure of that. How could I possibly make sense of it when everywhere I looked there were things I'd never seen before but thought I recognized and things that seemed familiar but turned out not to be? All around me was a bewildering mixture of similarities and differences, with a line between that was constantly shifting back and forth. Which should I concentrate on? Which, if I looked hard enough, would provide the thread that would lead me through the labyrinth?

When I'd arrived, I remembered, all those months ago, I'd been struck immediately by the similarities. The air was air. The water was water. The trees, though mostly of unusual shapes and sizes, were nonetheless trees.

The people, I had assumed, were also just people. They went about their lives the way people did. They planted crops and gathered in the harvest. They bought and sold, smiled and argued, hoped, despaired, and died. But, I had come to realize, they looked at the world through quite different eyes, their thoughts shaped by the beliefs they shared with those who had gone before.

And yet there were ways in which these people and mine were very much alike. One of the strongest of these common threads was certainty. Moving through the chaos of this conflict were two—or three or maybe even four—sides, all fighting for what they believed to be right, but, I knew now, with startlingly different ideas of what that "right" might be. Two distinct cultures faced each other across an abyss, each certain that its view of things was, self-evidently, the way the world was and ought to be.

Nhan and I had somehow found a way to reach across that abyss and touch each other, mentally as well as physically. His mother and my mother might have succeeded in communicating, finding common ground in how it felt to raise sons they would never entirely understand. But my grandfather and his great-great-grandfather, though they were both self-made men, could have come from different planets.

My grandfather. I hadn't thought of him for months, but he was an extraordinary man in his own right. He'd always inspired more respect in me than love, I realized. Why was that? Recent experience told me it might be worthwhile to look and see.

What did I remember about my mother's father? That he had lived all his life in a small town in east Texas. That he'd pulled himself up from one of the poorest families in town and created one of the most financially secure. And that he'd done this by making deals. People could never stop speculating about how he learned to do that. Shrewdness and plenty of common sense had been my guess.

Real estate, stocks, utilities, mineral rights, oil and gas wells, rental units, small office buildings—he did it all. It seemed inevitable that the town bank would ask him to be on its board of directors. Like everything else he touched, the bank flourished under his guidance.

In all the time I spent with him and Grandmother, I remembered, the only lack of harmony I ever saw in their marriage was that he was a Baptist and she was a Presbyterian, and they went to separate churches every Sunday of their lives. I'd never known much about his theology, since when my brother Paul and I were with them every summer, Grandmother was in charge of our religious instruction, but I'd gathered somehow that it involved a big chunk of God's helping those who helped themselves. The successful Baptists in town, of whom there were a good many, had given off the impression that the extent of their well-being was in direct proportion to the approval they received from God, which seemed to depend on the amount of effort they were willing to expend and the degree of devotion they were able to show toward God. I wondered now which had come first, the devotion or the success. Maybe they hadn't been sure either.

What all this meant in practical terms had been clearest to me on Sunday afternoons. Sitting around in a little white sailor suit with new shoes pinching my feet listening to aunts and uncles and cousins talk about who was doing poorly and who had passed on was holy. Getting comfortable in a pair of shorts and playing a snappy game of Old Maid or Go Fishing or, worse yet, going down to the picture show to see Roy Rogers or Hopalong Cassidy would have been sinful. So sinful that I'd understood quite clearly—though I'm not sure I was told it in so many words—that if Grandmother ever heard of my doing something forbidden on the Lord's Day she would never want to see me again. Never smile at me or hug me to her soft and ample chest. Never fix the cornbread and black-eyed peas I loved so much. It was fear of her disapproval more than God's that had kept me in line.

One positive side to all this holiness, I suddenly realized, was that people had been required to be kind and understanding to those less fortunate than they were. The ones whose ancestors somewhere way back had either disappointed God or hooked up with the Devil to such an extent that they were born poor or given dark skins so that everyone would know right away that God was displeased with them.

I couldn't say for sure about anyplace else, but in Texas the people I'd known had thought of colored folks in a vaguely paternal sort of way. It wasn't their fault they were slower, lazier, more childlike, less trustworthy than we were, and it was our Christian duty to do what we could for them. Be sure there were leftovers in the refrigerator for them to eat when they came to clean our houses. Pass on clothes that no longer fit or had one too many rips to be worth patching. Put canned goods in the cardboard box at church just before Thanksgiving and Christmas. Take care of them, in other words, since they weren't much good at taking care of themselves.

I'd been especially fond, I remembered, of the dignified old colored man who came in once a week to clean my grandparents' house. I would always run to say hello when I saw him coming up the driveway to the back door, and he'd always ask gravely what I'd been doing "to keep out of mischief." He called me Master Matthew, and I called him George. My grandfather called him "the boy." Even in George's presence. "I hope the boy won't forget to sweep the sidewalks," Grandfather would say to Grandmother, "the way he did last time." With George standing right there. It seemed to me like a strange way of getting a message across.

Of course, I'd known all about colored toilets in public places, and colored waiting rooms in bus stations, and colored balconies at the picture show, which they got to enter by a different door and up a hidden stairway. I'd always thought they just preferred to be by themselves, since they sure seemed to have more fun when they were together than when they were mixed in with us. I thought it was another of our kindnesses to them, letting them gather like that with their own people so they could feel comfortable enough to laugh and smile.

For all those years, I realized, I'd lived in a glass-domed, hermetically sealed, happy little world. But one day a crack had appeared.

It was the summer I was seven, and Paul and I had been at our grandparents' for a month or so. A neighbor was taking her son to meet his aunt and uncle for lunch in Dallas, and she asked if I could go along. My grandmother said yes.

I was thrilled. It seemed like such an adult thing to do. I wore long pants, a white shirt, and a clip-on bow tie. The five of us sat around a big table and ordered from a huge menu that folded three times. I ordered a cheeseburger, french fries, and a coke. I always did that when neither Mother nor Grandmother was there to make me eat something sensible.

But getting to eat a cheeseburger wasn't the important thing. Not that day. What I remembered most vividly was the waitress. She was a heavy-set colored woman with a face so kind you wanted to smile the minute you saw it. I must have done just that because she looked right at me, grinned, and said, "Well, sir. If you're not the handsomest, most grown-up-looking boy I ever did see, I don't know who is. You just tell me what you're most hungry for, and I'll see they fix it up special just for you."

Just for me. She didn't even know me, never saw me in her life that I could think of, and here she was saying such nice things to me before she even said "boo" to any of the others.

"What's the soup today?" said Billy's aunt in a loud voice, drawing attention to herself the way older people had a habit of doing. The waitress knew what was happening as well as I did because she looked at me and winked and then said, "Vegetable beef." Billy's aunt arranged it so we went around the table giving our orders, and she made sure she gave her order before anyone else. But the waitress knew how to shift things back. She put my cheeseburger in front of me first, and then tended to the others.

"If that's not the best cheeseburger you ever ate, sweet chile," she said, "you just let me know, and I'll whip it back to the kitchen and bring you another." She set the plates in front of the others without a word. Even if that cheeseburger'd had cockroaches crawling out of it, I wouldn't have sent it back for the world.

Grandmother didn't like to be disturbed while she was fixing supper, so I couldn't talk about my adventure till we were all sitting around the table. Grandfather told about his day down at the bank. Grandmother said Cousin Opal had been by and wished we'd all drive out on Sunday afternoon to sit with them a while. Grandfather said he thought that would be right nice.

Finally Grandmother turned to me. "And how was your lunch in Dallas today, Matthew?" she asked.

"Great!" I said. "We got waited on by the nicest colored lady I ever saw."

Grandmother sat straight up in her chair. "Shame on you, Matthew. You know better than that."

I was confused. "I don't understand," I said.

Grandmother held tightly to the arms of her chair. "I don't like you to say things that aren't so."

"About the colored lady? She *was* nice. She smiled at me and everything."

"She may well have been a nice enough person," Grandmother said, "but she was *not* a lady."

"Course she was," I said. "She had on a dress and a white apron."

"Don't be impudent with me, Matthew," Grandmother said. "I understand that she was a woman, but she couldn't possibly have been a lady. The word 'lady' means something special."

"But, Grandmother, she *was* special. You didn't see her. How could you know?"

Grandfather slapped the table. "You apologize to your grandmother this instant," he said. "How dare you question what she says?"

"I'm sorry, Grandmother," I said.

Paul snickered into his napkin.

"Well, you should be," she said. "Now say you're sorry you mistook a nigra woman, however nice she may have seemed to be, for a lady. Say you understand now there's a difference."

I looked at her. Her stern face made me sad. I wanted to make it soften to the way it usually was, but, even though I had no idea what this was all about, I somehow realized that something important was at stake.

"I can't," I said.

Grandmother's face got even harder. "Then you'll leave this table and go to your bed with no supper. You'll need to learn better manners than that if you expect to eat with us."

I went to the room Paul and I shared, sat on my bed, and tried to think. Why on earth would Grandmother, normally the kindest and most loving of people, have gotten so angry? From somewhere came the idea that, even if I didn't know why, that sweet-faced waitress did. She must have seen it day after day in the eyes of firmly corseted, tight-lipped women in hats who sat at her tables. Seen it and understood.

## 39

Every time Nhan and I made love, I felt more and more satisfied in a place deep inside me. The excitement I had expected, and at least some of the fever of mounting and subsiding passion. But the lingering contentment afterward was a surprise to me. We would lie together for as long as we could, touching softly here and there, kissing gently.

Nhan liked to snuggle face-down in the curve of my arm, his legs stretched out across the bed. I could look over the tangled hair of his head and see the lovely lines of his back. The way his smooth skin was indented a little along his spine, dipped in around his waist, and rose triumphantly over the mounds of his buttocks. I wondered each time I looked at them how it was that this exact combination of size and curvature and outward thrust could have come together to produce two such perfect shapes. They were an unsettling blend of utility and extraordinary beauty. For Nhan, they were something to carry around behind him and sit on. For me, they were one of nature's sublime creations.

It struck me that his skin was exactly the color skin should be. I looked at my own, pale beside his. Freckled and dotted with red pimples and sunken pores. His was silky and unblemished, and the candlelight gave it a soft kind of radiance. The decision that white skin was superior to darker ones was clearly not made for aesthetic reasons.

"We are very different, you and I," said Nhan.

I was so startled I jumped.

"In what way?"

"Many ways. You are tall. You see everything over heads of other people. I see only crowds of faces everywhere I go. You see far away, past cars and jeeps and people trotting through these streets. I see only what is between me and next person. When you talk, you look down, comfortable for you. I must always twist my neck and look up.

"You are strong. See these muscles of your arms and legs?" He moved his hand over them. "Mine are small and weak. You could with no trouble lift me over your head. I could not move you off the ground.

"You are rough. Big hairs on your chest and small hairs on

your arms and legs are exciting for me. My own body is plain and empty like skin of babies. When I touch your face late at night, hairs that start to come out scratch my hand. My own little hairs are soft and do not scratch."

He stopped. It seemed that he was thinking, so I didn't interrupt.

"But for us. . . . , difference have been good. I have learn from you, and you have learn from me. We are better now, we both, from this learning. Yes?"

"Yes."

# 40

One afternoon, Boots and I had taken a break, put our feet on our desks, and lit up cigarettes. Boots cleared his throat.

"Can I say something personal, Cap'm?"

"Of course. This is our own private world back here, Boots. You can say anything you want."

"I thought so, but I figured I oughta check." He took a long pull on his cigarette and blew two smoke rings, one inside the other.

"What I was wanting to say is, I'm glad you've found yourself a woman, Cap'm. Real glad."

My face felt hot.

"What makes you think that?" I asked.

He smiled, shook his head, and took a puff.

"I know the signs, Cap'm. Specially in someone I. . . . Well, someone I like. These last couple weeks you been more relaxed. The lines around your eyes are smoother, and you smile more. A lot more. My experience says it's good lovin' does that to a man. So I just wanted to tell you I'm glad.

You're all right, Cap'm, and you oughta have some good lovin' in your life. It's an area where I know what I'm talking about."

"So I hear. You're famous around Headquarters, you know. They say you stick with one woman instead of cruising the bars."

"That's right, I do. I met Lee the last time I was here, and we had some real good times. When I got back, by god, she was waiting for me. We took up right where we left off."

"Sounds pretty amazing to me."

"Me, too, come to think of it. Loyalty's not something you find a lot of in this world."

"*You*'ve got more than your share, seems to me."

"Depends."

"Meaning?"

"I've got a lot, that's for sure, but I'm real choosy where I put it."

I grinned. "Thanks, Boots."

"My pleasure, Cap'm."

# 41

Twice a week for eight weeks. Sixteen times we were together. My god. Three hours at the most each time, so forty-eight hours. Two days. Nhan and I were with each other for only two days. But when we were there, we were *there,* in a way I'd never experienced before. If, as I suspect, most people manage to be completely conscious of the present moment for no more than, say, a few minutes out of any given day, then for Nhan and me, each hour was more like a week. So . . . forty-eight weeks. Nhan and I had almost a year together, crammed into those few hours. Well. Almost a year. That wasn't so bad, I guess. After all.

I waited as long as I could to tell him about the move out to Long Binh. It was not so much to spare his feelings as mine. As long as I didn't have to say it, as long as we didn't have to talk about it, both of us hear the words, I could believe that he and I would just go on as we were. But the time came when I couldn't wait any more.

"My headquarters is moving away from Saigon. A little ways north to a place in the country called Long Binh."

"Ah, yes. I have heard of this. But now?"

"Friday."

"So." He nodded. "I thought it would not come so soon." He nodded again.

I was suddenly furious. "Don't you know what that means?"

He looked up at me, startled.

"Of course I know what that means. We will see each other not much, if at all. Yes?"

I wanted to shake him. "After all we've been through, this is the best you can do?"

He narrowed his eyes and looked at me steadily. "Speak clearly, Mah-tyew. Say what you mean. What is this 'best you can do'?"

"This is the end of our little affair, so far as we know. I thought you'd at least be upset."

He reached out his hand and put it on my cheek. I hit it away. He put it back, and I hit it again.

"This is what mean 'be upset'? Kick your feet against the gate of heaven and say, 'I do not want this to be. Make it to be some other way.' Is this it?"

I leaned my head on his chest.

"Is a thing GIs say when someone is not enough aware. They say, 'Pay attention.' Is good way to say this, I think. *Pay* attention. Spend time to see what go on around you. You must learn to pay attention to life, Mah-tyew. It will be what it will be. We are small ants in the great wideness of this world. This world do not care what happen to us. It will turn and turn in its own time, with no thought of what we wish for.

"World will be what it will be. We make our choices when we can, when what to do is in our hands. But we must learn to know which are those things we can make choice about, and which are not. Care about you so much? Yes, that I can choose to do. Keep you here with me forever? No. Is not my choice to make."

He kissed me softly on the forehead.

"If 'upset' mean to wish what will be will *not* be, then no, I am not 'upset.' I see too much in my life to think this would do some good. But will I be sad when I can no more touch you like this? Oh, yes, I will. I will be sad to the bottom of my heart for the rest of my life."

He held me tight and rocked me back and forth. Then he put his hand under my chin and lifted my head so he could look in my eyes.

"Are things to feel that are good and have a value, I believe. Upset is a useless one. What is, is, Mah-tyew. What is not, is not. Upset, to my thinking, hang between like unhappy child. 'What is, I wish not to be. What is not, *must* be or I hold my breath and cry.' Or do I not understand this word?"

"No. You understand it very well."

"Good. Instead of useless thing, make more sense to feel value one. Like thankful. I am thankful so much I can know you. I have pleasure to touch every part of you, and I know I forget none of them. When I close my eyes, I can see you lie beside me. When I shut out noise around me, I can hear you say my name. I can remember way you have touch me, softness that change your face when you look at me, heaviness of your step when you must go. You have give to me gifts of such value that when I think of you late at night when I cannot sleep, I will smile.

"I will be unhappy, too, Mah-tyew. Never forget this. Unhappy I cannot kiss your mouth or put my head on your chest. But unhappy is good, too. Everything that is, is good in its own way. And unhappy is a thing that is. Upset is a thing we create, and it fill us up with. . . ." He looked at me and blinked. "I do not know this word. Is a thing that turn in circles inside you and make you think, 'If this were not so, all would be well.'"

"Frustration," I said.

"Oh, yes?" He smiled. "Big fat word. Frus-tra-tion. Yes?"

I smiled, too.

"You're wonderful," I said. "You know that?"

"I hope no one ever make you think different."

"How could they?"

I put my hand between his legs and felt him grow hard instantly. He giggled and rolled over on top of me. We came together twice and still couldn't let each other go. I would get up, fully intending to put my clothes on and head back to the BOQ. But, before I knew it, I'd be back in bed, holding him, brushing my hands all over him, kissing him everywhere I could think of. He alternated between gentle and passionate in a way that drove me crazy.

As midnight—and final curfew—approached, I somehow managed to get dressed and made it to the door, Nhan standing naked and beautiful beside me.

"I'll try to get back in to see you," I said.

His arms were around my waist. He tightened them.

"I know," he said.

"I don't think letters are a good idea, but if. . . ."

He put his hand on my lips.

"I know, Mah-tyew."

I ran down the block to the main cross-street and hailed a cab. No need to tell the driver to hurry. Full-speed was the only way they ever drove. As we roared through the quiet, empty streets, I pressed two fingers hard into the bridge of my nose. It worked. I was dry-eyed and composed when I paid the taxi driver and returned the MP's salute.

"Cutting it a little close, sir," he said.

"Just under or just over?"

"Just over, sir. But we'll call it even."

"Thanks, Sergeant. I appreciate that."

He grinned. "Hope it was worth it, sir."

I laughed.

"Yes," I said. "I believe it was."

# 42

Living in the barracks at Long Binh was exciting in a way that surprised me. I loved being in the middle of so many male bodies, nineteen of them, so often barely clothed or naked. But all I did was look and laugh at their antics. It was the most aggressively masculine among us who did the most teasing.

Whenever someone came in from the showers outside, towel wrapped around his waist, one of them would whistle from his bunk. "Sweetheart," he would say. "My heart's pounding. Come on over and let me kiss you." Someone else might pull the towel off, and the whistles would grow louder.

"Seven inches! Darling, you didn't tell me. I'll be over as soon as the lights are out."

A bare butt rarely went by without getting whacked with a towel. A bare penis *never* went by without its size and presumed proficiency being discussed. They said it was all "good clean fun," and I believed them. No one who was really interested would have dared to act like that.

The most flamboyant of all was a tall, muscular, crewcut major named Dubinski, who had a wife and three sons back home in Colorado. Most times when he came back from the shower, his towel would be not around his waist but wrapped around his head like a turban. He would stretch out one arm, hand dangling limply from the end. He'd sway his hips from side to side as he came toward his bunk. He'd flip his long, attractive penis up and down and yell, "Daddy's home, girls. Come and get it. Don't be shy. It's playtime. Come and get it." We'd all laugh.

Another guy, just as big and brawny, a first lieutenant named O'Reilly whose bunk was across the aisle and about halfway up, liked to wait till the lights were out and we were drifting off to sleep. "I'm lonely," he would say in a high singsong voice. "I'm soooooo lonely. Who wants to come and cuddle?"

Then there were the three guys down at the other end who had masturbating contests after lights-out on "dirty sheet night," the Thursday night before the mama-sans brought in clean linen on Friday morning.

One of them would start to talk, loud enough that the rest of us could hear. "I'm hard already. You guys hard yet?"

"Yeah, I'm hard. I feel her mouth licking around on me. Sucking up and down right at the tip. Oh, man. You feel it?"

"Oh, yeah. I feel it. She's got those soft lips and that busy tongue. Oh, yeah. Keep that tongue moving. Oh, man."

The point of the contest seemed to be to see who could creak the springs on his cot the most strenuously and who could moan the loudest when he came. Little telltale squeaks elsewhere let me know there were others taking advantage of the highly charged erotic atmosphere. But it was always the he-men in the barracks who let off tension in these ways. Those of us who were queer would never have dared.

# 43

I missed Nhan. Not every minute. Nothing quite so romantic as that. But a good part of every day. It was knowing I couldn't just run down and see him in a night or two that made me feel anxious.

Everyone was rushing around, trying to get settled into the huge, not-yet-completed Headquarters building, and I rushed with them. When I was busy, whatever I was doing took all my attention. If I slowed down a little, though, it wasn't long before I was thinking about Nhan. What I missed most were his smooth, soft skin and his sanity.

Boots and I worked hard at putting together the new secure room. Money was no object, so we asked for everything we could think of. Track lighting with rheostats aimed at much bigger maps, all carefully matted and framed. No more thumbtacks shoved into wallboard. Built-in audiovisual equipment and a screen that pulled down from the ceiling. Our own padded leather chairs and room to leave them in place all the time. No more rearranging furniture whenever a briefing came along. Built-in speakers that filled the room with music while we worked. We even had thick carpeting and an air conditioner that didn't hum.

It was all very elegant, much more impressive than the old room, and the CG took to bringing most of his visitors by to see it. Staff officers from the Pentagon. Division commanders. Air Force and Marine brass who'd stopped by to check on the progress at Long Binh. I saw more stars those first few weeks than I ever had at Boy Scout camp. Boots and I got very good at impromptu tap dances around the room, me with my pointer, Boots at the rheostats.

Then, as quickly as it had arisen, interest subsided, and we went back to a more normal routine. Boots and I stuck tape up every morning, I briefed the colonel, the colonel briefed the CG.

# 44

"Pack your duffel, Captain," said Col. Dunhill.

"Where to this time, sir?" I asked.

"Danang, first off. Then out to some pissant village near there."

I sat in the chair beside his desk. He pulled at his mustache and stared out the window.

"What is it you want me to do, sir?"

"*Do*?" he said, turning to glare at me. "*Do*? I want you to tell me what the fuck is going on in this shitass place. That's what I want you to *do*."

Uh-oh, *that* mood, I thought. Open my mouth, and he'll nail me to the wall. Wait, and he'll tell me what I need to know. I waited.

He slapped both hands down on his desk, hard.

"It's driving me frigging nuts," he said. "Wars I know about. Find out where the enemy is and blow him the fuck up. Right? I do the finding. I tell the CG. He gets someone to go blow the bastards up. Simple. But *this* place. Christ!"

He rubbed his hand across the bald spot on the top of his head. I waited.

"Trouble is, Fairchild, this isn't a war we got here. It's a goddam schizophrenia ward. I mean, if you're gonna fight a war, you gotta know some things. A few, at the very frigging least. And the only thing, the only one lonely godforsaken thing I can tell you for sure, right here today, is that we're going *nowhere* unless we get a little help and support from these fucking ingrates we're surrounded by. We aren't getting any now, that's for goddam sure. And if we don't find a way to get some *quick*, we're dead in the water. You hear what I'm saying?"

"Yes, sir."

"'Hearts and minds.' That's what MACV's calling it. We've gotta find out what these people are all about. Figure a way to reach them. They don't think like we do, that's for damn sure. We've always known that. But there's gotta be a logic to how they *do* think. If we could just get a handle on that, Fairchild, maybe we could get through to them. Convince them what we're trying to do over here is make a better life for *them*, for Christ sake."

"Assuming we are, sir."

His head snapped up.

"What the fuck is *that* supposed to mean?"

"Well, sir. You just said we don't know how they think. So how can we know what a better life for them might be?"

He stared at me.

"Sometimes, Fairchild, you take the frigging cake. That's the fuzziest goddam bunch of mush I ever heard! A better life's a better life. Everybody knows what *that* is. Peace. Prosperity. A chance to choose your own leaders. Hell, you know the drill as well as I do. *And*, I might add, a house with a floor that isn't packed-down dirt and a fucking plumbing system that keeps your shit from floating down the goddam street. You can't tell me they don't want that. I don't believe it. I mean, they must want what we *all* want. No, it's not what a better life *is* that's the problem. It's figuring out ways to make them believe we're trying to give it to them."

"And how do I go about finding that out, sir?"

"By asking the goddam people themselves, that's how. That's what 'hearts and minds' means, Fairchild. Find out why they aren't willing to help us do what we know needs to be done."

"Find out from whom, sir?"

He pulled a paper off a pile in front of him.

"Two district officials, a village headman, and an ARVN colonel."

He handed the paper to me.

"They speak English?" I asked.

"All but the headman apparently. For him we've got you an interpreter. Some man from the embassy named Lewis. Speaks fluent Vietnamese, so they say. Supposed to be an expert in the culture. Whatever that means."

He looked up, squinted at me, and pulled at his mustache.

"Find out what all you can from him, Fairchild, but do your own asking and your own concluding. These embassy people don't always have a particularly military point of view, if you get my meaning."

"I do, sir."

"So." He slapped the desk again. "Get your sergeant squared away to handle things back in the secure room, and be ready to leave at 0800 tomorrow."

# 45

I flew up to Danang on the CG's private jet. It was a classy little plane with eight big, comfortable seats, and I was the only passenger. It was quiet, a different world entirely from the noisy, rattly choppers. And it was fast. The sergeant on duty barely had time to serve me a drink and a bag of peanuts and chat with me for a while, and we were there.

The driver assigned to me in Danang was a Spec5 named Gresham. He and I had been waiting beside his jeep almost half an hour when a chubby man in slacks and a short-sleeved Hawaiian shirt walked up. He stuck out his hand.

"Arthur Lewis, Captain," he said. "Call me Art."

"Matt Fairchild."

I shook his hand.

"Ready?" he asked.

"Sure."

I waved to the sergeant in charge of the security guards. He nodded and climbed into the first jeep with three of the guards. Art and I got into the back seat of Gresham's jeep, the second in line. Three more guards piled into the third. The MP at the gate saluted as we headed out of the compound. I returned it.

The mountains on the horizon were the hazy mix of green and purple I'd come to love. The sky was about half full of clouds, the friendly white kind that meant no rain for the next few hours at least.

"Ever been to Danang before, Captain?" Art asked.

"Matt," I said. He smiled.

"No," I said. "My first time this far north."

"You travel around a lot?"

"A good bit, yes."

"It's a beautiful country."

"Very."

"I came here first in '51. You should've seen it then."

"I wish I had."

He nodded.

"It was clean and orderly," he said. "And so beautiful. Saigon really was like Paris in those days."

"For the French."

He frowned.

"For everyone," he said.

"Oh? The way I heard it the French rule was pretty repressive."

"Repressive?" His eyes widened and then narrowed. "Not in the least. Well, those who preferred to remain stuck in the past may have thought so. But the rest, the ones with sense enough to look to the future, were all eager to join in and make something of themselves."

He sighed and shook his head. "It's the age-old conflict that's been Vietnam's curse. The classic confrontation of old and new. A very ancient, very rigid society faced with the necessity of living in the modern world. Unfortunately, their culture has always looked backward. Now it's got no choice but to look forward, and the people are finding that hard to do."

"Maybe they just want to be left alone," I said.

"Not possible. Not one of the options. They're in the twentieth century whether they like it or not. But some of them've got this maddening kind of stick-in-the-mud attitude that keeps getting them into all kinds of trouble."

"Like?"

"Like their aversion to modern technology, for instance. Their intellectuals are still geared far more toward poetry and philosophy than science and technology. Bad business, Matt. Puts blinders between them and what they need to be doing. They just look back all the time at the way things have always been done. See no need to change."

"Yes, but. . . ."

"But what?"

"Well, couldn't there be a stability in the old ways that too much change destroys?"

He cocked his head and looked at me. "You some kind of radical thinker, or you working at playing devil's advocate?"

"Neither. Just curious."

He looked out his side of the jeep, and I looked out mine. The countryside was quiet, almost serene. The war hadn't come much to this area, so far as I could tell. Rice paddies stretched, yellow-green and sparkling, in all directions. I saw no craters, no defoliated trees, no outposts surrounded by barbed wire.

The day was hot, but the water in the paddies gave at least the illusion of coolness. Small figures in black pajamas and cone-shaped straw hats bent and straightened, bent and straightened. I couldn't tell which sex they were. My guess was both. On the far side of the road, two boys wearing shorts and no shirts stood beside a massive water buffalo. One boy held a huge upturned hoof against his leg and was poking at it with a stick while the other watched. As we passed, the boy dropped the hoof, and the two of them jumped up and down, waving both hands. I waved back.

I glanced at Art. He hadn't acknowledged the boys and seemed to be consciously not looking in my direction. The silence was taking on an edge of tension. I scrambled around in my brain for a way to break it.

"So Vietnam is a specialty of yours?" I asked.

He turned toward me. "Yes. It's always fascinated me."

"I can see why."

"When I decided to major in Oriental studies, everyone else was choosing either China or Japan. But I found them both intimidating. China was so huge and so old, and Japan was already full of Americans trying to sort out the aftermath of World War II. Vietnam seemed just right to me. Oriental enough to be interesting, but small and manageable."

"Well, it's still small at least."

He laughed. "But not so manageable, you mean?"

He laughed again.

Off in the distance was a dark green rectangular wall. As we got closer, I could tell it was bamboo, maybe fifteen feet high, growing so close together you couldn't see through.

"That's it," said Art. "The village of Nghia An. Means Peaceful Righteousness." He chuckled. "Grand name for such a little place."

We stopped in front of an ornately carved gate. The guards parked their jeeps in the shade of the bamboo and lounged against them lighting up cigarettes. Art and I went to the gate, where he rang a little bell.

Immediately, an old man opened the gate. He bowed. We bowed. As he and Art talked in high-pitched, lilting Vietnamese, I watched the old man, trying not to stare. His skin was weathered and wrinkled, and his eyes were alert and wary. He was wearing a long loose robe, of a kind I'd never seen before. He had a good amount of gray hair on his head and a long, wispy gray beard on the point of his chin.

Art said something to him. He looked directly at me, placed his palms together near his chest, and bowed. Art turned to me. "This is Hieu Van Tuong," he said, "headman of this village." I put my palms together and bowed toward the old man. He looked up and smiled, just a bit.

He closed the gate behind us, turned, and walked, not fast but with purpose, down the central path behind the gate. Art and I followed. It *was* cool here, no illusion about it. Trees shaded both sides of the path.

We passed neat houses made of wooden sticks, some of them covered with a smooth coating of what looked like mud. Thatched roofs hung out several feet over the edges of the walls. Through the open doors, I could see women squatting flat-footed on the ground and a few tiny children walking or crawling around.

On our left was a large building with big open windows. Through them I could hear voices. First an adult voice, then a chorus of children's voices. Then the adult, then the children. The old man turned to me, held his hand out about waist high, and pointed at the building.

I nodded. "Children, yes," I said. "In school."

Art translated. The old man crinkled his eyes at me and smiled.

Across from the school was the largest building I had seen in the village. We stopped in front of it. As the old man talked, Art spoke softly to me.

"This is the *dinh*," he said. "The center of village life. Here all important events take place. Feasts. Ceremonies. Meetings of the council of notables. Sacrifices to the spirits."

In front of the *dinh* were a large chair and four smaller

ones. The old man sat in the large one. He motioned me toward the one on his right. Art pulled another up beside us.

"The *dinh*," I asked, "is it a religious building or a meeting house?"

As I talked, Art leaned toward the old man and spoke softly to him.

"Both," said the old man through Art, who leaned back toward me. "It is a religious building at some times, and a governing building at others. The pagoda, for Buddhist worship, is there." He pointed down the path to his right. "Here in the *dinh* we have ceremonies, religious to us, to honor the guardian spirit of our village."

I was looking at Art as he translated this and saw him roll his eyes slightly. I frowned at him. The old man looked from me to Art and back at me.

"Have you not understood?" he asked.

"It was a new idea to me," I said. "I'm sorry. Please tell me more."

"Each village has a guardian spirit," he said solemnly, "given to us many hundred years ago by the emperor. It is the sign that we are a village, a place that governs itself. The spirit protects us, and we give it honor and thanks for this."

He moved his hand from right to left.

"As you see, our spirit is a strong one. In the middle of much destruction, we remain peaceful and prosperous. We have enough to eat, and our children are intelligent and obedient. There are not many villages left, I am told, for which this is so. Thus we believe our spirit is very strong." While the old man talked, Art leaned toward me and spoke quietly. He couldn't have been more than two or three words behind. It was a surprisingly efficient and satisfying way of conversing.

A young man came out of the *dinh* carrying a round wooden tray, which he placed on the low table in front of the old man. He bowed and went back inside. On the tray were a tall pottery decanter and three pottery cups. The old man poured a liquid into each of the cups. He held one of them out toward me.

"Will you take a small drink of rice wine?" he asked, smiling.

I glanced at Art. He shook his head. I raised my eyebrows. He shook his head again. I looked at the old man.

"I'm sorry I must say no," I said.

When the old man heard Art repeat this to him, he looked sharply at me, his eyes wide. He pressed his lips together and put the cup down on the tray.

"Please," I said. "I understand that this offer is a sign of hospitality on your part. And that to refuse it is a sign of great disrespect on mine."

He looked straight into my eyes.

"But," I said, "in these terrible times I find myself always in danger, and as a habit I must be very careful. I mean no offense to you, or to your village, or to the powerful spirit that protects it."

Art must have been faithful in his translation, because the old man's eyes softened a little.

"I understand, young soldier," he said. "The times are evil."

I nodded.

"May we talk now about your village?" I asked.

"With pleasure," he said.

"Most of your people grow rice?"

"Yes. We have many fields that, with hard work, provide us with much food. Enough for us to eat and more to trade."

"Do your men farm, or do they go off to fight?"

He looked at me steadily. "Some farm, some fight."

"And for whom do they fight?"

He looked directly into my eyes, then off toward the schoolhouse.

"When a man asked if an American officer could come here," he said, "I did not know what would be the purpose of this visit. No one has come before to ask what are my thoughts. I said, 'Yes, I will talk.' But still I did not know what we would talk about." He looked back at me. "Now I begin to see that you want to know what are the beliefs of the people of this village. Am I correct?"

"You are correct."

I tried to think how to proceed.

"We are foreigners," I said. "We've come from a long way off to a place we don't understand. I myself feel shame that I don't understand more. Even so, I'm asked to advise men who make decisions that affect the lives of many people like you. If I could understand a small part of what you think, I could give better advice."

The old man looked at me, then down at his hands.

"You say you feel yourself in danger," he said. "Just so do I. Not only for myself, but for all the people it is my duty to protect."

"Yes," I said. "I respect that. But I want only to talk. To try to know you and your people better. Not to harm you or anyone else. Can we just talk?"

He continued to stare at his hands.

"Words are powerful things, young soldier," he said quietly. "Once said they cannot be unsaid. And they can kill as surely as a bullet."

He squeezed his thin wrinkled hands together. I felt an urgent need to reach him. I was sure he knew a great many things I ought to know. I searched hard in my brain for something to say that might get through.

"We are in the same position, you and I," I said. "We want to help those who rely on us. But to do that we have to take some risks. Since I don't know you and you don't know me, the risks look very large. But. . . ." I hesitated. His face, still bowed, was impassive. "If we let this fear defeat us, there is no hope for any of us, your people or mine. We will go down parallel roads, never talking, never reaching out. And at the end of those roads will be destruction. For all of us. If we do talk now, you and I, maybe harm will come of it. I can't promise it won't. But if we don't talk, harm will come for sure. I do know that."

He looked up and stared hard into my eyes. He turned away, took a deep breath, and looked back.

"What you say is true, young soldier," he said through Art. "Everything we do in these evil times is dangerous. We must look for those things that have a possibility to make the danger less. Please. Ask me again what you would like to know."

"The men from your village who go off to fight. Do they fight for the government, or for the Viet Cong?"

He breathed in and out several times before he answered.

"Those who have fervor in their souls fight for the Viet Cong. Those who wish to be left alone are taken away by the government."

"None of them go willingly to the Army of South Vietnam?"

"None."

"Can you tell me what their reasons are?"

"Surely. They believe this government in the south, which changes so often now, does not have the mandate of heaven."

He stopped and watched my eyes.

"This, again, is something I don't understand," I said. "Will you explain it to me?"

"I will try. We have believed, since the first emperors ruled us thousands of years ago, that the authority for a man's rule over other men comes down from heaven. He does not choose it. Heaven chooses him. So long as his rule is just and the people benefit from what he does, we are content. When events begin to go against him and the people suffer, we know that he has lost the mandate of heaven. Another will arise, and the mandate of heaven will come to rest on that man's shoulders. This is the way of the world."

"You don't believe you should help decide who that next leader will be?"

"In the village, yes. We have always chosen. We live with these men. We know them. We choose the wisest to lead us. But the emperor was father of us all. Choose the emperor?" He waved his hand at me. "This is foolishness. Does a man choose his parents? He does not. He arrives on this earth through the gift of his parents. A gift of so great a value that he can never repay it. He remains in debt to his parents all the days of his life. It is his *on*, his greatest obligation, to revere them for as long as he is alive.

"He spends his life trying to repay the debt of this gift, but he cannot. Even by pleasing his parents in every way, making them always comfortable, doing as they wish, working beside them when they are strong and caring for them when they are weak, even doing all this every day of his life, it is not enough to repay this great debt. After they have gone, he must continue to pay the debt by honoring them, by remembering them, by inviting them back to join him on special occasions. He must honor not only them but their parents and their parents' parents. Only in this way does the proper order of the world unfold. To interrupt this natural order, to look for this 'change' you Americans talk of so easily is to invite disaster. Not only onto your own head but onto the heads of your family, those it is your sacred duty to love and protect."

"So you think doing things in a different way brings disaster?"

"It is not a thing to think or not think. It is the way of the world. The way the world has always been and will be once again when this turmoil has passed and heaven restores order to our land."

"And there's nothing for you to do but wait?"

"You misunderstand. To wait is not to do nothing. It is to do the thing that is proper. You Americans come here and tell us a thing utterly foreign to us. You tell us the mandate comes from *us*. That we are to tell heaven who will lead us. We are shocked at the impiety of this. At the affront you throw in the face of heaven.

"This is to turn the world upside down. It is for the small boy to say to his father, 'I do not like what you do. I will seek a new father.' This is an insult to heaven. Heaven selects the father. Heaven selects the ruler. And the duty remains with heaven to replace the ruler when his path goes astray.

"Here in the south, the natural order is out of control. A man seizes power. Another man seizes power from him. Those who please you Americans stay. Those who do not must go. Heaven is far from these arrangements.

"You ask if our people support such a government? Go willingly to fight for the army of such a government? No. How could they? To support a government that has no mandate is to spit in the eyes of heaven."

I nodded.

"And the ones who fight for the Viet Cong," I said. "They believe their leaders have a mandate?"

He thought for a minute.

"Their fervor," he said, "makes them wish to believe it is so."

We looked at each other without speaking.

"Thank you for telling me all of this," I said at last.

He bowed his head just a little. "I watched your face as I was speaking," he said. "It is my thought that you were hearing me."

"Yes. I think I was."

"Then my heart feels light for the first time in many months."

"You are a wise man," I said. "I can see why the mandate for this village has come to rest on your shoulders."

When he looked at me that time, it was as if a veil had lifted from his eyes and I could see much further into them. From somewhere far back, they were smiling at me.

I looked down at the tray.

"Is it too late for me to accept a cup of wine?"

Out of the corner of my eye, I could see Art shaking his head, but I ignored him. At least he kept translating.

"When the mind begins to open," the old man said, "it is never too late."

He handed me a cup, and I took it. He picked up another, and we held them out toward each other before we drank.

# 46

The next morning, I had an early breakfast so I could get started on my report. As I walked down the hall toward the secure room, I heard someone call my name. I turned and saw a sergeant I didn't know.

"Yes?" I said.

"Could I see you for a minute, Captain?"

"Sure."

"Look, I'm awfully sorry, sir. There's no easy way. . . ."

"What's happened?"

"It's your sergeant. Sergeant Anderson? He was wounded last night, sir. Bad."

"*What*? How could he've been?"

"There was a sapper attack over on the west perimeter. A big one."

"So? What's that got to do with him?"

"Well. . . . Boots was having a couple of beers over at the NCO Club with a bunch of us. It was late, but we were all schmoozing and having a good time the way we like to do.

Boots was entertaining us with his wild-ass tales, and everybody was laughing and hooting." He stopped. "You want to know all this stuff, sir? I'm kind of rambling."

"You're doing just fine, Sergeant."

"Well. . . . All of a sudden there was this whole lot of commotion. Somebody come running in, said there was this big attack, and all the security guards in there needed to head over and reinforce. Some of us started running out. Boots laughed real big, you know how he does, grabbed a rifle, and came along. 'Put my beer in the cooler,' he said as he went out the door. 'I'll be right back.' You know Boots."

"Shit," I said. My eyes were stinging, and I was fighting to keep control. "Sorry. I. . . ."

"That's OK, Captain. I know how you feel. Boots told us he and you were more like friends. That's what he always said. No offense, sir."

I rubbed my eyes. "Keep going, Sergeant. Please."

"When we got over there, we saw they'd blown a big hole in the perimeter fence and were pouring in. We were sort of disorganized at first, but we managed to push them back some. Then more of them showed up and pushed *us* back. One of Boots's drinking buddies had got hit and was laying on the ground between us and them. We were retreating, and they were moving towards his buddy.

"Boots yelled, 'What about Smitty?' Something like that. And somebody yelled, 'Can't help him. Too many. We got to regroup.' Next thing we knew, Boots was crawling out towards Smitty. He got ahold of him and was dragging him back when a automatic rifle opened fire. Kicked up dust all around them. They stopped moving."

"Christ," I said.

"We regrouped, pushed Charlie on out through the fence, and secured it. Smitty was dead, and Boots was. . . . well, full of holes. Six, I think they said."

"Where is he now?"

"Field hospital. Other side of the supply compound."

"Do me a favor?"

"You name it, sir."

"Tell the sergeant-major where I've gone."

I ran as fast as I could down the dusty road. As I passed the supply tents, I heard helicopters landing. By the time I got to the hospital, a stream of wounded men were being moved quickly from the helicopter in through the front door. I pushed past them and into the hallway. A nurse, a captain with long brown hair, was walking fast toward me.

"Where can I find Sergeant Anderson?"

"What?" she said.

"Sergeant Anderson. Kevin Anderson. He's a patient here."

"Please get out of my way, Captain. I have no time for you."

"But I have to see him. See if he's all right."

She moved by me. I grabbed her arm. She whirled and knocked my hand away.

"Get your fucking hands off me, Captain. I'm sorry for whatever's bothering you. I truly am. But I have a thousand things to do all at once. Do you understand me?"

I stepped aside, and she was gone.

The wounded men were all being carried down the hall to the right. I turned to the left. A corpsman brushed past me.

"Excuse me," I said. "Do you know where a Sergeant Anderson is?"

"No, sir," he said. "We're more likely to know them by condition than name."

"He was hurt last night. On our perimeter. Six bullet wounds, they said."

"Recovery room, sir. Past the entrance. Second door on the right."

He ran off down the hall.

The room was eerily quiet after the chaos outside. Beds were jammed together almost touching, and bags of blood and clear liquid hung over them. The door banged open, and a different corpsman wheeled a wounded man in. The nurse I'd seen earlier was right behind him.

"You're haunting me, Captain," she said.

"I'm sorry. I was told Sergeant Anderson was in this room."

She rubbed her temples with her fingers.

"It's about to be fucking mayhem in here, but I'll give you two minutes. Anderson?"

"Yes."

She walked to a station across the room, circled the beds, stopped at one, and came back to me.

"Sorry, Captain," she said. "I'm moving him to expectant."

"You're what?"

"My judgment is he's not likely to make it. We have to give our attention to those with a better chance."

"'Likely'? You're not sure? I mean, he might make it if. . . . ?"

"If he were the only one in here, and we could do everything in our power? Yes. But he isn't, and I have to do what I have to do. We've got seventeen more men moving through the OR on their way here. Seventeen, Captain. I have two corpsmen and one of me. You figure the odds."

"You're just going to let him die?"

She rubbed her temples again.

"Look," she said. "We have only so much time and attention to give. I decide who gets it. Today, with all this, it's not going to be him. Tomorrow, who knows? But this is today."

"God," I said. "I'd hate to have to make choices like that."

"I'm not real happy about it, Captain."

We looked at each other.

"Well," I said. "Thank you for your time."

She put her hand on my arm and turned away.

"Hanson," she said in a loud voice that echoed around the quiet room. "Move seven to expectant. Give me as much more room as you can."

She turned back to me. "You can stay with him a while if you like. Just keep out of our way."

The corpsman wheeled a bed to a far corner behind a screen. I followed him. Another bed was already there. The corpsman left.

Boots lay silent and motionless. His head was wrapped in bandages, his face was white, and his eyes were closed. This time I didn't bother to keep back the tears.

"Goddam hero," I whispered. "You had to go be a goddam hero."

He didn't move. There was no place to sit, so I stood by the bed looking down at him. I couldn't really see the blood moving through the tube into his arm, but the bag got slowly emptier. I put my hand on his arm and left it there. I didn't know if he was conscious at all, but if he was, at least he'd know someone was with him.

On the other side of the screen, periods of noise and confusion alternated with periods of quiet. I heard the nurse being tough and efficient. She seemed to be moving a great many men in and out. After a while, she came and gave Boots a new bag of blood. I wondered if that was normal procedure for "expectants."

When that bag had drained to half full, the corpsman came back, checked the man in the other bed, looked at Boots.

"He's gone, sir," he said. "I'm sorry. We have to move him out and make room for another."

"How can you tell?" I asked. "He looks the same to me."

"It's my job, sir."

I squeezed Boots's arm and took my hand away.

"Nice of you to stay with him, sir," the corpsman said. "I hate it when they have to die all alone."

## 47

The next day, a replacement for Boots reported for duty. First Sergeant Daniel Miller. His friends called him Payroll, from his job back in the States. I called him Sergeant.

He was nice enough, hard-working, and eager to please. In awe of secret things he never knew existed. But I kept a distance. Not intentionally. I just couldn't risk it. Besides, he didn't smoke and stepped outside every time I pulled out a cigarette. I tried not to light up too often.

## 48

Colonel Dunhill summoned me. "Jesus fucking Christ, Fairchild," he said. "You taking some kind of dope on the side?"

"No, sir."

"I ask for 'hearts and minds' stuff, and you give me fucking 'mandates of heaven.' I can't make head or tail out of the whole fucking thing, start to finish."

"Shall I try to explain it to you, sir?"

He narrowed his eyes and took a deep breath.

"You starting to like living dangerously, Captain Fairchild? I do *not* need you to explain it to me. You tried it once, right here." He tapped the cover of the report. "And you didn't succeed. What makes you think you can do any better with me looking at you?"

"Sorry, sir."

"You're goddam right you're the one to be sorry. I called that Lewis idiot went up with you, and he says it's all your fault. He says he tried to set you straight after he translated all that horse-shit, but apparently you paid him no mind. That correct?"

"Yes, sir."

"Then here's what you're going to do, Captain. You're going back out, *not* to a village recommended by some embassy retard, but to one the ARVN commander's come up with, over near Chu Lai. And you'll talk *not* to some wine-swilling, hallucinating old has-been, but to the district administrator and a couple of the ARVN village coordinators. And, Fairchild. . . ."

"Yes, sir?"

"Do me a goddam favor and try to recognize the difference between something worth reporting to me and the inside of a fortune cookie. Can you do that?"

"Yes, sir."

"I'll believe it when I fucking well see it."

# 49

A huge box from my family brought all the trappings of Christmas. A small artificial tree. Cute little ornaments. A tiny creche. Lots of carefully wrapped presents. I cleared off a table in the corner of the secure room and loaded it up with holiday cheer. The effect was eerie and unsettling. Like those long-ago peaceful days in Penang. Too clear a reminder of home in a place too much unlike it.

Mail calls became longer and longer. We all got a great many packages and avalanches of letters. For many of those back in the States, remembering their boys overseas seemed to fit right in with what the holiday season was all about. My mother organized a card-writing campaign that included relatives and friends I'd forgotten I had.

The parties around Headquarters—a long series that began

well before Christmas and culminated with a raucous New Year's Eve—were more to the point. We pooled the nuts and cookies and canned hams and fruitcakes that came pouring in and drank ourselves silly. The irreverent ones among us, the ones who'd kept us sane all along by never running out of things to joke about, were the stars of this movable celebration. With their help, we laughed our way out of the old year and into the new.

Even so, the holidays brought with them a homesickness I'd somehow escaped all those earlier months. Alone in the secure room, our splendid new tape system cranked up and running, I thought about turkey and dressing and pecan pie. About cornbread and black-eyed peas. It was Tchaikovsky, though, his sixth symphony full of longing and an ache he knew was there but couldn't quite reach, who took me back to the woods of East Texas.

The cabin was cold when we got there, but I'd expected that so I didn't complain the way my brother Paul and my cousin Jim did. I might as well have, though, because Grandfather didn't appear to notice. He went right over and made a fire in the little stove in the corner, and the room warmed up fast. Paul and Jim, who'd been before, knew just what to do. They sat down on their cots and started cleaning their rifles. I took mine, the one Grandfather was loaning me, out of its long leather holder and sat down too, as if I'd known all along this was what came next.

I whistled as I worked. More air than music, as usual, but I liked the overall effect of nonchalant concentration. I rubbed the outside of the barrel with a soft cloth I'd found in the case. Mostly I looked straight at the rifle, frowning and nodding, but every once in a while I peeked at Jim, to see if there was something else I wasn't aware of.

Sure enough, he stuck a small piece of cloth on the end of a long metal rod and started pushing it in and out of the barrel. I kept on with my outside rubbing for a while before I looked in the carrying case and found my own rod and little cloth. I cleaned the inside of the barrel, polished the stock, and oiled things in what I hoped were the right places. I must have been doing all right because when I glanced at Grandfather, puttering around over by the stove, he did smile at me, the first I could remember aimed in my direction. One of the secrets of life had been revealed to me that afternoon—pretend you know a whole lot more than you really do.

I was a smart and diligent boy, and I'd discovered early that making good grades at school was not only easy but fun. I got to find out all sorts of interesting facts and read lots of books in which people did the most amazing things. Trouble was, only the women thought this was a worthwhile way for a boy to spend his time. For the men to want to pay any attention at all, I'd have to excel in at least one sport, whether organized, like baseball or football, or outdoor, like hunting or fishing.

I wasn't much good at the organized kind. I could run fast enough, probably because I had long legs and didn't weigh very much. But most games also involved catching something and holding on to it, and I could never quite get the hang of that. I wasn't so awful that I should just give up sports altogether, but I was nowhere near good enough.

What I *could* do was shoot a gun. With my better than average eyesight and my intense concentration in full force, I could hit a bull's-eye nine times out of ten. Or, better yet, a whole row of tin cans straight off the top of a fence.

Pistol. Rifle. Shotgun. It didn't matter. I was a virtuoso with all of them. This was the way, I realized with secret satisfaction, that I was finally going to make my grandfather proud of me. He wouldn't look askance at me any more, with one eyebrow slightly raised. He would be glad to see me, the way he was with Paul and Jim. He would pat me on the shoulder and tell his cronies down at the bank what a great hunter I was.

While we worked on our rifles, Grandfather heated up some beans on the top of the woodstove. After we'd eaten, he sat us down for a lecture on what to expect the next morning. Come on, said Paul. Don't treat me like a little kid. I know all that stuff. You be quiet and listen, said Grandfather.

We'd be out long before sunup, he told us. We must be sure to dress warmly. He would take us to the places where we would sit and wait, each of us all alone. He would point out the directions in which we could shoot. We must under no condition move around—or shoot in any other direction. If you should get lucky and see one, he said, aim for the heart, in the center of his chest. The head's good too, of course, but then you have no trophy.

He looked at each of us in turn. Did we understand what he'd said? We nodded. All of it? Yes. Were we sure? We were. Then get some sleep, he said. I'll wake you up at five.

I took off my heavy wool shirt and my Levis and, snug in my long underwear, crawled into the sleeping bag Grandfather had spread out on top of my cot. I was so wide-awake with excitement I was sure I'd never sleep. It wasn't killing a deer I was looking forward to. That I could do without. The great thing was that this time tomorrow, I wouldn't be a sissy any more.

I guess I fell asleep right away because the next thing I knew, Grandfather was shaking my shoulder. When I looked up, he put his finger to his lips.

We'll start out being quiet, he whispered, so we'll all be used to it by the time we get to the woods.

I nodded.

He had bacon and scrambled eggs cooking on the stove. Paul and Jim were already halfway dressed.

When we had our coats and hats and gloves on, he lined us up by the door. Remember what I told you last night? he whispered.

We nodded.

Good, he said, and smiled.

The air outside was cold and damp. There was just enough faint gray light for us to see where we were going. Grandfather went first, then Jim, then Paul, then me. We came to a structure I figured must be a blind. Its three walls were made of dried sticks. One corner was attached to a tree, and inside was a little bench. Grandfather pointed at Paul and then at the blind. Paul went in and sat on the bench.

At the next blind, Grandfather pointed at Jim, who went in and sat down. Grandfather and I walked a long time to the next blind, which was smaller and had no bench. Grandfather motioned to show me where I could shoot and where I couldn't. I walked inside, and he went away.

What was I supposed to do? Just stand there? I tried that for a while, but the gun was heavy, so I sat down on the ground. It was cold, and pretty soon I felt the dampness creeping through the seat of my Levis. I stood up again and leaned the rifle against the tree in the corner of the blind. The stock would get wet, I knew. Probably ruin it. But I couldn't think what else to do. There was no way I could hold it for long, not all by myself.

Very slowly, the woods got lighter, and a few birds started to sing. The air was so heavy you could see it. Not a fog exactly, just wisps of thick air. Moisture condensed on the bare branches of the trees and dripped to the ground. Every once in a while, a breeze blew past. Just enough to make the cold air seem even colder. I moved my weight from one foot to the other, as quietly as I could.

The cracking of a branch startled me. I froze. Another crack. And another. A long pause. Then another. I stuck my head up, slowly, and stared hard. A loud crack, and the head of a deer appeared between two trees. My heart stopped beating, then pounded against the side of my ribs. I counted the points on his antlers. Six. He was a big one. He took another step, and I could see his shoulders and front legs. He stood still, took a step, and moved his head from side to side.

Behind me was the direction I mustn't fire, so he was standing in exactly the right place. I eased the rifle up to my shoulder. He looked around, calm but wary. Don't wait too long, you idiot, I told myself. He'll spook soon and run away. But I couldn't shoot. I hadn't expected him to be so—what? So real.

He took another step. Suddenly he tensed and jerked his head up. I fired. The rifle slammed into my shoulder, the smell of burning powder hit my nose, and a high sharp ringing filled my ears.

The deer lay on the ground, bright red blood pouring from a hole in his spine just at the base of his neck. His legs were twitching, and he kept making a kind of moan, over and over. I dropped the rifle and started to run toward him. I stopped. Grandfather said don't move under any circumstances. But surely he didn't mean this.

I ran to where the deer was lying. The one eye I could see looked straight up at me. He stopped moaning but couldn't stop twitching and looked straight at me.

"Oh, my god," I said. I knelt beside him.

I looked in his eyes, expecting to see fear there. But wasn't any. He just rested his head on the ground and looked at me.

The others came crashing up behind me.

"You got him! You got him!" yelled my cousin.

"A six-pointer," said my brother. "Wow!"

Grandfather was frowning. "Where's your rifle?" he asked.

"Back there, I guess."

"Go get it."

I shook my head.

"Go get the rifle, Matthew, right now." His face was hard, and his mouth was tight.

I walked to the blind, picked up the rifle, and took it to where they were standing.

"Shoot him in the back of the head," said Grandfather.

"What?" My mouth hung open, and I couldn't seem to make it close.

"You heard me. Put the barrel of your rifle at the back of his head and shoot him."

My head started shaking from side to side. "No," I said. "No. I can't."

I heard a giggle and turned to see Paul and Jim grinning at each other. I looked back at Grandfather.

"Please," I said. "Don't make me do this. I know he's hurting, and I know we have to do what you say. But you do it for me. Please. I can't just. . . ."

"Stop this foolishness, Matthew. It's your responsibility, not anyone else's. You're the one who missed. Now get on with it."

I put the barrel of my rifle at the back of the deer's head. He tried to move out of the way but realized he couldn't. He stopped twitching and looked up at me. Not at the others. Straight at me. I knew that he knew.

I pulled the trigger, and his head exploded.

# 50

As long as I was heading back out to a village, I figured I might as well go during Tet, the Lunar New Year celebration that was the most important holiday, by far, for all Vietnamese. If I really wanted to know what Vietnam was all about, seeing at least a part of Tet was essential. Nhan had talked about it a number of times, and it sounded like a fascinating combination of Thanksgiving, Christmas, New Year's Eve, and the Fourth of July. The religious, patriotic, cultural, and familial high point of the year. An added advantage of being out in the countryside at that time was the annual Tet ceasefire, proclaimed by both sides, which allowed most of the South Vietnamese Army, the Viet Cong, and—who knows?—maybe even the North Vietnamese regulars who'd infiltrated south to go home to be with their families at this most special of times.

In past years, I understood, the South Vietnamese Army had practically disbanded during those couple of weeks, but this year there'd been some disquieting developments. The little colored dots on our big new maps in the secure room had shown movements and unit concentrations we couldn't quite figure out. The enemy was clearly getting into position for something, but no one I knew of was quite sure what. When I got back from Hoa Binh, Miller and I would have to get the coordinates updated fast to see if the changes in positions could tell us anything. I heard that MACV was asking for some ARVN units to be called back, those stationed around Saigon in particular, just to be ready when Tet was over and the fighting started up again.

I wanted to see some of the celebrations, but I also wanted to be sure I wasn't interfering, so I decided going early in the week was the thing to do. I would watch the preparations on the first morning of Tet and talk with a few people in the village, meet with the district officials and ARVN commanders that afternoon, and fly back to Long Binh that night. In order to be at the village early in the morning, I arranged to stay at a base camp nearby.

The officers were hospitable, supper in their mess tent was delicious, and, after the dishes had been cleared away, four of us played bridge till after eleven. My partner was a first lieutenant with a degree in mathematics and phenomenal card sense. He and I mopped up the floor with our opponents. I was feeling very good, and a little cocky, as I went off to brush my teeth, pull the mosquito net down around my cot, and drift off to sleep.

Sometime after midnight, the world fell apart. A barrage of loud explosions brought me straight upright in bed. Fireworks for Tet? I wondered. In a base camp? I heard high-pitched whines before the next barrage shook the earth, and I knew it wasn't fireworks. I threw the mosquito net aside, slipped on my fatigue pants, grabbed my T-shirt, and stumbled out of the tent. People were running and shouting, fires were burning all around, and the sky was full of flares and the luminescent tracks of tracer bullets. The ceasefire had lulled us all. I'd forgotten to ask where the bunkers were, and no one had thought to tell me. I stood outside the tent like a fool, not knowing which way to run.

A sergeant came racing up.

"CO sent me to get you, sir," he said. "This way."

We ran off toward the perimeter and jumped down into a covered bunker piled high with sandbags.

"Thanks, Sergeant," I yelled.

"No sweat," he yelled back. He jumped out and ran away.

I sat in the bunker and watched through the narrow opening across the front. The two machinegunners to my right fired almost constantly. My reactions astonished me. I was frightened and exhilarated. Eager not to miss anything and scared shitless. It was glorious and insane, heroic and so sad I couldn't comprehend it, all at the same time.

A man can get used to anything, I quickly discovered, even terror as all-encompassing as that. After a while, it eases off to a constant, bearable level, like the dull throb of an abscessed tooth. No way you can forget it's there, but you can continue to function. So, anesthetized by fear, I sat and watched.

What I realized most clearly was how useless I was. I didn't know what needed to be done, and even if I had, I wouldn't have known how to do it. The men all around me knew, because their lives depended on it. Had for as long as they'd been here. The decisions that got them into these horrendous situations were made in my world, the world of staff cars and Monday morning band concerts and officers sunbathing on roofs. The decisions that saved them, if salvation was possible, were made in their world, the world of mud and heat and jungles and death.

Throughout those next hours, enlisted men risked their lives to take care of me. First they brought my boots and fatigue jacket. Then they came with C-rations twice and a canteen of water.

On the second day, around noon, the assault eased up. Even I, still sitting there watching from the bunker, could sense the pressure slipping away, the level of sound dropping, the smoky air clearing.

A sergeant ducked into the bunker, out of breath.

"Up and at 'em, Captain," he said. "A supply chopper's just landed and'll take you back. The CO's talked to HQ, and they think it's safe enough to try. You got to hustle, though, sir, cause soon as the stuff's unloaded, they're taking off, whether you're there or not."

The most perverse feeling I've ever had in my life came over me. For a day and a half, I'd been making almost constant silent prayers to I don't know who to get me out of there. Now that they'd been answered, I didn't want to go. It was too easy. Nowhere close to fair. I could pick up and leave, just like that, but all these other guys, heroes and cowards, supermen and crybabies, here only by the luck of the draw, had to stay. Soon I'd be there in that air-conditioned, sealed-off room, and they'd be here. Stuck without a hope, here. If they didn't die this time, they'd just have to sit and wait for it to begin all over again. Even though I knew it was insane, I didn't want to go away and leave them here to that.

But I was being stupid. Beyond stupid. Ridiculous. For my staying to be worth anything to them, I'd have to have something to offer. And I had nothing. I was far more of a hindrance than a help. Less than that. I was all hindrance and no help.

The sergeant was staring at me.

"Captain?" he said. "We gotta move it."

"Thanks, Sergeant. You lead. I'll be right behind."

Up at ground level, the living were beginning to drag the dead away from the places where they had fallen. The sergeant and I dodged around those who had not yet been reached. The chopper's blades were turning and the pilot was revving the motor as we ran up. I leaned toward the sergeant.

"Tell the CO I said thanks for the hospitality," I shouted at him.

He laughed. "Right, sir," he yelled. "We pulled out all the stops for you."

As soon as I was in, we took off and climbed fast. An explosion off to our left side rocked the chopper. We dipped and fell sideways toward the ground, but the pilot righted us and kept climbing. Looking past the gunner's shoulder, I could see flashes of fire and puffs of smoke outside the perimeter.

The assault was beginning again.

# 51

As we neared the landing pad at Long Binh, I saw an enormous blackened crater. I turned to the sergeant behind me.

"What's that?" I yelled.

"*Was* the ammo dump, sir," he shouted. "Sappers got it, first night of the attacks. Biggest explosion there ever was. Like Hiroshima."

Even here.

Once we'd landed, I headed for the barracks, showered, shaved, put on clean fatigues, and then went over to Headquarters. No stubble on *this* chin, I thought.

I went straight to Colonel Dunhill's office. His desk was piled high with papers. He looked up.

"Fairchild, you bastard," he said. "What the hell good are you? The whole fucking lot of you. Coordinated goddam attacks across the whole fucking country, and *no one* knew they were coming? Not *one* fucking person in this gigantic-ass intelligence network we got here had the tiniest fucking *hint* that anything that big was up? You were all sitting around with your heads up your asses licking your prostates while *thousands* of slope-eyed little gooks were getting themselves into position all over the goddam fucking country. Padding around in their sandals carrying fucking *howitzers* on their backs. And no one saw a motherfucking thing? I don't enjoy being made to look that shit-eating stupid."

He slammed his fist onto the top of his desk. A pile of papers slid off onto the floor. I started to move toward them.

"Leave it, Fairchild, for Christ sake. None of them make the least particle of fucking sense.

"And *you*, you bastard. I counted on you to keep me abreast of what was happening in this godforsaken hellhole. And what do you bring me but 'mandate of heaven' horseshit? Village fucking social structure and *spirit* worship, of all the crazy-ass pieces of cowdung I ever heard. If you'd done your job, soldier, on all these goddam pleasure trips you been taking all over the country. Kept your fucking eyes and ears open instead of getting taken in by some decrepit, betel-chewing old con man, you might have found out something worth reporting to me."

I stood there waiting.

"So?" he said. "What have you got to say for yourself?"

"Nothing, sir."

"No excuses?"

"None, sir."

"Well, that's a fucking goddam relief. All I've heard for the past two days is one lame-ass, crappy excuse after another. 'If this one had that' or 'if that one had some fucking other.' Christ. Makes me puke."

He pulled a handkerchief out of his pocket and wiped the sweat off his bald head. "So. . . . If you haven't got any excuses, do you have any fucking *ideas*? How come we didn't have one motherfucking clue that all hell was about to break loose?"

"They didn't want us to know."

His mouth dropped open, and he stared at me.

"Say that again."

"They didn't want us to know anything about it. So we didn't."

He continued to stare, and then he laughed. Hard.

"By god, that's a good one, Fairchild. 'Didn't want us to.'" He laughed louder and slapped his desk. More papers slid off. "You had me going for a minute there. I almost thought you were serious."

He smiled and pulled at his mustache.

"You got good instincts, though," he said. "I did need a little levity right about then. I was wound up too fucking tight. Christ, you look beat!"

"I haven't slept much for a couple of days, sir. We were under attack pretty much all the time."

"Oh, shit. Of course you were. Up by Chu Lai. I'm gonna want to hear all about it in a day or so. When things cool down. First-hand report from the front lines, so to speak."

"Yes, sir."

"Right now, though, get the hell back to that fancy-ass room of yours and get a briefing together for the CG. All the latest stuff. You know what he likes. He's madder'n a longhorn steer with barbed wire up its ass. Can't say I blame him."

"Yes, sir."

# 52

In the days that followed, G-2 crept back toward normal. Information again flowed in and up. Summaries went from the teletype to the colonel to the CG. Colored trails wandered around on our wall-sized maps. Vugraph slides lit up, and pointers pointed.

It didn't matter so much *what* was flowing, so long as the apparatus was back in gear and clicking smoothly along. In that place, I was beginning to see, appearance won out over substance every time.

Before long, the crisis had passed, like a pig digested slowly but inexorably by a boa constrictor. Every ass in the place was once again safely covered, as the consensus formed that whatever failures there had been were clearly the fault of those below us—or above.

I knew Saigon had been hit hard, and I was worried about Nhan. I wanted more than anything to know if he was all right, but I couldn't think of a way to find out. Nothing that wasn't critical was moving between Long Binh and Saigon.

Learning about Brent was easier. It took three days to get through to Cu Chi, but word came back that he was unharmed.

# 53

Other villages in the area had been battered, but Hoa Binh was pretty much intact. HQ smelled VC infiltration, which made it a perfect candidate for the kind of operation Colonel Dunhill wanted me to report on.

The impact the Tet offensive had had on everything and everybody, especially back home, made the "hearts and minds" idea even dearer to the brass than ever. We had to have the Vietnamese people on our side, and, by god, we were going to find a way to get them there. The "or else" wasn't exactly stated, but it hung in the air like stale cigarette smoke.

Security was to be much tighter this time. No staying in base camps for Headquarters personnel. And no flying back at night. I would go out to the village by armored convoy, watch the operation there, talk with district and ARVN officials at the big compound at Chu Lai, stay there overnight, and fly back to Long Binh the next morning.

The convoy from the chopper pad at Chu Lai out to Hoa Binh moved slowly. Armored personnel carriers at the front and the rear clanked along at what seemed like five miles an hour, but may have been ten. In between were three jeeps. I rode in the middle one. The canvas top, secured on all sides, closed me in. I could see nothing of the sky. Nothing of the countryside we were passing through. Nothing but about six feet of the edge of the road on my side of the jeep.

We stopped at the outskirts of a village that I assumed must be Hoa Binh. As I got out of the jeep, I saw American soldiers pouring out of the lead APC, Vietnamese soldiers coming fast out of the one at the rear. The Americans set up a perimeter around the entire village. Their rifles and machineguns were aimed at the village, ready to fire.

"Any fucking VC still in there, we'll get 'em as they try to leave," said Captain Ziegler, my guide for the day.

Why any halfway intelligent Viet Cong would stay in a village being approached by a slow-moving, loudly clanking convoy was more than I could imagine, but I had sense enough not to mention it.

The ARVN soldiers rushed into the village, and Captain Ziegler and I followed. The soldiers, rifles at the ready, herded the people out of their houses and toward the center of the village. The soldiers snarled as they barked out their orders.

The faces of the people were blank and impassive. When they reached the open space at the center of the village, they stopped and stood around looking at nothing. When someone yelled at them, they moved again. If no one yelled, they stood obediently. Several ARVN soldiers passed through the crowd checking identification cards. Others walked behind them handing out pieces of paper.

"Chieu Hoi pamphlets," said Captain Ziegler. "Sets out the advantages of supporting the government and tells them where to go to turn themselves in. Or identify VC infiltrators in their village."

The people took the pieces of paper and held them dutifully in their hands, but none that I could see were reading them. Right next to me, two Vietnamese men in business suits had unfolded a table and were piling it high with toys and candy bars.

"For the kids," said Ziegler. "They love that stuff."

I nodded.

On the far side of the open space, in the shade of two large trees, three more men in business suits were setting up a projector and a portable screen.

"What in god's name is going on over there?" I asked.

"We've added a propaganda film to these little shindigs," Ziegler said. "Put out by the Saigon political operations guys, with our help, of course. Just got the battery-operated projectors last month, but they've already been a big help. Keeps the peasants occupied while we search their hootches for weapons, documents, hidden tunnel entrances. Stuff like that. Works real good."

Sure enough, ARVN soldiers, waving their rifles, started barking orders again. The people moved over and squatted in front of the screen. The projector clicked on, and an image, dim and indistinct in the flickering sunlight, appeared on the screen.

I was in Hoa Binh for more than three hours. I spoke to no one but Captain Ziegler, and no one else spoke to me.

We clanked back to Chu Lai for the afternoon discussions. They were formal affairs, me on one side of a long table, them on the other. The district officials were arrogant. The ARVN colonel was condescending. I was polite, took notes of what I thought Colonel Dunhill would be most interested in hearing, smiled and nodded, and said little.

After supper, another stilted affair, I excused myself and went to the tent assigned to me, off down a dark, dusty road. It was stuffy inside, so I took a folding chair and a lantern outside and made a halfhearted attempt at organizing my notes. I sensed more than saw someone walk up to the edge of the circle of light.

"Captain?" he said.

I squinted at him.

"Creeper?"

"You got a good memory, sir." He hesitated. "Look, could I talk to you for a minute? Kind of off the record like?"

"Sure. Want to sit down?"

"I better."

He sat on the ground beside me. He was quiet for a long time, looking down at the ground and fiddling with the dog tags around his neck.

"How can I help, Creeper?" I asked.

He breathed in and out a couple of times.

"I can't sleep, Captain. That's the awful thing. Not only cause I'm so tired all the time, but cause. . . . Well, being back here on standdown for a while, I got so much more time to think."

"About what?"

He stared at the ground. "Something really bad. So bad you don't want to know about it."

"I've heard plenty of bad things by now. I can handle it."

He looked up, creased his forehead briefly, and looked back down.

"Maybe," he said. He kept pulling the chain through his dog tags. He looked over his shoulder, off past my chair, and back down.

"I shouldn't be talking about this, I know that. They all say we should just leave it be. But when I saw you back up here and off by yourself like this. . . . Well, I remembered the last time I saw you, you seemed like somebody knows how to listen. Not like most officers, you'll pardon me for saying."

"It's all right."

"You got to understand, though. I'm not a snitch or anything. I'm as loyal as the next guy. But if I don't do something about this, I'm gonna go crazy, I'm sure of it. Everbody else just says, 'It's over. Forget it.' Thing is, Captain, I can't. It shouldn't've happened this time, and it sure as hell shouldn't happen again. So I thought, when I saw you here, if you could tell them, higher up, they could see to it."

He flipped his tags around and around. "Maybe you could not say who told you. . . ." He shrugged. "But if you have to, that's OK too."

"You can trust me, Creeper."

He glanced up and back down. "I hope so, Captain. I don't have too much of that left."

He stared off into the darkness outside the circle of light. He took a deep breath. Then another.

"We were out on patrol, the whole platoon, so the lieutenant was in charge, not the sarge, like on a smaller patrol. We came to a village with nobody in it. The lieutenant went over to a fire still going with a pot of rice boiling on it. 'They're here, all right,' he said. 'Hiding in their hootches.'

"The lieutenant yelled for everbody to come out. The Vietnamese words they teach you for 'come out.' Most of them did. Young women with kids. Old women. A few old men. They stood by the doors of their hootches staring at us. Nobody came out of the hootch the lieutenant was standing by, so he yelled into it. I was standing right next to him, and I could hear a baby crying inside. But nobody came out. The lieutenant had his pistol in his hand, and he went in and drug out a woman with a baby in her arms. The woman was young and real scared."

He stopped and pulled at the chain around his neck.

"Go on," I said.

He shook his head and looked at the ground.

"I can't."

"He raped her. Is that it?"

His head swung up, and he stared at me with wide eyes.

"Raped her! Jesus Christ. *Raped* her! She shoulda been so lucky."

"What are you saying?"

"I don't think I can do this. . . ." He rubbed the back of his neck. "But I know I gotta. If I'm ever gonna sleep again."

I had the sense to just wait.

"The woman was so scared she started screaming. She screamed and screamed. The lieutenant told her to shut up, but she wouldn't. So he put his pistol in his left hand and hit her across the face with the back of his other one. The rest of us, the sarge, everbody, just stood there watching him. He hit her again, but she just screamed louder. Then he. . . ."

I waited.

"He put his pistol back in his right hand and shot her in the stomach. She fell on the ground and dropped the baby. It started to scream too, so the lieutenant shot it. Then her, then it, then her, then it. The other women started to sort of moan and cry, and people started running away.

"'They all saw it,' said the lieutenant. 'We can't let 'em get away. Any of 'em.' He shot an old man running slow past one of the hootches. Then we all started in, stabbing the ones closest to us with our bayonets and shooting the ones running away.

"'Fan out,' said the sarge. 'Be damn sure we get 'em all.' So we fanned out into the jungle and tracked down the few that had got that far. It wasn't hard. They were all old or carrying kids in their arms. We pulled their bodies back into the village and piled 'em with the rest.

"'Torch 'em,' said the lieutenant. 'Them, the hootches, everthing. Make it look like a air strike.' We flipped open our lighters and lit the thatch of the hootches and the clothes of the bodies. We stayed till it all burned down, just to be sure.

"'Let's move on out,' said the lieutenant, and we did."

He was staring past my shoulder. I couldn't imagine what there was I could say.

"That was over a week ago, Captain," he said, "and I haven't slept since. I swear to god I haven't. Not a wink. And worse than that is, I haven't cried either. I feel so sad I wish I could die, but I can't cry. I just think about it all the time."

"Are there any others who'll back you up? I can't report something like this with just one witness. No one's going to want to believe it as it is."

He looked at me hard for a minute.

"Yeah, you're right. One guy coulda gone nuts and made it up, I guess. So yeah. There's a couple more guys I know feel pretty bad about it. I'll see how they feel about backing me up."

In the end, two others came to see me that night, one at a time, and told the same story. They had the same far-off look in their eyes, and the details didn't vary. Much as I didn't want to, I had to believe they had done what they said they'd done.

Like them, I was too horrified to sleep and too sad to cry.

# 54

The next morning, I flew from Chu Lai to Long Binh. As soon as I got to Headquarters, I thought about going right to Colonel Dunhill's office to tell him what I'd heard. The sooner he knew, the sooner he could get the CG to do something about it. But I was afraid to try to talk to him about it like that. Afraid my emotions would get the better of me, and Colonel Dunhill wouldn't like that.

Better to go right to the secure room, get out my typewriter, and put the story in some kind of coherent order. A carefully prepared report would do more good than a rambling verbal description. Besides, if I hurried, Colonel Dunhill could have the report that afternoon, and the CG could begin making his inquiries the next day. I would say nothing to anyone until I had the facts all straight.

A good plan, I thought.

I worked the rest of the morning, writing and rewriting, pulling sheets of paper out of the typewriter and tearing them up. I skipped lunch and kept going. Finally, about two-thirty, I gave the report to the sergeant-major.

Forty-five minutes later, Colonel Dunhill sent for me. When I walked in, he was sitting very still, some papers on the desk in front of him. He looked up slowly.

"Sit," he said.

I sat.

"I think you're losing the few marbles you had left," he said. "I keep giving you simple assignments in the plainest language I know, and you keep coming back with the wildest frigging fairy tales I goddam well ever heard. But this. . . ." He tapped the papers under his hand. "This pile of shit is the fucking limit. I send you out to try to recover your fucking 'mandate of heaven' fumble and do your feeble-minded best to tell me why the goddam Vietnamese are not supporting us. And you come back with some crock of camel dung about a fucking *alleged* massacre."

"You don't see that the two things could be related, sir?"

"I ask the fucking questions in this room, Captain."

"Sorry, sir. But in my opinion, I can't think of a better reason for the Vietnamese *not* to support us."

"Your opinion, Captain, is worth about as much as a flea's left gonad. You think because I put you in charge of a high-level, top secret, important-as-hell project you've suddenly inherited a whole new set of brains?"

"No, sir."

"You're fucking right, 'no, sir.' Now you take this fucking piece of slander and you rip it up and burn it."

"I believe that report is true, sir."

"I don't care if Moses wrote it on fucking stone tablets, that report is going nowhere. You hear me?"

"I don't understand, sir."

"You are not paid to fucking understand, *Cap*tain. Your job is to do exactly what you're told. And I'm telling you to tear up that report and forget you ever wrote it."

"Whether this happened or not, sir, is for someone else to decide, I agree. But these are serious allegations. They should be investigated."

"They should be dropped and never mentioned again. Do you hear what I'm saying?"

"I hear you, sir, but I don't see what the problem is with sending the report on up the chain of command. People ought to know."

"The problem, Fairchild, is that you are practically at the *top* of the fucking chain of command. This is the Headquarters of the United States Army in Vietnam, in case it had escaped your waning attention. A report out of here gets looked at by DOD, which means civilians get their hands on it, which means leaks to Congress, which means headlines in every bleeding-heart liberal paper in the frigging country. We're fighting a war here, Captain, and it behooves us to keep our dirty laundry to ourselves."

"If you agree it's dirty laundry, sir, then it should be investigated. If we just ignore it, it could happen again."

"If you don't stop playing games with me, Captain, you're going to be in more trouble than you ever knew existed. I've spent this much time trying to talk sense to you because of the good work you've done for me in the past. But just because you've been the fair-haired boy around here doesn't mean you can start running the frigging place. I am your commanding officer, and I am ordering you to fucking tear up that report."

I could see the muscles of his jaw working up and down. I tried hard to steady my breath.

"I'm sorry, sir," I said. "But I can't do that."

His eyes widened, and he pulled at the corner of his mustache.

"I didn't quite hear what you said."

"I said, no, sir, I can't do that."

The silence in the room took on a weight that pressed on the top of my head.

"Then, *Cap*tain, I will tear it up for you."

He looked straight at me, his eyes hard. I looked straight back, determined not to blink.

"May I ask, sir, what route I should follow to bypass you?"

The room was so still I could hear the ticking of the big clock on the wall. When he spoke, his voice was soft.

"I'm going to forget you said that, Captain Fairchild. And you are going to forget you ever said it. You are going to leave this room and spend a long time thinking about the responsibilities of an officer to his superiors, about comradeship and esprit de corps, and, most especially, about the remedies provided in the Code of Military Justice for insubordination."

I stood up, left the room, and walked upstairs to the Office of the Inspector General.

## 55

Colonel Dunhill's face was stony, and his voice was quiet. "Your ill-thought-out visit to the IG's office yesterday was a big mistake, Captain. He and I think of ourselves as being on the same team, even if you don't. He's no more likely to help you cripple the war effort over here than I am. All you accomplished by that very stupid visit was to declare war on me.

"Surely you know me well enough by now to understand that I'm not accustomed to losing wars, large or small. And I have no intention of losing this one. Consider this your fair warning, Captain. I'm going to get you if it's the last thing I ever do, and I don't care who I have to step on to do it. Is that clear?"

"Perfectly, sir."

From that moment, everything around me changed. The sergeant-major sent word that the colonel would not be needing daily briefings—for a while. Sergeant Miller, more distant than usual but still efficient, helped me keep the wallmaps up to date. But no one came to look at them. Officers moved away when I sat down at a table in the mess, and a hush settled over the barracks every time I walked in.

Not many knew for sure what was happening, I was confident of that. The brass would be holding the details as close as they could. But the knowledge that I had seriously displeased the higher-ups, and was somehow too stubborn to back down, was widespread. People knew and disapproved. The idea that I'd thrown in my lot with the peaceniks back home was mixed up in it. I heard the words "traitor" and "pinko" a couple of times, after I'd passed groups suddenly intent on what they were doing. No one said anything to my face. Nothing was clear-cut enough for that. Still, averted eyes and stiff silences were eloquent enough.

I thought of the Amish farmlands I'd visited in Pennsylvania. Those people lived in extraordinary harmony with their land, with their God, and with each other. Except when one of them stepped out of line, refused to obey the rules, shattered the peaceful progress of their ordered lives. When this happened, when someone committed an act of flagrant willfulness, the community turned its collective back on the transgressor. Left him to meditate, outside the warm circle of human companionship, on what he was doing. And what he was about to lose.

It was called shunning. I was being shunned. I saw immediately what a powerful weapon it could be for promoting conformity. I was lonely, discouraged, and so sad I could barely comprehend the extent of it. I wanted back in. What abstract ideal of right and wrong could possibly be worth such total isolation?

My initial certainty, the certainty that had given me the strength to defy Colonel Dunhill, began to fade. Being alone so much gave me plenty of time to think, and the thing I thought mostly was that I was a fool. If I was the only one around who thought a thing, what arrogance gave me the temerity to believe I was right and the rest were wrong? With all my strength, I wanted to go back to the time before this soul-searching was necessary. To a time when I didn't know what I knew now. Not knowing was safer, easier. I wouldn't have to choose. The responsibility wouldn't be mine. I could believe again in choices made for me by others.

Was it too late to go back to that time? I began to believe it wasn't. This was a war, after all. A particularly ugly and brutal one, but had wars ever been pretty? I doubted it. Maybe this one seemed ugly to me because it was my first, because I was in it. Maybe it seemed ugly to people back home because, in all the ways that really mattered, it was *their* first. The first they'd ever seen close up, on their television screens. Maybe all of us were judging it too harshly. Maybe we should move back from the *things* that were happening and look instead at the goals we were hoping to achieve.

We were trying to bring the peace and order of that Amish farmland to a small country that had known nothing but turmoil for thousands of years. Wasn't that a thing worth doing? Even if many of them had to die, even if many of *us* had to die, wasn't that a goal worth pursuing? Didn't we in America believe that the quality of life was more important than life itself? That a life without liberty and freedom of choice was not worth living?

That's what our whole history had been about. "No taxation without representation." "Life, liberty, and the pursuit of happiness." "We, the people of the United States, in order to form a more perfect union. . . ." "One nation, under God, with liberty and justice for all." "Give me liberty or give me death."

Of course. Those were not just empty words to recite on the Fourth of July. They were the principles on which we had founded the freest, most just, most prosperous country ever seen on this Earth. God's country. If He approved of it and its endeavors, who was I to stand in the way of His purposes?

Then my mind played a trick on me. It showed me something I had never seen in real life, but showed it to me as clearly as if I'd been there when it happened.

I saw a young woman, dark and frightened, holding a baby in her arms. She was screaming, and the baby was crying. I saw a man, just like me, my age, skin the color of mine, raised by a mother and father like mine, familiar with church pews and impassioned old hymns. I saw that man shoot that woman, not just once but time after time. I saw him shoot her baby, again and again. I saw grandmothers and grandfathers, little boys on short stubby legs and little girls with black hair flying out behind them, all running panic-stricken from the shots that hit them in the back, from the bayonets that stopped their running forever.

And my mind played another trick on me. It told me why their terror was so great. Why their eyes grew so huge when they saw those bullets tear into the young woman's stomach. Why it took them those few fatal seconds to begin to run. They had not believed we would do it. Others, maybe, but not us. Not the big, lumbering Americans.

Rape, sure. Rape was common. Rape happened. Men did it, and women endured it, in the villages and on Tu Do Street. They were used to that. But a bullet in the stomach of a woman and her baby? That was a thing beyond comprehending.

Accidents from the sky? Of course. Bombs and napalm that fell randomly on soldiers and old women. That happened, too. That they'd come to expect. The men who dropped them couldn't see where they landed. Too bad.

But this. This man saw. He saw the frightened face of that young woman. He saw her stomach spout blood, and he kept on shooting.

Those were the tricks my mind played on me, and once they'd been played, I saw it *was* too late. I could never go back to the time before I knew. I was outside, pressing my nose against the window, and I could never go back inside again.

# 56

I ate lunch alone, as I'd been doing for days, and walked back to Headquarters. On the stairs I passed a sergeant I'd seen around the building but didn't know.

"Captain Fairchild, sir?" he said.

I stopped.

"We can't talk now, sir, but please believe I'm trying to help. You know the supply tent beside the mess hall?"

"Sure."

"Meet me behind it at twenty-two hundred. No one'll be around then."

"What's this all about, Sergeant?"

"Not now, sir. Please. Just believe me. Twenty-two hundred."

He walked quickly down the steps.

What are they setting me up for now? I wondered. Nothing that's for my benefit, that's for sure. And who is this guy anyway, out of nowhere? I'm not about to go off behind some dark tent in the middle of the night to find out.

Miller and I stuck tape on maps all afternoon. I ate supper in the mess hall at a completely silent table and drank two beers alone in the Officers' Club. Conversation and laughter swirled in all directions but never came near me. A space surrounded me that no one was willing to cross. I was in quarantine as surely as if I'd had smallpox sores oozing all over my face or leprosy eating away at my fingers. God dammit, I thought, I'm as healthy as they are! 'Healthier,' said a voice off in the corner of my brain, but that was too radical a thought for me to deal with.

I looked at my watch. Nine-forty-five. Twenty-one-forty-five. Fuck it, I thought. Fuck all these self-righteous bastards. What the hell have I got to lose?

I took what we'd learned in intelligence school to call a "circuitous route," so it was after ten when I got to the supply tent. The sergeant was standing in the shadows.

"Over here, sir," he said. "I thought you might not come."

There was barely enough light reflected off the mess hall to see his face.

"I almost didn't," I said. "Tell me what this is about."

"My name's Woodruff, sir. Nick Woodruff. I work in counterintelligence. You and your report are just about the only thing anyone's talking about in there. The brass are convinced you're going to try to find a way around them, and they're determined to stop you. The CG's ordered us to see to it, but he didn't really have to. For most of the guys in G-3, it's like a labor of love. 'Get the pinko.' That kind of thing."

"But not you."

"Not me."

"Why not?"

"Two reasons, sir. First, I've read a summary of your report, and I think what you're trying to do is a really gutsy thing. I admire the hell out of you."

I wanted to hug him.

"Do you know, Sergeant, that's the first friendly thing anyone's said to me in almost a week?"

"I can imagine, sir, and I'm sorry. It may seem like you're the only one who thinks the way you do, but you're not, sir. Fear is a powerful weapon, you know."

"Oh, I *do* know. Believe me. And you don't have to keep calling me 'sir' out here in the dark."

"I figured that, but it's a hard habit to break. Sir."

I laughed.

"Good," he said. "Hang onto your sense of humor, if you can. You're going to need it."

"Any particular reason?"

"Yeah. Reason number two why I want to help you. G-3's decided maybe you're gay, and they're about to turn the base upside down to prove it."

"'Gay' meaning queer?" I asked.

I could see he was startled. "Gay meaning queer, yes."

"Jesus Christ. Is there no limit?"

"To stop you, sir? And what you know? None."

I swallowed hard. "Why would they think I'm. . . . that?"

"Their kind of logic. You're not married. You never went to Tu Do Street in Saigon. A number of guys swear to that. You don't go to the whore houses out here. Open and shut, in their eyes. Oh, and poor Colonel Dunhill's had to admit he waived your polygraph exam. He's in a big pile of trouble over that."

"But why go to such lengths?" I asked. "There's no way I can get that report out of here over their objections. I tried the one route I could think of and hit a brick wall."

"But you still *know*, sir. That's the scary thing. Everyone else who knows they're pretty sure won't talk. But you they can't be sure of. They want to make it worth your while never to open your mouth. Not now. Not ever."

"Why are you letting me in on all this?"

"I told you, to help you if I can. If you know what they're up to ahead of time, you can be as careful as you need to be. Stay away from people, if that's appropriate. What I'm here to tell you is, don't try to warn anyone. Don't say anything, even to me. Just keep your eyes open, and don't do anything that'll give them ammunition."

"But I still don't understand your angle in all this."

"You don't?" He hesitated. "I'm asking you not to tell me anything about yourself because the less I know the better. But I'll tell you something about *my*self, in hopes it'll help you decide to believe what I'm saying. I'm gay, Captain. Queer. Not actively now, but I was before and will be again, if I'm lucky enough to get back home."

"Jesus." I couldn't imagine someone just coming out and saying a thing like that, especially to a stranger.

"But if you'd. . . . already done things," I asked, "how'd you ever sneak through?"

"The polygraphs, you mean? I lied."

"And it didn't show up?"

"Apparently not. I kept telling myself it was none of their goddam business. Maybe that helped."

"I wish I'd known that. I might have saved myself some sleepless nights."

"I'd say it's just as well, sir. You might not be as good at lying."

"And they stuck you in counterintelligence?"

"Yeah. Ironic, isn't it? But I've worked out a very satisfying revenge."

"What's that?"

"Doing exactly what I'm doing tonight. It's a kind of mission I've taken on for myself. If I was going to have to be in this rotten war, I figured I might as well try to help my people. *My* people, Captain. You know the old Army motto, 'Take care of your own'? Well, that's just what I'm doing."

"And you've been successful? Warning guys about stuff like this?"

"A good many times, I'm happy to say. You'd be surprised how many leads can go astray. How many memos can get lost. They're proud of the ones they catch, and I'm proud of the ones that get away."

"But that's dangerous work, isn't it?"

"Very. But rewarding. I intend to keep at it till I either slip up and get caught or finish out my year. One or the other."

"And you were willing to take a chance on me? Without knowing for sure?"

"Yes."

"Jesus," I said. "Take care of yourself."

"Thanks. I will."

"So what shall I do? This is all new to me."

"First of all, do you trust me now?"

"Yes. I'm not exactly sure why, but yes."

"Good. That instinct is correct. Now make me a promise, sir. Please."

"What?"

"That you won't trust another living soul. Not old friends,

not people you've just met, not your co-workers, not your superiors. From now on, listen to that feeling in your gut that told you not to come meet me tonight. Let me make this as clear as I can, sir. What you know is a serious threat, and they're pulling out all the stops. They've gotten to everyone else who was at that village or who knows about it outside of Headquarters. They're sure they've plugged all the leaks. Except you. You're the only one who hasn't agreed yet to play along, and they'll do whatever it takes to see that you do. Do you understand me, sir?"

"I hear what you're saying, Sergeant, but no, I don't understand it. It sounds melodramatic to me."

"In a place like this, melodrama and reality bump into each other coming and going. Who's to say which is which? All I know is, you're a threat to everything they hold dear, and they're not about to let you mess things up. Period."

"Tell me what to do."

"The important thing is to be careful. Starting tomorrow, you'll be followed wherever you go. Your locker in the barracks will be searched every day, and your desk in the secure room will be searched every night. And you'll never notice a thing out of place. Every phone call you make, every piece of mail in and out will be monitored. Every note to yourself, every doodle, every laundry list. You tear it up, they'll patch it together. *Nothing* will escape their notice."

"Can they do that?"

"This is a war zone, Captain. And you've pissed off some very talented people. They can, and will, do anything they damn well please. They need to find something concrete to nail you with. And you need to be sure they don't. Look, I don't know if you've been seeing anyone. . . ."

I nodded.

"I *don't know* if you've been seeing anyone," he repeated, "but if you have, don't try to warn him in any way. That would lead them right to him. Just let everything rest, nice and easy. Go on about your business. Don't suddenly start visiting the whore houses, like you know something's up. And just hope there's a god somewhere who watches out for fairies."

"Isn't that who you are?"

He laughed. "Bravo," he said. "Good for you. If you can see the absurdity of it all, hang on to that. It'll go a long way toward preserving your sanity."

# 57

"You will report to G-3 at 0900."

The message was terse and to the point.

When I got there, I was shown into a large room. Seated behind a rectangular table were five officers—Colonel Dunhill; the head of counterintelligence, a colonel named Briggs; a lieutenant colonel; and two majors. Several other officers sat in chairs along the walls. My chair was in the center of the room. I saluted in the direction of the table.

"You may be seated, Captain," said Colonel Briggs.

I sat down.

"We have been shocked and greatly troubled, Captain Fairchild, to learn some distressing things about your conduct. In a willful flaunting of the Military Code, the generally accepted norms of civilized behavior, not to mention the teachings of the church, you have been committing sodomy right here under our noses. Not with a fellow soldier, which would have been disturbing enough, but with a known Viet Cong agent named Tran Le Nhan.

"In short, Captain, you have been sleeping with the enemy, an act of treason against the United States. What do you have to say for yourself?"

There was no way I could speak. My throat seemed not to be connected to my brain.

"You have nothing to say?"

He waited again.

"Perhaps you're not aware that we know everything about this little affair of yours, Captain. *Every*thing. Shall I read part of a report to you?"

I still couldn't speak.

He opened a file on the table in front of him and turned over a page.

"'The first time was on or about 14 July,'" he read. "'Captain Matthew Fairchild came into the restaurant in Cholon where I am a busboy. It was about nineteen-thirty. I was surprised to see that he was alone. He had usually come in with other Americans, in particular a tall man with sandy-colored hair.

"'As he ate, I noticed that he kept looking at me and smiling. Since my assignment for the Viet Cong is to entice American soldiers to my bedroom in hopes of learning valuable information, I went over to Captain Fairchild's table and engaged him in conversation. I told him I got off work at twenty-one hundred and would meet him on the corner out back, if he liked. He said he would like that very much.

"'We walked a few blocks to a Viet Cong safehouse, which I told Captain Fairchild belonged to a friend of mine who worked nights in a hotel. I should say here that Captain Fairchild was one of the easiest assignments I have ever had. It took little effort to convince him that I was sincere and trustworthy and only interested in him because I liked him.

"'We arrived at the apartment, and I asked if he wanted something to drink. He said no. I moved some pillows off the bed in the corner of the room, lit a stick of incense and three candles, and initiated sexual activity by beginning to unbutton Captain Fairchild's shirt. I believe it was blue.'

"Shall I continue, Captain? There's a great deal more."

"No," I said, in what came out as a hoarse croak. I cleared my throat. "No," I said again.

"Good." Colonel Briggs straightened the papers and closed the file folder. "Now," he continued. "As you can see, we have a complete and detailed file on your homosexual activities with this Viet Cong spy. We suspect that he was not the only one and are at work attempting to determine if there are more, either Vietnamese or American. If there are, you can be sure we will find them out before much longer."

He stared at me, letting the weight of the air in the room become more and more claustrophobic. Suddenly he smiled and leaned forward.

"Look, Captain," he said in a soothing voice. "We are not cruel men, or unkind men. We understand how lonely a young officer can be, far from home and his loved ones. We understand how impulsive and unthinking youth can be, and how easy it is to make mistakes that we come to regret."

All five officers at the table nodded gravely.

"It is our mission," Colonel Briggs continued, "to ensure the security of all our brave men fighting over here. But we want to be reasonable in carrying out that mission. You've done some fine work here, Captain. Setting up the CG's briefing room and that excellent report on the Soviet rockets. We don't forget things like that, do we, gentlemen?"

The other four officers shook their heads solemnly.

"So." Colonel Briggs interlaced his fingers, set his hands on top of the file folder, and leaned forward again. "We want to do what's best for everyone concerned here—for the security of our troops, for the war effort as a whole, and for you, Captain Fairchild. Now, how can we do this?"

He leaned back and waited a few seconds. No one spoke.

"How?" he repeated. "By a synthesis. You've made two mistakes, Captain. Two youthful, impetuous, foolish mistakes. Luckily, one can cancel out the other. You have insisted on sending forward a report that could have serious, even disastrous, consequences for the war effort in this country. And you have given in to the weakness of the flesh and had sex, repeatedly, with an enemy agent.

"Now. By synthesizing the effects of these two mistakes, by your forgetting about that report and our forgetting about your. . . . shall we say, activities, we can all come out ahead. The war effort can continue unimpeded, and you can serve out your time here, in a less sensitive assignment, of course, and go home without the disgrace of a court-martial and possible imprisonment."

He leaned forward. "We're fair men here, Captain. No one else needs to know about all of this. Your family. Future employers. All those people you'd like never to hear of this." He smiled. "So. You help us, we help you. It isn't often that unfortunate, even tragic, turns of events can be arranged with so much positive benefit for so many people."

He settled back into his chair.

"What do you say, Captain Fairchild?"

I sat for what seemed like an hour. No one moved. This time I cleared my throat before I even attempted to speak.

"I thank you for your concern, sir," I said. "What you've told me makes me realize just how foolish I *have* been. But—"

All five officers leaned forward.

"But a lot of this has come as quite a shock to me. I was not aware of some of the things in your report, the true nature of the man who gave that information to you. And I really need some time to think. Am I pushing too hard to ask for a day or two to try to sort things out?"

Colonel Briggs huddled with the other officers, first on one side of him, then the other. When he looked at me again, his smile was positively benign.

"Of course not, Captain. As I said before, we want what's best for *you* as well as for the war effort as a whole. We can't allow you to continue working in the secure briefing room. Too much at stake. You understand that. Colonel Dunhill has agreed to give you a desk in the big room outside, where you can help with the weekly briefings."

"I understand, sir."

"Good." He smiled. "Now, you take a little time to think things over, and let us know when you've decided."

I stood, saluted, and walked out the door.

# 58

I went up the stairs and down the hall to the secure room. I clicked the buttons and pulled, but the door wouldn't open. I tried again. It didn't move. A sergeant from G-2 walked up.

"The combination's been changed, sir," he said. "Your new desk is in here."

He led the way into the big outer room and over to a desk in the far back corner. A cardboard box sat on top.

"Your personal effects from the secure room, sir," he said. "Now, if you'll excuse me."

I put the box on the floor and pulled out the chair. They've done it, I thought. They've got the upper hand. In spades. There's no way I can beat them. I turned away from the room and sat staring at the wall.

I'd just been forced out of it two minutes before, but already I missed the secure room. Back there, with soothing music playing, alone with my thoughts, I could have worked out what I needed to do. But here, out in the open, with prying eyes and hostile looks following my every move, it was too hard. One thing was certain, though. The shunning I'd been through up to then—and hated—had been a picnic compared to what I'd have to deal with for the rest of my life. If everywhere I went people knew what I really was. And what I liked to do.

Maybe half an hour later, a PFC handed me a note and walked away. "Captain Fairchild," it said. "You don't know me, sir, but I work in G-3 with Colonel Briggs. I know you are faced with a difficult decision, and I think maybe I can help. I am aware of some of the facts of your case, and I'm told I'm a good listener. At 1030 hours, I will be on the walkway between Headquarters and the mess hall, where we won't be disturbed. If you think talking with me might help, please meet me there. Staff Sergeant Nicholas P. Woodruff."

I read it again, and it still said the same thing. What the hell was going on? Then I realized that nothing had made sense for days. Why should this? At ten-twenty-five, I walked out the door of Headquarters and up toward the mess hall to where Sergeant Woodruff was standing.

"Aren't you taking an awful risk?" I asked. "I'm a confirmed queer, you know."

"It's a gamble, I guess, but I wanted to see you. Sneaking around would never work now, so I figured, what the hell? Why not just be direct? I told Colonel Briggs I'd be glad to talk with you and try to impress on you how serious your situation is. One-on-one with a noncom, I said. Much less threatening than with another officer. It just might work."

"And he bought that?"

"My degree in psychology impresses the hell out of him."

"And that's what you're here for? To help me decide?"

"No. That's up to you. I wanted to tell you about your friend Nhan."

"Some friend!"

"You have no idea, sir."

"What I know is he told them everything. Some deal to save himself, no doubt."

"I was afraid you'd see it that way, and it isn't true. They tracked him down, took him somewhere, and he refused to talk. For days, Captain. Do you know what that means?"

"Come on! What about that report? He told them everything that happened. How many candles he lit, for Christ's sake!"

"Of course he did. Pain is a great persuader."

"Pain?"

"*Lots* of it. The more pain, the more detail. And as you must have heard, sir, that's a *very* detailed report."

"You're saying he wasn't a Viet Cong agent after all?"

He put his hand on my arm.

"Keep your perspective, please, sir. He's a busboy in a Chinese restaurant who went to great lengths to protect you."

Shit, I thought. I remembered his Uncle Kim. Of course he wasn't anybody's spy. But all it had taken was for someone to suggest it, and I'd been ready to accept it in a second. Were they killing my ability to believe in people, or had it died from lack of use?

"Is he all right?" I asked.

"No."

"Oh, my god. Will he *be* all right?"

He hesitated. "I *think* so. He's young and strong, I gather. The breaks will heal, but. . . ."

"Tell me."

"But there'll be scars. There'd have to be."

"They beat it out of him?"

"Every word."

Screaming would have relieved the pressure on my brain. I wanted to scream and just keep on screaming. Sergeant Woodruff was looking intently at my face.

"Don't break down now, sir," he said. "You've got to save it for later. Please."

"I'd like to kill the bastards."

"For all the good that would do."

"Maybe not. But I'd sure feel better."

"Would you?"

"But how could they do something so awful to a sweet, gentle man like that?"

"My guess is his being sweet and gentle was as great a provocation as his refusing to talk. Who knows?"

"I hate this!"

"Don't stop. It's seeing it and *not* hating it that's causing all the trouble."

I closed my eyes but felt dizzy, so I opened them.

"God," I said. "How little faith I had in him."

"Don't blame yourself, sir. It's in damn short supply around here."

"Can you at least get a message to him? Tell him how sorry I am?"

"No, sir. That's the last thing I could do."

"There's nothing I can do to help him?"

"Absolutely nothing. Staying far away is the best thing you can do."

"But I can't just leave him like that. Without knowing I'd be with him if I could."

"I expect he knows that, sir."

"He is an amazing man, Sergeant."

"I believe that."

"And I did this to him."

"I don't think so, sir. I imagine he was a willing participant."

"I don't mean our making love. I mean his refusing to talk. I told him the first night we were together that I'd been hesitant to come. That I was afraid he'd betray me. He was angry and said he never would. So he kept on holding back. For me."

"And it was a heroic effort, sir, from what I hear. Futile, of course, but heroic. He has that to remember."

"There was no way he could keep from telling, then, was there? Really?"

"None."

"So might always wins in the end."

"You think they've won?"

"Haven't they?"

"Not yet. From what I've heard, Nhan strikes me as a survivor. I'll bet there are thousands more like him. We hurt them, but they survive. And, of course, you still know what you know."

I nodded.

"You can still blow them out of the water."

"But if I did that, and they were angry enough, they might beat Nhan again, even kill him. Mightn't they?"

"They might. There's nothing to stop them. What's one Vietnamese more or less? Or they might not. When all *that* shit hits the fan, they'll have a lot more on their minds than him."

"All of a sudden I'm walking around in a nightmare."

"All of a sudden, sir? Where've you been these past nine months?"

"Fighting a war that didn't exist, I guess. Certainly not this vicious, insane one."

"Maybe you just weren't paying attention."

I snapped my head up and stared at him. "That's something Nhan might have said."

"Well, then. He sounds like a wise young man."

"Wiser than me, you mean."

"Very likely."

I looked hard into his eyes, and he didn't look away.

"You're a good man, Sergeant. I hope you know that."

He shrugged.

"I wish. . . . ," I said.

"What?"

"I wish I'd known you somewhere else. Somewhere sane."

He smiled. "I'd've liked that."

"Look," I said, "I've no idea where I'll end up, but my parents will know. Everett Fairchild. San Antonio, Texas. He's in the phone book."

I hesitated. "You can't write it down, can you?"

"You're catching on fast, Captain. My hopes for you are rising all the time."

"But you'll try to remember?"

"I'll remember."

We stood looking at each other for a second or two.

"If there's any way you can help Nhan. . . . ," I said.

"You know I will."

"Thanks."

"Well. I'll be getting back now. Tell them I've made my pitch and you're thinking it over."

He started to salute, but I reached for his hand and shook it instead.

"Take care of yourself," he said. "It's not going to be easy, whatever you decide."

I nodded.

He walked a little ways away, stopped, and turned.

"Everett Fairchild," he said. "San Antonio. Right?"

"Right."

He winked and headed off toward Headquarters. I watched him go.

It's not what we pretend it's about at all, is it? I thought. It's not about bullets or bombs or strategic alliances. It's really about hurting and being hurt. If we can hurt the Vietnamese enough, in enough ways, they'll stop doing what we don't want them to do. If they hurt us enough, we'll pack up and go home. Hurt one man enough, and he'll tell you everything he knows. Hurt another, and he'll shut up and never say a word.

All I wanted, right then, was for no one to be hurt that much, ever again.

# 59

I walked into Colonel Dunhill's office. He looked up and stared at me.

"I've done a lot of thinking, sir," I said, "and it's clear to me you're right. I'll stop trying to have my report read by anyone further up the chain of command."

His shoulders relaxed. He smiled. "Thanks, Fairchild," he said. "I knew you'd see it our way. Eventually. If enough people explained it clearly enough. And we gave you enough time."

I nodded.

"You've destroyed the copy I gave you?" I asked.

He smiled again. "Yes, long ago. And the copy you had in the safe. And all your notes. You'd've had to write it from scratch again, you see, if. . . ." He raised his eyebrows. "But that's all over now, isn't it?" He frowned. "Unless you've got something else tucked away."

"No, sir," I said. "I haven't."

He got up and came around from behind his desk. He put his hand out toward my shoulder but stopped before it got close enough to touch me. It hovered there for a second. Then he patted the air in my general vicinity and lowered his hand.

"This has been an unpleasant experience for all of us, Fairchild," he said. "But I think we've all learned a great deal."

"Yes, sir. We certainly have."

"I'm not all bluster and foul mouth, Captain. I do know about loneliness and the things it can make a man do he would never do otherwise. You just got caught up in a lot of things you didn't understand, that's all. Experimented with stuff you should've left the hell alone. It screwed up your thinking, and everything just got out of hand."

He pulled at his mustache.

"We never wanted to mess up your life, Fairchild. I hope you know that. All we've ever wanted was for you to leave us free to do what we came here to do. Not fuck things up with stuff that don't amount to much in the overall scheme of things. You understand what I'm saying?"

"I understand, sir."

"I've been pretty pissed at you, I don't mind saying. And shocked as hell at what you'd gotten yourself up to. A clean-cut young man like you. That fucking queer stuff makes my skin crawl. But the important thing is that you've come to your senses."

"Yes, sir."

"And you won't regret it."

"I hope not, sir."

I went right to work on that week's briefing. Viet Cong ambushes. B-52 strikes. Success stories about villages that had been secured. I was diligent and studious and said very little.

After the briefing on Friday, instead of going back to my desk, I wandered out the door of the Headquarters building and down the road to the right. I came to a tree, one of the few left standing inside the compound. I sat on the ground and leaned up against the trunk. It was hot and still. No breeze stirred the thick red dust that covered everything.

Across the road, an old mama-san squatted beside the steps of a barracks shining shoes. A portable radio on the top step was playing a Vietnamese song that sounded strange to my ears. The singing was so high-pitched and nasal it was impossible to tell if the singer was a man or a woman. Although I couldn't understand a word of it, the song sounded old to me. Maybe ancient. The odd tonality and unfamiliar harmonics created a barrier I couldn't penetrate, behind which was a world I would never know.

We'd all be gone some day, I thought, this new horde of foreigners who'd come to rearrange things. The barracks would be gone, and the mama-san would no longer shine shoes. But she'd still listen to that song. And not a one of us who'd come and gone would have the tiniest inkling of what the song meant. Or what went through her mind as she sat there listening to it.

## 60

Getting into town was the problem. Ever since Tet, travel from Long Binh to Saigon had been restricted. I would need a pass, and no one was about to give me one. I decided brazenness was the only way.

That Saturday, around midmorning, I showered, put on civilian clothes, looped up behind the NCO Club, and came out on the main road a few hundred yards inside the gate. I waved to a jeep headed out, and it stopped. Two sergeants in uniform I'd never seen before were in the front seats.

"Saigon?" I asked.

"Yeah," said the sergeant on my side. "Got a pass, soldier?"

I patted my empty hip pocket. "Lucky me," I said.

"Hop in," said the sergeant.

He leaned forward, and I crawled in back.

At the gate, the driver waved his middle finger at the MP on duty and said, "Jenkins and me'll fuck one each for you, dickhead."

"Yeah, yeah," said the MP. "You and what squad of Greenie Beanies? All talk and no action. That's why they let you go to town in the first place."

They all laughed, and we drove on through.

While the two of them bragged and razzed each other, I watched the side of the road. What had once been a beautiful drive was now a horror. All the vegetation on both sides of the road had been cleared far back. No more havens for snipers there. Thick red dust blew fitfully across the rubble. The few trees that survived were covered with it and seemed to be gasping.

Saigon was almost as bad. It was a nightmarish blend of burned-out buildings and barbed wire and life-as-usual. The cyclos and mopeds and jeeps all fought for space on the narrow streets, each one adding to the noise and the thickening of the air.

The sergeants let me out near the park. I quickly saw that during the months I'd been away, the atmosphere had changed. People on the streets no longer smiled at me and bobbed their heads. Most turned away. Some stared hard, their lips pressed tightly together.

I had lunch in a little cafe I'd never seen before and walked once around the zoo. Only a few small animals were left, monkeys mostly and a couple of sad-eyed rodents. The bear's cage was empty.

Just after two, I walked down Le Thanh Ton Street and turned left on Tu Do to the Continental Hotel. A few men were in the lounge, and a few more were at tables by the windows. I waited at the end of the bar until the bartender came over. He was a young and slender Vietnamese with a bright smile. He pointed to a man sitting alone at a table writing with one hand and holding a pipe in the other.

I walked over.

"Excuse me," I said.

The man looked up.

"You're with the *Times*?"

"That's right."

"Got a minute?"